Michael and Mollie Hardwick have been working together as writers, dramatists, reviewers, producers of radio plays and gramophone records, and in other capacities for a number of years. Together or individually they have written over thirty books, chiefly on literary or historical themes, and are best known for their work on Charles Dickens and Sherlock Holmes. Northerners by birth (Michael is from Leeds, Mollie from Manchester) they now live in London.

Michael and Mollie Hardwick

Charles Dickens:
The Gas-Light Boy

Futura Publications Limited
A Futura Book

A Futura Book

First published in Great Britain in 1976
by Futura Publications Limited

Copyright © Michael and Mollie Hardwick 1976

ISBN: 0 8600 7383 1

Printed in Great Britain by
Richard Clay (The Chaucer Press), Ltd.,
Bungay, Suffolk

Futura Publications Limited,
110 Warner Road, Camberwell,
London SE5

CHAPTER ONE

Outside the Westminster Hotel, in Irving Place, New York, the normal peace and quiet of that establishment was disrupted on a bitter cold night of 1867 by the babble of voices and the uneasy shiftings of a strange and motley crowd. Some of them were in fancy costume – a Red Indian chief, a shabby George Washington, a Sam Weller even more raffish than the book illustrations, a grotesque, pot-bellied Pickwick wearing a mask. They were ticket touts, trying to cash in illicitly on the enormous demand for seats for the dramatic readings of the world-famous author Charles Dickens, known to be staying at the Westminster together with his tour-manager, George Dolby.

In the fitful gas-light, the stout figure of Dolby appeared and began to force his way through the throng, tightly clutching a wash-leather bag. Hands clutched at him and voices clamoured.

'Three dollars a ticket over the public price, Mr Dolby, and a dollar apiece for yourself, sir.'

'Scandalous.' Dolby elbowed a man aside. Another brandished a fist.

'This is the United States of America, Mr Dolby! This ain't no rackety old queened-over state. This here is a democracy, sir.'

'There's three thousand queueing outside the Steinway Hall, Mr Dolby. Give us a chance!' Another tout was growling threats, physically barring the manager's way.

Dolby pushed his way through. 'I'll take my chance, sir, as you must take yours – at the box office with the rest of the citizens of your wonderful city. Excuse me!'

At last he was through them, in the hotel, in the ante-room

where somebody was always stationed to guard Mr Dickens's sitting-room door and to supply anything he might want. Tonight it was a French waiter, Lasalle, hired specially by the manager, Mr Palmer. He greeted Dolby with a patient smile. He had been there a long time, and his services were beginning to seem redundant.

'Has Mr Dickens taken anything, Lasalle?' Dolby asked.

'I bring him some oyster, sir, and a very excellent bottle of Veuve Clicquot – an excellent year, the 1852 . . .'

Dolby slipped past him, quietly entered the sitting-room of Dickens's suite, and went towards a curtained alcove that served as the bedroom. Dickens lay on the bed asleep muttering fitfully. Dolby gazed anxiously at the lined twitching face, the face of a man looking ten years older than his fifty-five. The bushy grey beard jutted, the still-thick hair had retreated from the high noble forehead, the brilliant eyes, now set in a network of wrinkles, were shut. He had caught a cold – the true American catarrh – on the journey from Boston; Dolby hoped it was not turning to influenza. Heaven knew, his beloved Chief suffered sufficiently from the affliction in his foot which he thought to be gout but which might well be something more serious. He had never been wholly well since the terrible railway accident in which he had been involved in 1865, and which had shattered his nerves.

Nor had his now-established series of dramatic readings helped. A failed actor himself, the Chief threw all of his wasted talents into bringing to life the characters he had created: the comic and the tragic: Sam Weller, Tiny Tim, Little Nell, poor Nancy brutally murdered by Bill Sikes, Mr Pickwick and his friends. His wonderful interpretations of them seemed to drag something out of his very being and bring him near to breakdown. He was 'better than the play', people said. Cries of 'Dickens is coming!' were raised when news got about that he was to visit a town. When he appeared on a platform, in England or America, a surging, roaring sea of people overflowed the hall, the chairs, the platform itself, tearing to ribbons the clothes of the attendants, the spectators screaming and fainting in their seats as emotion overcame them. Dolby congratulated himself that he had helped to control the worst of the excesses by his managership, and spared his poor Chief's feelings as much as possible.

He eyed with concern the bottles of medicines beside the bed. All drugs, opiates. The oysters and champagne were untouched. Gently he spoke.

'Mr Dickens?'

The figure on the bed stirred uneasily. 'The Mask, the Mask!' it muttered.

'What do you say, sir?'

Dickens struggled up on his elbow. 'Dreams, Dolby, dreams,' he murmured. 'There's a curiously powerful – as my father might have said – quite extraordinarily remarkable and even – yes – evanescent quality to a dream, which no words may catch.' He smiled. 'My dreams have brought me a great fortune, Dolby.'

'Yes, sir.' Dolby indicated the oysters and champagne, and the contents of the wash-leather bag, £3,000 worth of Yankee greenbacks. 'And another three thousand to come, sir. For only two recitals.' Dickens's eyes were alight, he swung his feet to the floor, seeming a new man.

'I think I could put down a few oysters now, Dolby.'

'Wonderful, sir, but stay in bed and I'll bring them to you.' But when Dolby, bustling about with plates and knives, turned round, Dickens had fallen back on the pillow, pale and sighing. After a startled glance, Dolby went off to call the doctor whose services the thoughful Mr Palmer had requisitioned.

When he came back he found Dickens still prone on the bed, while above him stood a nightmare figure: the mock-Pickwick of the crowd, monstrously padded, a great bald headpiece above a gruesomely bland, expressionless mask with a bulbous nose and false spectacles.

Dolby exploded. 'You devil! Get out of here, sir, instantly! Stop troubling us!'

The horrible face turned towards him. 'I have my rights, Mr Dolby,' it said nasally through the mask.

'You have no rights whatsoever in the matter. Get out, sir!'

As the ticket tout stared at him through the slits in the cardboard face, Dickens stirred convulsively.

'The Mask! Oh, no! Oh, God! Oh, no! It is the Mask!'

As Dolby hustled the protesting tout away, the figure on the bed went limp in a faint.

CHAPTER TWO

The Mask had first terrified him so many years ago. It had been at a Christmas party in the house where he had lived with his parents and brothers and sisters, at Chatham, the bustling Kent town on the Medway basin, where Charles's father, John Dickens, worked as a clerk in the Navy Pay Office. They were not very rich, indeed they were often in debt, but John Dickens was an incorrigible optimist delighting in the slightest occasion for festivities. And what greater occasion than Christmas ? Charles would never forget those Christmases in the neat little terraced house in Ordnance Terrace, set in pleasant countrified surroundings. This most genial, loveable family consisted of the young parents, Charles, the eldest boy, born in 1812, his sister and best playmate Fanny, the younger children, and the widowed aunt, Mrs Allen. So many for such a small house, with just two attic bedrooms for the children, and the basement for the servant, Mary Weller, and for Jane Bonny the little maid from the Chatham orphanage who helped her.

Christmas, so jolly with its turkey and plum pudding and holly-tree, decked with glorious toys of all kinds, the donkey with the real hide, the little lady in the blue silk skirt who danced, the miniature volumes in which the book-mad Charles delighted . . . what richness! Except for the Mask.

When did it first look on him ? Who wore it ? Why did it frighten him so ? It was not even particularly hideous; indeed, it was probably meant to be funny. But for some reason it struck terror into his childish heart. He was never to be good at analysing his own feelings and motives, but he came somewhere near to discovering the secret when he wrote one day, for all the world to read: 'Perhaps that fixed and set change

9

coming over a real face, infused into my quickened heart some remote suggestion and dread of the universal change that is to come on every face, and make it still?'

Charles Dickens loved Life too passionately to accept the face of Death.

There was so much to do at Chatham. Fanny and he played with their toy theatre, enacting the stories Charles devoured so eagerly, especially The Arabian Nights. Always he was the dominant figure: manager, script-writer, voice behind the scenes. Fanny timidly tried to assert herself, but it was as though a star had tried to vie with the sun. Where books and the theatre were concerned, Fanny had to take a back place. There was a real live theatre only a few minutes from their house, the Theatre Royal at the foot of Star Hill, where Chatham merged into Rochester, and where Charles, speechless with ecstasy, watched drama and comedy and slapstick and rubbish played by every variety of performer, from the great to the insignificant. Once he was even taken up to London to see the fabulous, the matchless clown, Joey Grimaldi, the memory of whose humour was to stay with him for life.

Charles was a quicksilver child, sharp, witty, emotional, imitative, quick to laugh and to cry. Neatly and elegantly made, he was sprightly though not physically strong, with an elfish face, a sweet mouth, abundant brown hair, and eyes about which in years to come nobody would be able to agree. Were they light blue or dark blue, brown or hazel or steel-grey? What all agreed was that they were as bright as the morning, brimming with life and light, the eyes of a lover, a visionary, a hypnotist. Look into them and you were lost.

When Charles was nine the merry life at Ordnance Terrace altered. His father's 'never very stable pecuniary circumstances' were the cause of the family's moving to a rather less smart address, St Mary's Place, The Brook, near the Dockyard. Aunt Allen married a Dr Lamert, whose son James came to lodge with the Dickenses and, himself stage-struck and years older than Charles, exercised a strong influence on the boy. He had seen all the great ones play at the Theatre Royal. He showed Cousin Charles how they did it. Siddons as Lady

Macbeth, for instance. And Macbeth himself – not Garrick, but someone dashed good. Charles imitated him.

'"Is this a dagger which I see before me? A – something – before my hand".'

'Handle towards my hand,' James prompted.

'"Come, let me clutch thee,"' went on Charles with realistic gestures, and continued the speech, unaware of the presence of his father leaning in the doorway, watching appreciatively; the little servant Jane (who was rather unkindly nicknamed The Orfling) lurked wide-eyed beside him. John Dickens was thirty-five, a man of presence, flair and dash, not handsome but striking of face, humorous of eye, with a nose which gave the simultaneous impression of being both aquiline and tip-tilted. He wore smart clothes and a superfluity of rings, stock-pins, and fobs, most of which found their way to the pawnbroker's from time to time. His speech was rolling, fruity, genial of tone, in quality similar to the port he relished. A smile spread over his face as he heard James praise his son.

'Excellent, Charles. First class. A little more polish, a few more touches here and there, and I think we shall have it.'

John Dickens was beaming and clapping. His son's delicate skin flushed with pleasure.

'Admirable, admirable! But if you will permit, my dear James, just one observation from one, who, like yourself, has admired the Thespian world and would, in other circumstances, all things being equal, have ventured, perhaps, not to put too fine a point to it, into that very arena himself – well, in brief...'

He launched into a demonstration of the Dagger Speech which was colourful but would have given the late Garrick considerable pain.

'Feeling, my boy!' he cried. 'Emotion! Heart!' He beat his breast in the approved barn-storming manner.

John had no intention of hiding his son's theatrical talents under a bushel. The Mitre Tavern in Chatham was the town's principal inn and posting-house, a rambling, romantic ancient building which had once been a manor-house, and still owned beautiful, tree-filled gardens. Its landlord was the amiable Mr Tribe, whose children were playmates to Charles and Fanny, and whose pretty youngest daughter was one of Charles's childhood sweethearts. In the cosy bar-room, surrounded by friendly patrons, John Dickens and James Lamert spent many a happy evening 'presenting' Charles and his accomplishments. Together they would swing his slight form up on to the large table which served as a stage, and John would make his customary speech, to the approbatory rattling of tankards.

'Gentlemen, gentlemen! The lights are about to be put out to aid your concentration upon a singularly important artist. Gentlemen, there is not, as I say, the slightest cause for alarm, but I crave your indulgence while the house-lights are dimmed and the floats reveal your own – your very own – Mister Charles Dickens!'

The house-lights, which consisted of two candle-branches, having been duly extinguished, another candelabrum discreetly placed below the level of the table lit up the small form in its tight long trousers, nautical short jacket, and frilled shirt. An old man by the fireside struck up on his hand-accordion the prelude to that well-known tune 'The White Cockade', and Charles, after a slightly false start which did not deter him at all, gave a spirited rendering complete with an authentically Cockney accent and lively gestures, of the ballad which had replaced the original words of Burns's song.

> In Gray's Inn, not long ago,
> An old maid lived a life of woe;
> She vos fifty-three, vith a face like tan,
> And she fell in love with a cats'-meat man.
> Much she loved this cats'-meat man –
> He *vos* a good-looking cats'-meat man;
> Her roses and lilies vos turned to tan,
> Ven she fell in love vith the cats'-meat man.
>
> One morn she kept him at the door,
> Talking for half-an-hour and more;
> For, you must know, that vos her plan,
> To have a good look at the cats'-meat man.
> "Times is hard," says the cats'-meat man;
> "Folks get in my debt," says the cats'-meat man;

Then he took up his barrow and avay he ran,
And cried "Cats'-meat!" did the cats'-meat man.

He soon saw vich vay the cat did jump,
And his company he offered plump;
She couldn't blush, 'cause she'd no fan,
So she sat and grinned at the cats'-meat man.
"If you'll marry me," says the cats'-meat man,
"I'll have you," says the cats'-meat man;
For a qvartern of peppermint then he ran,
And she drank a good health to the cats'-meat man.

There were a good many more verses, telling the sad tale of
how the deluded lady lent her swain a five-pound note, only
to learn from friends that he had a wife and seven children.
Charles gave it every ounce of value, and received a tumultuous ovation and a kiss from the barmaid. 'The Cats'-meat
Man' was always to be one of his favourite party-pieces. He
had not learned it from his erudite, elegant mother, who had
been in charge of his education until he went to Mr Giles's
school nearby, but from the servant and nursemaid Mary
Weller, a plain young woman with a fund of stories and
ballads, and she in turn had learned it from her sweetheart,
Tom Gibson, a shipwright at the dockyard. Mrs Dickens
instructed her son in much more refined items, such as Dr
Watts's highly moral poem "Tis the Voice of the Sluggard'
which was not, understandably enough, quite such a favourite
with the Mitre's customers as livelier numbers. Sometimes
Fanny performed as well. The pretty little girl had always
shown a talent for music, and she and Charles would sing duets
together, quite charmingly, very often songs of the sea such as
'Long Time I've courted you, Miss'. There were other per-
formers at the Mitre, of course; music was as important as
liquor in that highly respectable tavern. Elizabeth Dickens was
often persuaded to accompany her husband to one of the
musical evenings, though her instinct warned her that more
would go out of John's pocket and into Mr Tribe's till than
they could possibly afford. It was she who counted the pennies,
she who saw the resentment on the faces of unpaid tradesmen,

she who bore child after child, each one an added drain on the family resources. She came of a better family than her husband, her father having been Head of the Moneys Section in the Navy Pay Office; he had caused a terrible scandal by embezzling almost £6,000 and escaping overseas with it. She had felt that disgrace deeply, as she felt John's extravagance. But he was her husband, he adored her and said so often, and she could never resist him or reproach him for his extravagance.

They were going to the Mitre. Elizabeth stood in front of the long mirror, arranging a shawl of Indian silk around her shoulders. Her dress was low-cut, revealing pretty white shoulders and a long slender neck with a necklet of tiny pearls and turquoises round it. That had seen the inside of the pawnshop, too, in its time. Her waist was still slender after ten years of childbearing, her hair clustered in luxuriant ringlets about her heart-shaped, almost colourless face. Twenty-nine years old, nearly middle-aged, she thought. And haggard; not just thin, haggard.

John came up behind her and kissed the nape of her neck, his arms round her shoulders.

'How pale and beautiful you are, my Moon.'

'Pale, indeed.'

'And beautiful.'

She gave a short, bitter laugh. 'Kind of you, my dear, to overlook the wear and tear.'

'Wear and tear? I'm not aware of the wear and tear. Yet life goes on, my dear, and family life has its strains for both of us. Things become more expensive. Salaries lag behind. Tradesmen gather like vultures overhead.' He assessed an imaginary flock of predators hovering somewhere above the four-poster. 'Away, all you vultures! All you black birds of prey, keep away from the Dickens family or we shall blast off your feathers with the radiance of our joys!'

Elizabeth turned and laid her head against his shoulder. 'Oh, John, John!'

There was a little group of musicians playing at the Mitre that night, and a very large lady soprano warbling an Italian song. John Dickens applauded her warmly and heaved a theatrical sigh.

'Ah, Naples, Naples! How I blame myself that we have never seen Naples together, my love.'

His wife smiled and pressed his hand. 'I forgive you.'

'Of course you do, Angel of Light. But can I ever forgive myself?'

'Saw Naples myself once,' Mr Tribe said, drawing on his pipe, 'on a packet steamer. It was very misty – smelt bad. Bessie! Another jug of punch, and make sure it's well spiced.'

John beamed. 'Tribe, your generosity is beyond reproach.'

'Nothing to my pleasure in your company, Mr and Mrs D. Your health, coupled with that of our late great patron Lord Horatio Nelson.' Mr Tribe raised his glass towards a bench. Nelson had used the Mitre as his headquarters when at Chatham, and the room he had occupied was known proudly as Nelson's Cabin. 'He sat in that very place, Mr D. Lord Nelson his very self sat there.' All the company turned reverent eyes towards the spot.

Next day, at his desk in the Navy Pay Office of the Dock-yard, John was regaling two younger clerks with Neapolitan reminiscences which the previous evening had aroused in him.

'Oh yes, indeed, my dear chaps. I would give my eyes rather than have missed the sight of Naples Bay in that unbelievable sunset.'

They were credulous young fellows. It said much for John Dickens's charm that they were still wide-eyed at his tales. 'You really are a travelled man, Mr D,' commented the elder.

'Special courier for Lord Nelson, you says you was, Mr Dickens?' queried the other.

John shook his head sagely, 'Don't ask me to be too specific and all that, my dear boy, I beg of you. Even at this distance in time the matter is of the utmost secrecy. I was a mere boy, of course.' He would need to have been, as the year he was recalling was 1798, when he would have been exactly twelve.

'Secret business, was it, Mr D?'

John sighed sentimentally. 'The most secret. A matter of the heart.'

The younger clerk clapped hand to head. 'Of course! Sir

15

William Hamilton was Ambassador to Naples.'

John waved him away. 'Please. I beg of you, say no more.'

'And Lady Hamilton – the infamous Emma.'

John was genuinely indignant. 'Sir, don't speak that name in such a manner!'

The elder clerk sniggered. 'I say, what a lark, carrying letters from Lord Nelson to you-know-who. Well, Mr Dickens, you certainly are a dark horse.'

Modestly the dark horse replied, 'What can I say? A simple matter of duty. I did what I had to do. Danger of no account. Reward, a lock of the lady's hair.'

The younger clerk's brow furrowed. 'Hold on now. Who gave you the lock?'

John laid his finger alongside his nose, in the manner popularised by Mr Grimaldi when wishing to convey a matter of great intimacy to his audience. It would have taken a fair degree of even his imagination to supply the answer, for the nearest he had ever come to Lady Hamilton was to be employed in that same office, as they were themselves, with her cousin by marriage Frederick Newcombe, who had been a ship's purser at Trafalgar. He was a quiet man, stand-offish with juniors, and had said nothing to anybody in the office about his wife's cousin since her sad death in poverty at Calais, some five years before. He and Sarah had been good to her after Nelson's death, had entertained her and the little Horatia and had ordered in oysters for her; but by 1820 she had ceased to be news. Only to the expansive John Dickens, over a drink, would he sometimes talk of His Lordship and of the unquenchable charm of Her Ladyship. On this foundation the romantic John had built up a whole past for himself, and had infected his son Charles with a delight in all things smacking of the sea and ships, pointing out to him the very dock in which *Victory* had been built.

His 'memories' of Naples would have continued indefinitely if, at that moment, the door had not opened. A sombre-suited, sharp-faced man stood in the doorway. Behind him were three others, all grim of expression. The first man carried a paper, which he flourished as he entered.

16

'Yes, sir?' said the elder clerk.

'I've business with Mr Dickens.'

John was puzzled. 'Do I know you, sir?'

A sour smile crossed the man's face. 'Hardly, sir. But your domestic, Miss Mary Weller, knows me well. And you, sir, should know well enough, for you stand there, it seems to me, with some excellent meat on you.'

'I fail to get your trend sir. Am I to understand . . .'

'I'm your butcher, sir, and I want me bill for these last five months paid, sir. And so does me colleagues want theirs paid.'

The two clerks, embarrassed, pretended to scribble in their ledgers, while listening to every word. John Dickens's face was a study in helplessness.

'There must be some mistake,' he said. 'No doubt you have the wrong Dickens. We're a large family. Why not? Excellent thing. Can lead to misunderstandings, though.'

The butcher flourished the paper under his nose. 'This 'ere, sir, is a Deed, sir, what me and my colleagues has drawn, totally accounting all what's owed to us for domestic comestibles and etceteras of various kinds. We have to ask you, sir, to pay somewhat on account and after that something by the week. And meanwhile, sir, our services will be suspended.'

John flushed angrily. 'Insufferable! Unspeakable!'

He found the Deed being shoved into his hand. 'This 'ere Deed puts it all down very clear, sir. I think you will agree, Mr Dickens, it's better than a wind-up petition in bankruptcy. Good-day to you, sir.'

When they had gone John sat staring in front of him, blank-eyed. The scribbling clerks heard him muttering to himself.

'Some terrible mistake. Easily explained. No need for concern . . .'

Charles was sitting up in bed, Fanny in her nightdress perched on the end of it. Mary Weller was telling them a bedtime story. It was not a nice story, for Mary had a fertile imagination running towards ghoulishness, and liked nothing better than embroidering a simple enough sailor's yarn with grisly detail. Tonight it was about a ship's carpenter known as

Chips, who had offered his soul to the Devil.

'"How much will you give me for it?" says Chips. "I don't know," says the Devil. "For a soul in that kind of condition I'd give an iron pot and a bushel of tenpenny nails." "Add half a ton of copper and it's yours," says Chips. "I will do better than that," says the Devil. "I will throw in a rat that speaks." Says Chips, "I'll have no rat."'

Charles's eyes were wide and apprehensive, to Mary's gratification. She loved the boy, and all the children, and would have defended them with her life, but she simply could not resist making their flesh creep.

'But the Devil with his big eyes squinting and shooting out sparks of blue fire through his eyelashes, which were clanking together like iron pokers, says to Chips that he can't have the rest without the rat. So Chips gives way and takes it. And never afterwards could he get rid of it. He tried to kill it but it wouldn't die. He poured boiling pitch over it, but it liked the pitch. And soon it was joined by other rats that filled up Chips's pockets and got into his hat and into the sleeves of his coat, and they would all speak to one another and Chips could understand what they said and it was horrible.'

'What did they say?' Charles whispered.

'Rat talk.'

'What is rat talk?'

Mary made a prim mouth. 'I'm not repeating that kind of language before children.'

Charles nodded. 'I see. You don't know.'

'She does!' squeaked Fanny, huddled under the bedclothes.

'Anyway,' Mary continued, warming to her subject, 'they go into his bed. And into his teapot and into his boots.'

'Ugh!' Fanny shuddered. Charles had turned white. He could feel the rats among his own bedclothes, crawling over him, nipping him with long yellow teeth, chattering together in their horrible language. He wanted Mary to stop, yet a dreadful fascination kept him listening to her.

'And Chips was going to be married to the corn-chandler's daughter, and he give her a workbox for a present, and what happens but that a rat jumps out of it. And when he puts his arm around her waist a rat clung with him. So that was that and the marriage was broke off and Chips was broken-hearted and was pressed for a sailor. But the rats followed him and ate the planks and the ship sank and the crew drowned and was eaten, all except Chips who floated to shore with a huge great overgrown monster of a rat sitting on his chest and laughing.'

'That's horrible,' Fanny said. But Charles was too terrified to admit how awful it was to him. He had read plenty of stories, books by the dozen that were stored in the little room next to his; exciting adventures about swashbuckling heroes like Peregrine Pickle, Roderick Random, Tom Jones, and Robinson Crusoe. But none of them had ever got mixed up with devilish talking rats, not even in the often bloodthirsty tales of the Arabian Nights. That night he dreamed of the Mask, the hideous blank-eyed Mask on the Christmas Tree, and he woke, screaming and shaking.

John and Elizabeth Dickens sat up far into the night. It was not in John's nature to be daunted by circumstances. He showed Elizabeth the letter he had written to the Marquis of Crewe, that great nobleman for whom John's parents had been housekeeper and butler, and whose influence had got John into the Navy Pay Office. The domestic service relationship had been quietly played down in that erudite, suave, appealing letter, begging His Lordship to use his great charity, wisdom, and understanding once again on behalf of the Dickens family, this time to get John's ailing wife and children transferred to London. It was a letter few would be able to resist, John thought, though, as Elizabeth pointed out, it might very well occur to Lord Crewe that the air of London was considerably less salubrious than that of Chatham. John waved the objection aside, and his wife burst into tears.

'We have been so happy here, John.'

John, soon weeping with her, recalled jolly trips on the Medway in the Navy yacht with his eager son; recalled marathon walks with that eager small boy in the beautiful Kentish countryside, among the quiet lanes of the Isle of

Grain, flat and staid as Holland, between the flourishing hop-fields, over Rochester Bridge and up the hilly road to Gravesend, towards the place where Shakespeare had set that hilarious night-piece of the encounter between Falstaff and the rogues in buckram. They had talked as they walked (or rather John had talked and Charles had listened) of John's own rise to prosperity, of the two hundred sovereigns a year which was now his official remuneration, of the importance of a hopeful and open-hearted approach to life and fortune.

As they reached the top of Gad's Hill John had said, 'I see no reason why a young fellow of your abilities, Charles, should not, if he were to be very persevering and to work very hard – which is no very great difficulty for one of our breed – well, then, sir, he might, some day in the reign of our blessed and benevolent monarch come to live in even such a glorious pile as *this*, sir.'

They were looking at Gad's Hill Place. To the inhabitants of The Brook, Chatham, it appeared a mansion, but in fact it was a plainish square-faced house of red brick, dating from somewhere in the 1770s, set in good gardens with some fine cedar-trees and a handsome pillared portico. Charles looked on it and fell in love with it. He needed no persuading that one day he might live in it. There could be nowhere better to live. How happy they had been, ebullient father and lively son, on that walk to Gravesend. And it must all finish. They were going to London.

Lord Crewe had been most obliging. John Dickens was given a transfer to Somerset House, the London headquarters of the Navy Pay Office. To help pay the expenses of the removal John had taken Charles up to London to beguile his godfather, Christopher Huffam, rigger and block-maker at Limehouse Hole, with a brilliant display of his talents. Huffam was known to be 'a warm man'. But Charles's gallant rendering of 'The cats'-meat man', rounded off by a hornpipe, extracted only two sovereigns to ease John's 'purely temporary pecuniary embarrassment' plus a half-crown tip for Charles.

There had, of course, to be a celebration; just a short port of call at the Mitre, where the purchase of a bottle of wine took care of one of the sovereigns. Merrily dancing into his house in due course, John was greeted by the daunting spectacle of a grave man of law, calling to request the balance of payments in a certain Deed.

'You are some thirty-two shillings in arrears on your weekly payments. What of that, sir?'

'What of that, indeed, sir?' brightly retorted John. He flung down the remaining sovereign and a few coins on the table, with the gesture of one dispensing largesse to the multitude. 'I say to you, sir, take your thirty-two pieces of silver and leave my house forthwith.'

Taken aback, the legal gentleman did so.

''Twas a famous victory, guv'nor,' said Charles afterwards in the nursery, where he had expected to find his father full of exultation; but John was gloomy-faced, playing idly with a cardboard toy theatre.

''Twas,' replied his father. But there was no victory in his voice or his look.

'We shall do well in London.'

'We shall.'

'Let me just say two words, sir. *Somerset House.*'

'Somerset House it is indeed, my boy. At one hundred and eighty-six pounds per annum.'

'But that's less than here.'

John Dickens was musing. 'Earnings one pound – expenditure nineteen and sixpence – result happiness. Earnings one pound – expenditure one pound and sixpence – result misery.'

'Don't worry, guv'nor,' Charles said gently. 'We can always sing to the people and they will clap and give us lots of money.'

John looked at his son, his eyes beginning to well with tears.

'Was ever a man . . .' He choked and started to sob. 'Was ever a man more blessed?'

Charles stared at him, puzzled and distressed. John put his arms round him and wept unashamedly.

'Oh, my poor boy,' he sobbed. 'My poor, lovely, clever, bright, untarnishable, tragical, comical boy – what's to happen to us?'

His face was like a mask; a mask of blank misery.

CHAPTER THREE

Charles was home. At least, he was in a place which would have to be called home in future, because his family was there. 16 Bayham Street, Camden Town, north London, was a small terraced house, fairly recently built, in one of the areas where speculative builders were rapidly turning rural Middlesex into town. There were still fields and gardens, but they were not the fields and gardens of Kent. Hens pecked and clucked in the gutters, dirty bare-foot children played in the street, gawping as the obviously superior Dickens family went in and out of their new abode.

Charles looked round the small back garret which he would have to share with his little brothers. There were six Dickens children by now; the Chatham house had been a squeeze, but this one would be worse. It was a come-down, and young Charles's proud spirit did not like come-downs. His lip trembled. It would have been a luxury to give way to tears if he could have indulged in them alone, but in this house it would be impossible to be alone for long. Downstairs he could hear the younger children babbling away, with Fanny's voice trying to quell them. At least *she* would be able to get away from it: she had been accepted as a pupil at the Royal Academy of Music.

The door burst open, and John Dickens stood there, his arms wide, his genial face beaming.

'Charles! Charles!'

'Governor!' They rushed into an embrace, then shook hands. John held his son away from him.

'How *are* you, my boy? You look a little pale. Long tiresome journey, I expect.'

'Nothing much to bother about, Governor.' In fact, there

had been a good deal to bother about. Alone in the Chatham to London stage-coach he had sat with his feet in damp, stale-smelling straw, eating damp sandwiches and staring out at the ceaseless rain, thinking that life was sloppier than he had expected to find it. For part of the journey he had been joined by a large, grotesque-looking woman in black, who had muttered mad, resentful ramblings about her dead husband and the general rottenness of men. It was a journey he would never forget as long as he lived.

John drew his son down to sit with him on the narrow little bed, one of the relics of furniture left to them from the sell-up at Chatham, when so much had had to be sold off to satisfy the demands of the rapacious Deed.

'Trust you'll be comfortable here, sir,' he said cheerfully.

Charles swallowed. 'Very much to my taste, sir.'

'Simple chambers. Modest apartment. But peaceful. Harmonious. Just what the doctor ordered.'

'Just so, sir.'

John looked faintly relieved. 'Hear excellent things from your Chatham Scholasticum. Mr Giles very pleased with your progress. Calls you the Inimitable. Naturally, like myself you're of a studious turn of mind.'

Charles looked up at him earnestly. 'I've been thinking about schools here, sir. I mean, the London schools must be very worthy.'

'Oh, they are, they are. We'll come to that in time.' Obviously this was not the time. 'But all London is a great school, Charles! Whatever a man can learn he may study in the streets of London, my boy. As the great Doctor Johnson observed, "The man who is tired of London is tired of Life".'

'I see, sir.' Charles would have much preferred his father to talk about real schools, but John was carried away by enthusiasm.

'The theatres, the bazaars, the caravanserais! My word on it, Charles, there's no other place to live.' John ruffled the boy's hair.

'Yes, sir. But wouldn't a place that offered so much tend to be a leetle on the expensive side?'

'Possibly so, my boy,' John said and moved his hand to his waistcoat pocket, and very shrewdly observed. 'But consider the much greater field of opportunity – the streets paved with gold, the fortunes made daily. No, my boy, we were right to leave that petty Kentish village. Here's scope for great souls.' John turned towards the door. 'Cheer up, my lad. Hearts of oak, my boy. Something entirely unimaginable is likely to turn up every second of the day in this city of delights.'

'I expect it is, sir.' But the first cloud that had fallen on Charles's life was darkening the optimism his father had always instilled into him, and something unseen was telling him that whatever turned up was likely to be unimaginable in a sense not meant by his father. With relief, he turned to un-packing his small travelling bag and his parcel of books, his dear companions, the food of his imagination.

Dinner that evening was rabbit stew, cooked in a pot over the small fire-grate in the back half of the living-room. It was not a complicated dish, but it seemed to be giving more trouble than the most sophisticated meal likely to be prepared by an army of chefs at the best of London's hotels. Mrs Dickens, in a peignoir with floating ribbons which caught in everything and had already absorbed a fair portion of stew, was struggling to stir the mixture, hindered by a crowd of offspring who clung around her, refusing to be herded by Fanny into their seats round the table. Steam filled the room, onion-flavoured steam which created an atmosphere like wash-day. Mrs Dickens scolded, the children fought for precedence of place, and the Orfling scurried to and fro, threatened with scalding from an overturned dish, so small was she. This was not Jane Bonny, the Orfling of Chatham. She had gone to Ireland with Mrs Lamert, James's mother, as her maid. A new Orfling had been engaged for the London home, a child from the Foundling Hospital, stunted of growth and old-young of face, un-naturally knowing. Charles, in his new sensitiveness, felt a simultaneous revulsion for her and sympathy towards her; just as he felt a warm love for his mother, his sisters and brothers, and a fastidious horror at the scene of chaos before him.

His father appeared not to notice it, as he sat at the table, his napkin tucked into his collar.

'Good to be back in the bosom of the family, eh, Charles ?'

It was the Orfling who introduced Charles to those streets of London which, his father had said, were paved with gold. With the Orfling as his guide, Charles trailed for miles on countless errands. The paving-stones and cobbles between Camden Town and the Borough, over London Bridge, where cheap food was to be had, seemed, depending on the weather, largely to be covered with gritty dust or slimy mud, rotten cabbage-leaves, small flattened animals and pigeons run over by cart-wheels, and ordure. It was something of a revelation, as was the revelation of his family's poverty.

As they tramped over the Bridge, into the Borough High Street with its ancient galleried inns, the Orfling told him, 'We gets our bread no more 'an a day old at half price, 'ere. Then we gets our bit o' meat of a Friday, 'cos they slaughters on the Tuesday, and what they've still got left by Sat'dy, if it ain't gone in the pickle-barrel, stinks like I don't know what, so you gets your bit o' meat for a bargain. See ? Now, as to your few greens and that, you picks 'em up for nuffin' around by the greenery stalls and wiv a bit of luck you'll get a spud or turnip or what's over frown in.'

It was degrading, it was dirty, but it was undoubtedly instructive. Sitting on a pile of sacks in a corner, eating scraps with the Orfling, Charles frowned and said, 'I don't see the necessity for such excessive care.'

The Orfling snorted. 'Necessity indeed! The necessity is, we got moufs to feed, Master Charles, and precious little of the jingling stuff to do it wiv.'

'But my father has an important position in Somerset House, which, you know, is the heart of our great Navy.'

'So 'e 'as. Granted. But what he also 'as is the little matter of the Deed.'

'That foul Deed. It persecutes us everywhere.'

Gloomily he shared an apple with her. 'The thing is, Orfling, I am losing valuable scholastic time. You see, if I got on with my education, I should soon be able to settle the little matter of the Deed. After all, it's a mere matter of money, to the golden gate of which education is the key.'

She threw him a gap-toothed grin of admiration. 'You do talk nice, Master Charles. But it's all a lot of rot for all that, 'cos we need bread today. We can't feed the nippers on jam tomorrow, Master Charles.'

'I take your point, Orfling dear . . .'

Suddenly she flared up. 'Oh, drop it, Master Charles, drop it!'

He stared. 'What's the matter?'

'Nuffin.'

'Really, my dear Orfling . . .'

'If you *must* know, Master Charles,' she almost spat at him, 'it don't relish a person to be called Orfling all the time. Orfling, Orfling!' She threw up her hands and jumped down from the sacking.

It had never occurred to him. Perhaps the Chatham Orfling had felt so. 'I suppose not,' he said, slowly, climbing down. 'I never thought about it.'

'Well, fink about it, then.'

'All right. What is your name?' There was no answer.

'What is it, for goodness sake? What shall I call you? Miss Crumbs? Henrietta Apple, Lady Bluenose? What?'

She jerked round to face him. 'If you must know – I don't 'ave a bloody name.'

'Exactly why we called you Orfling.'

She began to cry. 'I may be an Orfling but I got me rights to 'aving a proper name like uvver coves do.'

'Why not, indeed? Perhaps you would like to pick a name for yourself?'

Delight shone through the tears on her grubby face. 'Oh, can I, Master Charles?'

'Certainly you can. What shall it be? Angela or Sophronia or Faustina or Julia?'

'Too stuck up.'

'Well, Betty or Molly or Lily or Polly?'

'Soppy girls' names.'

He shrugged. 'All right then. You choose.'

'Well . . . my werry favourite name is Charles.'

'You can't be Charles. I'm Charles. It's a man's name.'

'All right, then,' she said furiously. 'Sam!'

'*Sam*?'

'Well – can I?'

Charles smiled. 'Of course you can – it's a perfect name for you.'

'Perfeck. Sam will do werry well. Come on. If we get to the pie shop just before she closes you gets two meat pies for a penny. Uvverwise, you see, the old 'ore chucks 'em away. Come on – just follow Sam!'

He was reading in bed that night, by the light of a shaded candle so as not to disturb the slumbers of his small brothers, when the door creaked stealthily open and a shadowy figure appeared in the room. He sat up, startled and trembling, his head full of ghostly legends.

'Who is it?' But it was only the Orfling, a tiny form in a shabby flannel nightdress. She fiddled with the frill of one cuff.

'I – just wanted to say sumfin, Master Charles . . .'

'Well? What?'

'Well, Master Charles, you don't need to go telling one and all anyfink.'

He was now thoroughly irritated. 'All what anyfink, for goodness sake?'

''Bout my bein' Sam, a-course, for goodness sake!' Angry at his incomprehension of what seemed to her a perfectly reasonable request to keep their mutual secret, she turned and stamped out. Young Fred stirred in his sleep but subsided. Charles stared at the spot where 'Sam' had stood, and shook his head. 'Women!'

There was a crisis at Bayham Street. John Dickens arrived home one night to find his wife pale-faced and shaking, comforted by young James Lamert (who, as if the house were not crowded enough already, had moved in with them as lodger). They told John, and the awed, eavesdropping Charles, of the visit of a grim-visaged, threatening Scotsman, called

27

Kerr, or, as Elizabeth preferred to call him, Cur, who now held the dreaded Deed and was demanding payment of no less than forty pounds.

John, shocked but trying to maintain his carefree stand, waved his hand casually to the air. 'Forty pounds – four hundred – forty thousand – what is it to me?'

Elizabeth saw, behind him, the wide, frightened eyes of her eldest son. 'To bed, Charles,' she ordered.

He left, obediently, but went no farther than the lobby outside the parlour-door. The door was thin, shoddily-made; he could hear every word that was being said within.

'The time has come for us to face the truth, John.'

'Never!'

'Elizabeth is right, John. This Kerr is no petty Chatham tradesman.'

'James and I have been talking things over while waiting for you to return.'

'I hope you won't resent it, John,' said James apologetically, 'but I feel it for the best.'

Charles heard the squeak of a chair as his father subsided into it. 'Carry on, carry on,' he said feebly. 'I am in your hands.'

'I shall take up gainful employment myself...' began Elizabeth.

'Never, I say!'

She went on implacably, '... and Charles also shall help.'

'Never, I say, never, never, never!' This time his father's voice was even more vehement; but Charles, his ear pressed to the door, felt his heart turn to lead.

The gainful employment which Elizabeth Dickens proposed to take up was the management of a school for young ladies. It was a pity, as she said, for her to waste her unusually good education (which included Latin as well as the usual female accomplishments, painting on velvet, playing the pianoforte, and familiarity with the use of the globes, a polite sobriquet for geography) and there must be plenty of parents in need of genteel schooling for their daughters. Cousin Huffam had an excellent Indian connection, with his seafaring acquaintances, and people in the East Indies always sent their children to boarding establishments in England. The Dickens family fired each other with enthusiasm. They were to take a larger house, a six-roomed one in Gower Street North. It would cost fifty pounds a year to rent, in addition to the twenty-three pounds they were paying for one in Bayham Street; but Providence, in the shape of Christopher Huffam, came to their aid with the required money.

'We'll have a salon to launch the establishment,' declared John. 'Ask everybody. Announce the grand opening to the entire world. I shall publish a circular. *You* shall deliver it all over London, Charles.'

Charles's face fell. 'But won't I be in the establishment, Governor?'

'Tush and pish, my boy! I don't flatter myself by saying that I have already educated you far beyond the resources of any dame-school, even one conducted by so unusually highly educated a lady as Mrs Dickens.'

'But Father, any school would be better than none, if I could just be taught something, somewhere . . .'

His father was not listening. 'You have great things before you, Charles. Never belittle yourself, my boy.' He indicated the map he had just hung on the wall of the new schoolroom. 'There's the world. It's yours. Take it firmly in your grasp. Will you do that for me, Charles?'

'But . . .'

'But me no buts! Look at me. Do I allow a slight deficiency of formal academic education to hold me back? No, I do not. Our good James here, does he propose wasting his life waiting for an army commission to turn up? He does not, do you, James?'

James shrugged. 'No good waiting around for ever, Charles. Best take the bull by the horns.'

'Exactly,' John broke in. 'And James has done so, and become director of an important commercial enterprise.'

'Hold on, Mr D,' said James. 'I'll only be the manager.' James, who had passed at Sandhurst and whose ambition was to serve as an officer, had decided to fill in the waiting-time by going into business with his cousin George, who had put some capital into the blacking-factory run by Jonathan Warren, at 30 Hungerford Stairs, a tumbledown old building once a merchant's house, almost on the shore of the Thames at Charing Cross. A quaint rivalry existed between Jonathan Warren and a relative, Robert Warren, who also made blacking, a product much in demand for the shining of boots. The Lamert capital was to make Jonathan's variety of blacking pre-eminent, by widespread advertisement.

James talked privately to Charles, in the bookshop in the Hampstead Road where they had been buying, for a penny each, books for the library of Mrs Dickens's Establishment.

'At least,' Charles said, a bundle of shabby volumes under his arm, 'I shall have plenty to read in Mother's school.'

'Come, Charles. That's hardly a manly attitude in the circumstances. You must realise the Deed is still over your father. And now, of course, there'll be the extra debt to Mr Huffam.'

'But Father says Mother's establishment can't fail to make a great deal of money.'

'And I dare say he's right. In the meantime, would you not feel more satisfied to be bringing in a salary to the family treasury than to be a charge upon it?'

'But how?'

'As the rest of us do, dear boy. By taking a job.'

'My education isn't finished. How will I succeed if I'm only half finished?'

'A position with expectations is no bad thing, Charles.'

The boy's face flushed with emotion and his voice shook. 'But I want to write. I've written some small things already – plays for the toy theatre, and some stories – and I wish to go on, Cousin James, truly I do. So I must read more and more, mustn't I?'

James temporised. 'A salaried position will hardly prevent you from writing or learning, Charles.' He saw, apprehensively, Charles's anger, the violent emotion which shook his frail body, as he burst out, 'Damn it! Fanny's at school, and everybody is thoroughly pleased about it. Fanny's doing so well. Fanny's reading of the tonic-sol-fa is excellent. Why must it be only Fanny?'

James was not enjoying himself, but he was committed to try to persuade his cousin. 'Shame, Charles!' he forced himself to say. 'You surely won't be so girlish about this matter? A girl needs a little polish on her to attract a good marriage. But in a man's world a man must work – or so I've always been led to believe.'

'A *man* of only twelve? It is so damnably unfair.'

'I hope you'll watch your language at home.'

'Damn, damn and damn it to hell!' was the furious reply.

James sought about for inspiration. 'Perhaps you could write advertisements for Warren's. Robert, that's the rival Warren, has been advertising on a mighty scale with his little verses. Remember? "Warren's Blacking is the best; You can just forget the rest".'

'I've seen that in the newspapers. I thought it rather silly,' replied Charles loftily.

'Effective, though. And Charles, you could be earning six shillings a week – perhaps seven. Not a bad start for a young fellow of initiative.'

'No doubt. But quite the wrong position for me.' Charles clutched the bundle of books tighter.

Warren's Blacking. Warren's Blacking. Warren's Blacking. It went through and through his head like an ominous litany. It was there, in front of him, on the label of the bottle from which he was blacking his father's boots: that was the sort of menial job he was reduced to in the house at Bayham Street. They would not be there much longer, the Orfling was saying, from her place at the sink, scouring dishes. They'd all be up at Gower Street, pigging in with Mrs D's Establishment.

Charles was not listening. The smell of the blacking was a sickly stench in his nostrils. A sharp pain kept coming and going in his side and his vision was blurred; he was seeing huge, apparently endless rows of blacking-bottles, floating and dipping on a shelf. There was a picture on them, a trade-picture of a gleaming black top-boot and a cat, fur and tail

31

bristling with fright, spitting with anger at its own reflection in the boot's surface. Long years after, when the boy was a grown man and a famous author, the very image of that cat would appear, by his order, in an illustration to the most gruesome episode in all his novels, the horrible death by spontaneous combustion of Mr Krook, the rag-and-bone dealer. No detail of this traumatic twelfth year of his life was ever to vanish from the mind of Charles Dickens.

The pain grew worse, and as the Orfling cried out with alarm, he keeled over in a faint.

He was very ill. He lay in the garret-room, muttering in a high fever with the complaint which was to afflict him again and again. Visions flitted before him, nightmare shapes all in black: James Lamert's face, pitch-black, proclaiming the virtues of Warren's products, his father's face, black too, singing,

> Warren's jet blacking,
> The pride of mankind,
> Give it a try
> And your death you will find.

And somebody – who was it? – added,

> Warren's blacking is the best,
> You can just forget the rest!

But it was certainly his father, whose face was now a black, grinning mask, who amended this to,

> Warren's blacking is the worst,
> Blacks your heart and makes it burst!

'Call me Sam! Sam! Sam!' demanded a ghostly, black-faced Orfling, a miniature Sambo from a negro show. But the masks of his mother and Fanny, leering down at him, were stark clown-white, with coarse red lips like the gibbering woman in the Chatham coach, and they were cackling and singing,

> Do, re, me, fa, sol,
> La is lacking,
> You must go to Warren's Blacking!

'The Mask! the Mask!' shrieked Charles, and pulled the bedclothes over his head.

The Dickens family had moved to 4 Gower Street. There was plenty of room, for no young ladies had turned up at Mrs Dickens's Boarding Establishment for Young Ladies. The brass plate outside, so proudly put up, had been taken down. The books, the Latin and Greek primers, the histories bought for a penny each, had gone back to the bookseller to be resold. Worst of all, Charles's own books had gone too, all the old friends: *Peregrine Pickle*, *Roderick Random*, *Tom Jones*, *The Arabian Nights*, once so proudly housed on the little chiffonier which his father had called The Library. It was like taking pet lambs to the butcher's.

'Not much to this lot,' said the never-quite-sober bookseller of the Hampstead Road. 'Say two shilling'.'

'Ridiculous!'

'Good, are they?'

'First rate.' Charles eyed them like Agamemnon watching Iphigenia being led off to the sacrificial altar.

'Don't have much time for readin' myself. I might go three shillin', but only on your say-so mind.'

Charles sighed. 'All right. All but one.' He pocketed it, eyed suspiciously by the bookseller.

'Hold on, now, what was that? What was it called?'

'*Tales of the Genie*.'

'Girls' stories, I suppose. Can't be much.' A shaking hand tossed three shillings on to the table. The bookseller's wife's voice came from somewhere at the back of the shop.

'If that ain't the boy with the shirt cloth, what boy is it?'

The bookseller took a pull at his pocket flask.

'Just a boy, m'dear. Just a ordinary 'uman boy.'

Mr Kerr, that most fearsome of all the Genies ever mistakenly summoned from a magic jar, had visited Gower Street and thundered fire and brimstone at the improvident family of Dickens. Even he was not entirely proof against the airy declaration by John, made in the strictest confidence, that the family of the late Lord Nelson had approached him to act in

33

their behalf in the matter of a legacy relating to the late Viscount's Will. The question of the famous Bequest to the Nation of Lady Hamilton and her daughter Horatia was still a talking-point, wrapped in mystery. Mr Kerr wondered, just briefly, whether this specious, well-spoken debtor might not, after all, be concerned in it. The present Earl Nelson, His late Lordship's brother, was known to be a touchy character. Strange agents might be employed – even as strange as John Dickens.

'And do you tell me that all this farrago of matters will produce me an early payment?'

'A complete settlement, sir.'

Mr Kerr frowned and jammed his tall hat over his brows.

'Very well, Mr Dickens. I tell you once again, that time is running out for you. But as a Christian man I will give you yet one more opportunity to make good your word.'

He departed, amid cheers from the whole family, led by their father, who, when the door had closed on their awesome visitor, burst into invective against that Glaswegian Monster, and in the midst of his transports of ire went sprawling on the floor as one of the chair-legs collapsed under him. The smaller children laughed, Mrs Dickens wrung her hands, Charles ran to help him, and John Dickens lay weeping and humiliated on the ground.

That evening, restored to his usual spirits by a temporary loan from an office colleague, John was met by Charles as usual at the portals of Somerset House. It was an evening ritual they both enjoyed.

'Will you do me the honour of walking with me, sir?' formally enquired the father.

'I will, sir,' replied the son with a smile.

'Ah, walking, Charles! Walking is a great joy and blessing. It exercises the physique as nothing else does. It trains the eye to observe the world. And it costs nothing. Shall you remember that, sir?'

'I shall, sir.' They set off westwards down the Strand, the large figure and the small, at an equally brisk pace.

'Where shall we make for, Charles?'

'Hungerford Stairs, sir?'

John's dark eyebrows rose. 'Hungerford Stairs? A low area, Charles, but a slice of life. Lay on!'

The place they reached within a few minutes, beyond Charing Cross was indeed a low area. Night was drawing on. A lamp-lighter applied his torch to a gas-lamp which showed them the street-litter on the slippery cobbles; groups of poverty-stricken people huddled here and there for no evident purpose. The surrounding tenements had once been good dwellings. Between two high buildings a flight of stairs led darkly down to the ill-smelling river. Not far away a sewer discharged its contents. As the father and son, respectable enough figures, started off down Hungerford Stairs, a jeer came from one of the men idling on a corner. John Dickens shivered.

'Come, Charles, let's away to a friendly hostelry for a pie and a pint of porter. This is a depressed and depressing place.'

'Tell me, Father,' Charles asked earnestly, 'why does our blessed and benevolent monarch permit it?'

'Our B. and B.M. is no autocrat, my boy,' John said. 'We English will not brook a tyrant who tells us to live this way or that. We insist on a free choice.'

Charles looked back through the dusk at the jeering man pulling on a clay pipe and then spitting into the gutter, while his wife held a wizened baby to her breast under her filthy shawl.

'Do you say, sir, that these people *choose* to be poor?'

'No sir. They choose to be vicious, and thus become poor.'

'But surely, sir, not all the poor are vicious?'

'No, my boy. Some are merely weak.'

'Then what are we, sir?'

John stared down, truly amazed, into the enquiring face of his son. 'We? My dear boy, *we* do not belong to the "poor". A Dickens could *never* be such a thing!'

Picking their way down the dirty crumbling steps John's tone changed. 'Well, here's your precious Hungerford Stairs. A miserable, unsuitable place, and I can't think why you've insisted on walking us so far out of our natural terrain.'

Just visible by the faint gas-light was a sign chalked on the pavement: WARREN'S BLACKING IS BEST. 'Of course!' exclaimed John. 'Cousin Lamert's enterprise is in this vicinity, is it not?' He had known it was, of course, but his gift for banishing disagreeable facts from his mind had kept him from realising earlier where Charles was leading him. Disgust, shock, and shame filled him. He would have liked to stop his ears as he heard Charles saying, 'Cousin Lamert was good enough to suggest that there might be a position for me at Warren's. And I must conclude the business arrangements.'

'My dear boy...' For once his father was at a loss for adequate words. 'It was suggested – but at no time did such a course seem necessary to me...'

'But do you not think, sir, that man could rise from such a position to become a captain of industry? I believe the position pays six or even seven shillings a week. And, of course, that's only a start.'

John stared down the length of the stairs to the half-visible beach. A smell of rot and washed-up sewage rose to meet him. There was a stinging behind his eyes and an obstruction in his throat.

'Yes, indeed. I believe some such figure was mentioned. But, my boy, it is not what I would have wanted for you.'

'Nor I, sir,' said Charles quietly. 'But since, apparently, there is to be no other school for me. I had best help to keep us in our present station in life.' He began to walk down the stairs, leaving John standing half-way down. John's voice followed him.

'I'm sure it can be avoided! I'm sure something will, at any moment, turn up! Charles, my boy! I'm sure...'

But Charles was gone, a very small figure merging with the darkness below.

CHAPTER FOUR

He was sitting in an alcove on the counting-house floor of Warren's Blacking Factory. 'Nice view. Window all to yourself', he had been assured by the factory's foreman, Mr Gregory, known to the workmen as Slimy. This coveted position commanded a wide prospect of the debris-littered shore, picked over every morning by persons hoping to find something worth having among those heaps of boats abandoned as too far gone to ever take the water again. Grimy coal-barges passed by. The horribly bloated bodies of dogs and cats occasionally floated by, all four legs pointing to the sky.

The stench of decay outside was matched within the building. Between two and three hundred years old, it was riddled with dry rot, which diffused its sickly-sweet smell throughout the wainscotted, panelled rooms, once the parlours and bedrooms of comfortable London merchants. Down in the cellars rats swarmed, great grey well-fed rats whose squeaking was never still. Sometimes Charles would meet one and stand frozen with fear, Mary Weller's story about Chips the Carpenter still fresh in his mind. Suppose it were suddenly to begin to talk, in that rat-language which Weller had not been able to bring herself to repeat to the children? Suppose it were to leap upon his shoulder and cling round his neck? He dared not run past it. The only thing to do was to lay hands on something to throw at the rat. Once it was his precious *Tales of the Genie*, which he kept in his pocket as a talisman. He felt it to be tainted when he picked it up again after the rat had scuttled away.

Charles was not the smart little boy he had been. The apron he wore was stained with blacking, and his face was smudged with the stuff. The bright, eager look was gone from his face, for his heart was blackened with misery. His hands

37

were busy covering blacking-pots, first with oiled paper, then with blue paper, which was bound with a piece of string to produce a neat, unwrinkled appearance. He was being instructed in the art by a tall, big-boned boy called Bob Fagin, some years older than Charles, the son of a waterman. Of a mixed bag of men and boys in the factory below the counting-house, Fagin was one of the most amiable. He felt sorry for Charles and, unlike some of the others, respected him for his relationship to Mr Lamert.

'That's it!' he said. 'You'll get the idea soon enough. Werry good, Master Charles.'

Charles looked up wistfully. 'You couldn't call me Mr Dickens, could you? Or even Charles?'

Bob pondered. 'Spect I could. But wouldn't it be a bit off? What with fambly *being* fambly and that, and 'ow we all keeps our proper place in Warren's Blacking, the Pride of Mankind. Still, Charles let it be, mate, between ourselfs anyway!'

They shook hands on it. Bob looked round appreciatively. 'Nice place they give you 'ere, Charles.'

'Not bad, Bob. I'm to be trained for the clerical side of the business, you see. What's it like where the rest of you work?'

'Quite jolly, really. I mean, you can 'ave a bit of a laugh and joke when there's a few of you. And of course there's a better choice of wittles. If one 'as a saveloy and another 'as a meat pie and another a piece of cheese, it means all can 'ave a bit of each other's, and thus a more varied repast can be enjoyed by all. What I always say, Charles old boy, is look to your wittles and the work will look to itself.'

It was lonely, working in the counting-house with only one old clerk for company, if company it could be called, for he took not the least notice of Charles, but scratched away in his corner with his quill pen, endlessly book-keeping. Perhaps he was deaf. Perhaps he was mad. Charles made up his mind to join the others, in the factory.

In the room below – a large apartment, once the double drawing-room of the house, now a bare dirty place with a big table in the centre – half a-dozen youths, ranging in age from twelve to twenty, and in dress from shabby to ragged, were eating their dinners and engaging in horseplay. Charles had been formally introduced to them before, by Gregory, in an announcement which combined deference with sarcasm, but it was left to Bob Fagin to lead him into their midst and genially present 'Mr Charles Dickens, of the fambly of our respected management.'

There was Poll Green, Tom Sweedle, Tim Burrow, Bill Hodges, Bill Smelly, and 'Tiny' Tucker. The last two named were big, formidable, and surly. Smelly was heard to mutter that he was somethinged . . . if he would call the new recruit 'Mister.' Tucker agreed, and together they began to barrack Charles, mimicking his refined accent. He decided to leave, but Smelly was quick to intercept him at the top of the stairs.

'Don't like our company much, do you, your lordship? Not really what you're used to, I expec'. Well, you'd better know how fings get done round here. Slimy Gregory may be the bloody foreman, but when it come down to brass tacks, the gaffer 'ere on this floor is yours truly, William Smelly. Now, 'ow does that strike your lordship?'

Charles, his collar held in a vicious grip, said that he thought he saw what Smelly meant.

'See what I mean, do you? Well, that is really uncommon civil of your lordship. Now, 'ow would you like to smell this?'

A huge, dirty, ham of a fist was brandished closely in front of Charles's nose, while its opposite number prevented him from backing away.

'Ere, your lordship. Give it a good hard smell, because, mister or not, you get in its way and it'll draw off a pint of claret from your snoz before you can say "Pickens". Oright, yer lordship?'

Charles was terrified, but he found the courage to say 'The name is Dickens.' At that moment the voice of James Lamert came from above, calling 'Charles?'

'You'll be for it,' Bob Fagin threatened Smelly, 'if the young gentleman tells Mr Lamert.'

Smelly advanced his mouth to Charles's ear and muttered, 'The young gentleman ain't goin' to tell nobody nuffin'. Is 'e?'

'Nothing to tell,' said Charles, almost casually, pulling

himself away from the bully and hastening up to the counting-house.

By the time he got there he was crying and gasping with outrage. 'Villain, bloody villain!' he was saying to himself as he went towards Lamert, who viewed him with alarm.

'My dear boy, you are quite pale and shaky. Whatever is it?'

Charles bit back the tears. 'Nothing at all.'

'H'm. All rather strange here, I suppose. Well, soon get used to it. Where the devil is Gregory? In the nearest bar, I suspect. Never mind. Good day, Billings.' The old clerk neither looked up nor answered.

Charles followed James into his tiny office, the refuge he had made for himself in that evil-smelling, soulless place. It was cramped and shabby, cluttered up with old account-books and documents in which only mice and moths would ever again take any interest. But in front of the table was a comfortable old chair, and also visible were a sherry decanter, a small spirit-stove, kettle and teapot, and, most reassuring to Charles's eyes, a half-assembled toy theatre, with a heap of cardboard characters for it. It had been James Lamert who had made Charles's own beloved old theatre. They sat down together before this one, and discussed the next production, *Othello*. Mr Kean might be the Moor, Miss O'Neill Desdemona, and so forth. James tentatively voiced the suggestion that they might see a real *Othello* at Drury Lane, and he went on to discourse brightly of the great fun they would have together in London. He hated Warren's himself. For first choice he would have been an actor, for second an army officer. Well-meaning though he was, he could not comprehend what his unhappy little cousin might become, or wanted to become; but he sensed that it was he, James Lamert, who had got the child into this soul-eroding place, and he was heartily sorry for it. He patted Charles's brown hair, which no longer shone and crackled with life.

'There, there, Charles. We shall have no end of fun. You'll see.'

In one of the two upper rooms at 4 Gower Street North, all

that the Dickenses could afford to occupy, John Dickens was raving in a high style which would have given Mr Kean, as Othello, some cause for envy. Clutching alternately at a crumpled piece of paper and lumps of his own hair, he cried, 'The Deed! the Deed! the Deed!', while Elizabeth faintly restrained the youngest of her four offspring from either climbing up the chimney or falling out of the window.

'Oh, John, I cannot *abide* living so high above the street with such an over-active tribe as our dear children. Why can we not find a dear little house again?'

He flung the piece of paper on to the floor and aimed a savage kick at it. 'Because of the Deed, my dear. That is why we cannot have a dear little house.'

'But surely our present unsatisfactory and inadequate accommodation costs no more than a very little, tiny, small house in – say – Camberwell?'

'Camberwell? Why say Camberwell?'

Her voice rose sharply. 'Why not Camberwell?'

'What can Camberwell offer to compare with Mrs Dickens's Establishment in Gower Street?'

His wife's small fists were clenched white, and her drawn face flushed with rage and frustration. 'Damn Mrs Dickens's Establishment, my love! We have not had a single pupil since we opened the place.'

'And is that my fault, my dear?'

'No, it is not your fault. It is not my fault. It is the fault of no one I can name. But it is nevertheless – my love – and without one hint of criticism of yourself, a very costly and unnecessary luxury to keep a school without pupils. Is it not?'

He bowed his head. 'It is. It is.'

'Well, then. Why should we not move?'

'Move? Moving costs money, angel. Money, money!'

'But staying here costs money, too!'

And so the argument went on, until Elizabeth collapsed in tears and John stormed out, while the children watched and listened, open-mouthed.

The eldest of the sons (and he was not so very much older than the rest of them, after all) sat at his grimy window in the counting-house, staring out at the river, Charles was too lost in thought to notice the approach of the two bullies from the factory floor, Smelly and Tucker, until Smelly said 'Morning, your lordship.'

Charles spun round, to see them both touching their forelocks in mock deference.

'Don't honour us with your presence downstairs. Never come and see us since that first day, do 'e, Tiny?'

'Nah,' growled Tucker.

'Nearly a couple o' weeks his lordship's been with us, ain't it, Tiny?'

'Right.'

'Yus. And nary a good mornin' or a 'ow de do. We're a bit fed up about it, your lordship.'

Charles stammered. 'Well. I – I've been rather busy – you know – there's a good deal to learn and . . .'

Smelly mocked his accent. 'A good deal to learn! Rather busy! Truth is, we just ain't good enough for 'im, are we, your lordship? Even though you ain't making much of a job of it.' He grabbed one of Charles's neatly sealed blacking pots, ripped the label, and showed it to Tucker. 'Look at that. We got to go something to 'elp our young lordship feel 'e's one of us, Tiny. Eh?'

Before Charles could dodge he was caught in a huge arm and pinned against the wall.

'Now,' asked Smelly, 'are you going to take it off, or shall I 'ave to 'elp your lordship?'

'Take off what?' with the strength of desperation, he broke away from them and began to run, but he was cornered before he had gone more than a few steps. He struggled, but the two big lads had him down flat on the floor, stripping off his jacket, his collar, shirt, and trousers, until he was naked but for his under-drawers. They stuffed his mouth with the nauseous-smelling oiled paper used for labels.

'Very clean, ain't 'e?' said Smelly. 'Too clean for the likes of us.'

'Rather,' replied Tucker, and waved an opened blacking bottle.

'Right-o then. Dirty 'im up!'

42

Charles could not scream, could not cry out at all, as they poured the blacking over him, and rubbed it into his skin, his hair, smearing him until he looked like one of the grotesque black dolls which hung outside rag-dealers' shops as trade-signs. And all the time the old clerk, Billings, sat in his corner, scratching away at his books. It was the most degrading hour of Charles's life. It seared itself into his heart, his soul, his manhood to come. He wished he were dead.

The door was flung open and Bob Fagin was there, with two of the other boys behind him.

'You dirty brutes! Leave 'im be!' Fagin shouted. The three hurled themselves on to the bullies in a flurry of arms and legs. Smelly and Tucker swore, and hit out. As they fought, Charles spat out the oil-paper and clutched at his scattered clothes. Gasping, sobbing, he got out of the room and down the stairs, missing the sight of the punch Bob Fagin landed on Smelly's prominent nose and the gush of blood that followed.

When Charles went to James Lamert's office later that day he looked much as usual. Those whom the gods have bruised can remain outwardly untouched, if their pride is strong enough, and Charles's was very strong. But something showed, not merely the black mark on his face which had refused to come off when Bob Fagin scrubbed him under the pump. James looked at him with concern.

'What kept you, Charles? Having fun with the lads, I expect.'

Charles's reply was hardly audible. 'Yes.'

'Good. Good. Told you so. Very good. Er, look here, Charles. Got something to tell you. Now – how shall I put it? Thing is, Charles, your father, like all of us, has his problems. I'm afraid a – a little misfortune has overtaken him.'

Charles went paler than he already was. 'Oh God! The Deed?'

'Quite so, Charles. You're a bright little chap for your age. Well, then, here it is. The Deed has caught up with Mr D, and I regret to say that he's being held in the sponging-house, as it is rather unpleasantly called, and Mrs D has three days to raise the wind. A matter of some forty pounds, I believe. I . . . I only wish I were in a position to make more than a small contribution myself, but – not to put too fine a point on it – your father has been to the well more than once, and we are just at the present time a trifle dry. But count on me for a guinea or two, Charles.'

The boy sat down and began to shake. 'Oh God! Oh God!' was all he said, over and over.

He was in the small bare room in the sponging-house, comforting his father as though he were the elder of the two. John Dickens was in his lowest spirits, his head in his hands. 'Will this family of ours ever raise its head again?' he asked his son.

'It will, Governor. You have my word on it. I shall see everyone – all your old friends. And Cousin Huffam and Uncle William. I'll go to Grandmother Dickens, too.'

John's head lifted. 'Grandmother. Ah. A good thought, Charles. She is not in abundant good health, and sooner or later we must have expectations from the dear lady. Yes, your grandmother is a promising prospect, even though she has not proved herself excessively generous in the past. A wonderful woman, Charles, a great character – a trifle hard, some would say, but she has walked in the salons and drawing-rooms of the mighty of this land, and nobility is near her. Speak to her, Charles, of the shame that threatens the proud name of Dickens.'

And so Charles set out on his quest. It was fruitless. Trudging out to Limehouse, he was told by Godfather Huffam that 'John must learn his lesson the only way he will ever learn.' A gold sovereign found it way into Charles's pocket; that was all.

John's brother William, sitting in comfort in his well-furnished study, was not even good for a sovereign, merely for a lecture to Charles (as though it were all the boy's fault) concerning Aesop's Fable of the improvident grasshopper and the industrious ant.

As for Mrs Dickens Senior, that formidable and very sick old lady listened among her pillows to Charles's pathetic story, looking like the Wolf dressed up as Little Red Ridinghood's grandmother.

'John will be what he always has been – a spendthrift, happy-go-lucky, devil-may-care young jackanapes. And I hope you ain't cast in the same mould, young Charles.'

He was desperate. 'But Grandmother, what you say may be true . . .'

'May be? It *is* true, young man. I should know. Ain't I the young devil's mother?'

'Indeed you are,' the child said earnestly. 'And so you love him as we do, and when one loves one forgives many things, surely.'

In the dim light of the Oxford Street bedroom it seemed as though the old lady's gaze had grown a trifle less beady, as she heard the tears in Charles's voice and saw them start in his beautiful eyes.

'Now, Charles,' she said briskly, 'I'll have no blubbering in my bedroom. I ain't going to be put upon by John neither. But here, take this.' She fished out from under her pillow a large silver turnip watch.

'That was your grandfather's, and is to come to you in my Will, but you might as well have it now. Never part with it. It's a fine instrument.'

'Thank you, Grandmother – but we need money, and . . .'

'And I ain't a banker. Good day to you, Charles.'

The furniture began to go; what was left of it. Dreary trip after trip Charles made between the house in Gower Street and the pawnbroker's, with bundles of linen, small household articles, the brass coal-scuttle, the toasting-jack, a bird-cage whose inhabitant was long dead. Even his own little bed must go, his mother said, taking no particular regard of his expression as she said it. A barrow was borrowed from a neighbour, and on it Charles pushed the mattress on which he had lain, night after night, reading the books that, too, had gone as irrevocably as the bird from the cage.

In the wretched little room of the sponging-house, John frantically counted over the cash Charles had poured out on the table from the bag which had weighed down his slight shoulders like the Ancient Mariner's dead albatross. Yet, after all, it had not been really very heavy.

John was sweating, nearly hysterical. Charles, terrified and harrowed, had never seen him in such distress. 'It's not enough!' John cried. 'Not nearly enough. It's – ten – twenty – twenty-one and some shillings O, oh, my God, nearly twenty pounds short. Is that all your father is worth, Charles, to his family and his friends – twenty wretched pieces of gold? Oh, my God, why has thou forsaken me?'

He put his forehead down on the table and wept, and Charles wept too.

And so, after all, it was the Marshalsea Debtors' Prison for John Dickens. A gloomy barracks of a building in the Borough High Street, it was made up of a number of squalid houses, back to back, a paved yard round three sides of them, within high walls, which were spiked to prevent any unlikely attempt to escape. Next to the back wall, with its heavily barred windows was the burial-ground of St George's Church, where many former prisoners lay – one of them Mr Cocker, whose manual of arithmetic had given rise to the saying 'According to Cocker'. Charles had suffered from Cocker at school, but in his sad perambulations about the graveyard in weeks to come was sorry to think of him lying in that dreary place. There was a great brick vault by the gate, big enough for several ghouls to live in, Charles thought. He would sit on the tombstone and study it in morbid fascination. Perhaps one day he would write a story about such a vault and the dreadful secrets it held.

He did not cry much after that night when the great gate of the Marshalsea shut him off from his father and he heard that beloved voice saying, 'The sun has set upon me forever.' But his delicate constitution was breaking under all the strains of this terrible time. In the blacking-factory, some days after John's incarceration, he had a violent attack of pain and fever. The spasm in his side had never been so bad. He could barely drag himself from the door of the counting-house towards his window-seat, shaking and gasping, and before he reached it he collapsed.

Bob Fagin had seen him stagger in, and was at his side in a moment.

46

'Charles! What is it, mate?' He slapped Charles's cheeks lightly, alarmed. 'Come on, old feller – come on.'

Charles's eyes began to open.

'*There* you are, then,' said Bob. 'I knew you was all right. What was it?'

'The smell,' Charles muttered. 'The smell.'

Bob sniffed. 'I can't smell nuffin – nuffin, that is, 'cep Warren's Blacking, the Pride of Mankind!'

Charles tried to turn his mind away from the stench of the blacking bottles, which had been the last straw as he had entered the room, and caused his faint. He tried to get up, but the pain clawed at him, and he put a hand to his side. Bob watched him, worried.

'Got a pain, 'ave you? Yes, I can see. Oh dear. Oh lor'. What's to do? Slimy's dead drunk down in the yard. Mr Lamert ain't been in for days . . .' He called to the old clerk. ''Ere, Mr Billings! Mr Billings, sir!'

Billings made no reply. Nobody would ever know whether he were totally deaf or totally indifferent to his surroundings. Bob shook his head. 'I reckon he won't get 'is chin up until 'e's put in 'is coffin.'

Charles tried to laugh, but the pain overcame him again. Bob patted his shoulder. 'Nah, you just 'ang on for a minute and I'll make you a bit of a bed. No pasting up for you today, old lad.' He began to dart about the room, collecting straw from empty packing cases which had held bottles, and filling with it a long shallow box in a corner; a box not unlike, he reflected uneasily, the one he had just mentioned as the destiny of old Billings.

'What's it like, then, this pain?' he asked.

'It's . . . I can't describe it. Awful. A kind of – spasm.'

'Ever get it before?' The box was nearly full now.

'Well, a bit – on and off – just lately . . . but never – never so bad as this.'

'Reckon it's somefin' you ate?'

'I didn't eat anything today.'

'There you are then – that's wot it is! You got to eat somefin'. I'll give you a bit of my dinner. It's a nice wedge of pork pie.'

Charles shuddered. 'Thanks. But I couldn't eat anything.'

'Tell you wot, then. My old muvver always reckons if you got a pain you want to keep it warm. 'Ere, come on, old lad.' He half-carried Charles over to the improvised mattress and laid him gently down upon it. 'There. Nice 'ot water bottle, that's wot you need.' Bustling about, he went downstairs and filled a large rusty kettle with water, which he boiled on the stove where the blacking was prepared. Empty bottle after empty bottle he filled with hot water, applying them one after another to Charles's side.

''Ow does that feel, then? Better?'

It did. Charles smiled and thanked him.

'Why don't you cut off 'ome, soon's you feel able? Get your muvver to put you to bed.'

Charles turned his head away. 'I – my family have been obliged to move into new lodgings. They can't accommodate me there, at present.'

Bob just nodded. He did not want to be inquisitive. Neither he nor anybody else at Warren's, except James Lamert, knew anything of young Dickens's home circumstances. In fact, the dejected John Dickens, sharing a brew of punch with a fellow-prisoner, Captain Porter, and with the lady who was certainly the mother of that officer's two children but equally certainly not his wife, had been persuaded by them that the most economical and sensible thing he could do would be to move his family into residence with him in his cell, a normal enough arrangement. 'Prison for a debtor is freedom from his creditors, sir. Get 'em in!' And into the Marshalsea they had moved, Elizabeth at first dismayed and ashamed, but soon sustained by John's refreshed spirits when he found his family once again about him.

Only Charles and the Orfling were lodged outside; Charles in an attic in the house of a bankruptcy-court agent, in Lant Street, a little further down the Borough High Street, over-looking a timber-yard. It was not very grand, but Charles was glad to be there, near his family. He had breakfast 'at home' – in the prison – and went back there in the evenings. Any spare time he would fill in by discovering more of London; that London which lay about the Blackfriars Road, the Adelphi Arches, the sleazy, vice-ridden, prostitute-haunted London, a place where a child of Charles's years could, as he did, go into a public-house and order a glass of ale, receiving a pitying kiss from the landlord's wife.

So he could not let kind Bob take him back 'home', for he would not admit that it was the Marshalsea. Instead, when they left the factory, they went to Porridge Island, an area in the triangle of Charing Cross, St. Martin's Lane, and the old Royal Mews (one day to be replaced by the National Gallery). In a steamy coffee room, with two even steamier mugs of beef-bone soup, Charles, a little light-headed perhaps, stared over the thick rim of his mug at the reverse side of the glass door. MOOR EEFFOC, said the engraved letters, and Charles repeated it over and over to himself. Moor eeffoc. Moor eeffoc. It was set in an oval glass plate. He muttered it like an incantation, some magic spell from the *Tales of the Genie*. A good spell, or a bad one?

A huge man with a worried face was suddenly at their elbow.

'Did I leave a bag in that corner, boy?' he was asking.

Charles came out of his dream and looked down at the floor. There was a carpet-bag, in the shadows at his feet.

'Yes, sir. Here it is.'

The man, literally sweating with relief, mopped his brow. 'Thank God, thank God!' he said, flinging down a coin on the table before striding out. Charles and Bob stared at the coin. It was a silver sixpence – riches, no less. Bob was almost overcome.

'That's a saveloy each, Mr Dickens, and big lump of plum duff to follow. And enough change to buy bread and cheese for a week. Maybe our luck's changing, eh, Charles?'

'Maybe it is,' said Charles, silently mouthing 'Moor eeffoc,' If he said it often enough it might summon up a real Genie, a great black figure with eyes like glowing red coals and teeth white as pearls, who would salaam and call him Master, and grant any wish he expressed. He began to tell Bob the story of Sinbad and the Genie, and had the satisfaction of watching his listener's eyes grow rounder and rounder.

'Strewth!' said Bob. 'One of them wouldn't 'alf be useful. Think o' the wittles he could get you.'

And, indeed, it seemed that Charles's powers did summon up a Genie of good luck. Not long afterwards news came to John Dickens that his mother, the formidable old lady who had denied him help in his need, had died, and that from her estate would come the means to release him from the Marshalsea, and Charles from the blacking factory. The Dickenses did, in the words of the wholly imaginary family motto imparted to Charles by his exultant father, look after their own.

CHAPTER FIVE

'Times is hard,' said the cats'-meat man,
'Folks gets in my debt,' said the cats'-meat man . . .

It was not strictly true any more of the Dickens family.
Something had, as ever, turned up for John. The Navy Pay
Office had pensioned him off and he had found work reporting
Parliamentary speeches for his brother William's *Mirror of
Parliament*, the rival to Hansard. Because leopards do not
change their spots nor spendthrifts their habits, the Dickenses
were obliged to move fairly often from one lodging to another,
but without any particular hardship. Sometimes they were to
be found in Norfolk Street, Fitzroy Square, sometimes in
Bentinck Street – always in the modest but pleasant area of
Marylebone flanking Portland Place to the west and the New
Road to the north.

As for Charles, the days of the blacking factory were long
behind him. He was almost twenty, and as lively a young spark
as ever sang, whistled or danced in the streets of London. He
had, after the purgatory of Warren's, been sent to school at
last. It had not been a particularly good school, Wellington
Academy in Camden Town, and Charles had considered the
bad-tempered Welshman Mr William Jones a particularly bad
head-master; but it was education, and companionship, and on
the whole he was very satisfied that he had attended Wellington
House and rather distinguished himself there as a very bright
pupil.

He would never quite forget, or forgive, the fact that his
mother had been in favour of his returning to Warren's
instead of going to school. It set up a barrier between them
which would never be quite broken down. He was not unduly

grateful when she found him work as a law clerk in Gray's Inn, because he did not wish to be a lawyer. By means of intense hard work and study he taught himself shorthand, and followed his father into Parliamentary reporting, for his uncle's *Mirror of Parliament* and *The True Sun*, a new evening paper. He was an excellent shorthand writer and reporter, but he wanted to do something else. Write, perhaps? He was always scribbling down impressions of life, people, London. He might do very well in that line, he thought. But on the whole he felt he would come out strongest as an actor. The seed planted by James Lamert had grown into a flamboyant young blossom.

On this particular night, he was progressing somewhat drunkenly down a dark street in company with two friends, Henry Kolle, a bank clerk, and Jem, a law clerk he had known since his Gray's Inn days. Their female companion was a pretty young prostitute whom they called Dezzie, because she had just been playing (in a fashion) Desdemona to Charles's Othello in one of the private theatres run by enterprising managers, where, for a fee, stage-struck young men could satisfy their ambitions to perform leading roles. Charles had been a good, violent Othello, but not quite as affectionate as Desdemona would have wished. After all, if a feller had to die all over you, shouting 'No way but this, Killing myself, to die upon a kiss', you *did* expect a bit more than a peck, even from a young shaver like this lad who called himself Mr Belville and looked as if he was born yesterday, all big eyes and long brown curls. Dezzie was distinctly sulky as they swayed along Gray's-Inn-lane, singing:

> She went to seek the cats'-meat man,
> But she couldn't find the cats'-meat man;
> Till a friend gave her to understand
> He'd a vife and seven kids, had the cats'-meat man.

Dezzie brought them back to the serious business of the evening.

'Orlright, gemmelmen! Come one, come all! I'll take the three of you on for a sovereign!'

'Good lord!' exclaimed Kolle, but Jem declared it was cheap at the price. 'What do you think, Charles?'

Charles, however, was still chanting quietly to himself of the faithless cats'-meat man, and didn't seem to hear. Dezzie laughed.

''E's 'ad one over the eight, 'e 'as. I doubt 'e'll be a starter in the big race.'

Kolle, sobering up with nervousness, hastily consulted his watch. 'Look here, I really must be getting home. It's frightfully late.'

Dezzie pulled at his arm. 'Come on, matey, a quicky up the alley won't take much time.' She advanced on him, laughingly egged on by Jem, but he backed away like a frightened lamb confronted by sheep-dogs. 'No, no! You don't understand, Miss. I am affianced.'

Dezzie roared with laughter. 'Is you indeed? I thought you always walked like that. Come on, then, Jem – cut price. 'Alf a sovereign for you and the Blackie.'

Charles, reminded of his recent rôle, suddenly gave tongue. 'Down, strumpet, down!' he yelled, and flung himself on the cringing Kolle, who seized him with relief and began to hurry him down the street, leaving Jem and Dezzie in a dark doorway, haggling about half a sovereign.

'It is the cause, it is the cause, my soul!' exclaimed Charles to a gas-lamp. 'First-rate performance, wasn't it, Collie? Very moving, very moving. Absolutely first-rate. Put out the light, and then put out the light . . .' He was weeping with enthusiasm for the memory of his interpretation of the Moor of Venice, aided by several tots of Cream of the Valley.

Charles was weeping again the next morning, but for a different reason. In the Press Gallery of the House of Commons he was listening to the rolling, eloquent tones of Daniel O'Connell, the great Liberator of Ireland, pleading the cause of the oppressed Catholics.

'Did the Honourable Gentleman,' enquired O'Connell of his Tory opponent, 'never hear of the widow Ryan, who breakfasted in the morning with her two sons and a demand for four shillings and sixpence for tithes for a church which was not theirs ? And after the military protectors of that church had fired, ran out wild. "Where are my sons?" She found a dead body. She took it up to see the face. It was not her son; and she laughed – the poor woman laughed aloud, forgetting there was another mother to weep for that boy. Another body and another frantic laugh. And then a third, but now it was one of the boys who had left her a few hours before – a boy blood-boltered, still and dead.

'And this woman told this gentleman of Ireland, who tells you English gentlemen here in this assembly today, "I didn't cry," she said, "I never shed a tear. But my eyeballs are coals in my head and I shall never have them quenched on this side of the grave."'

He paused for effect. Charles's hand was flying over the pages, little black symbols pouring from his pen, but he was listening with all his soul, and the shorthand marks were blurred here and there by the tears which fell, unchecked, from his eyes.

In Bellamy's Kitchen, where the two Houses took their refreshment, a number of Members, friends and associates were eating, drinking, smoking, and talking. In this old Palace of Westminster, which in a matter of two years would be burnt to ashes, Bellamy's was a most valued institution. One of its waiters, whose memories went back to 1806, was fond of giving the lie to those who averred that the last words of Pitt the Younger had been: 'Oh, my country! How I leave my country!' In fact, the great statesman had roused himself enough to say: 'I *think* I could eat one of Bellamy's meat pies.' He, the waiter, had immediately been sent for in a postchaise to bring a consignment of the pies; but when he arrived at Pitt's house on Putney Common the great statesman was dead. 'Them was his last words.'

At one of the booth-tables sat John Dickens, greyer, plumper, more rubicund of nose than in the days of the Marshalsea. He was, very delicately, putting the touch on Sir Giles Watherspoon, a fat, unintelligent, but wealthy Member, on whom John's rhetoric was woefully lost.

'A gentleman like yourself, sir,' John was declaiming, 'who has, as I have pointed out often enough in the Press, stood all his life for fair play and the highest principles of this great realm of ours: would such a man see an old friend torn to shreds by harpies for a few miserable sovereigns? For the sake of my "friend", Sir Giles, I ask you, as one who has had the honour of reporting your quite superb principles often enough – I ask you, sir . . .'

Sir Giles slammed his mug of porter down with something between a sign and a belch. 'Need money again, do you, Dickens?'

John began to talk himself out of a direct demand, to point out his influence with the Press. 'Not to mention my son Charles, who is already turning his pen to finer things. You've seen his reports in *The True Sun*, sir?'

'Twenty pounds and that's the last of it,' was his benefactor's reply. At that moment John caught sight of his son, looking round for him at the door, red-eyed and generally snuffy of appearance. He beckoned him over.

'My dear boy. Been listening to that wretched Irishman again, have you?'

Sir Giles bridled. 'Irishman? Damn my soul! Blasted O'Connell!'

'A great advocate of the human heart, for all that, Sir Giles,' said Charles gently.

'Can always tell by your eyes when you've been listening to the Holy Roman from County Clare,' John said with a smile. 'You've met my sensitive son Charles, Sir Giles?'

Sir Giles grunted and re-lit his pipe. Charles turned to his father and handed him a wad of papers. 'Lord Gray's speech.'

John beamed, 'Excellent! I see some things have gone well with you today, my boy.' He winked. 'Some have gone well with me, too. Take a hot chop with us, my boy. I'd like Sir Giles to get to know you better.'

'I would be honoured, but I have a prior engagement. Sir Giles – Governor.' He flicked the brim of his tall hat in salute, and moved away, a slender, neat figure, not tall but undeniably elegant in line, dressed colourfully in the highest style

55

he could afford: swallowtail coat, pegtop trousers, bright embroidered weskit, and high cravat. He had a fondness for rings, decorative pins, and fobs. Sir Giles watched him depart, with a suspicious eye.

'Bit of a dandy, that boy of yours, ain't he, Dickens?'

The prior engagement was with Henry Kolle. Together they were bound to No. 2 Lombard Street, in the City of London, for there lived Anne Beadnell, Kolle's betrothed. Kolle was warning his friend not to let anything drop about the Dezzie incident.

'The Beadnells are a highly respected family, Charles. My engagement to Miss Anne is of inestimable value to my career in the bank.'

'Love at last, Collie?'

Kolle shot him a reproving look. It was nothing to be sarcastic about. 'Her uncle is manager of Smith, Payne, and Smith, and her father, Mr George, will probably succeed him.'

Charles looked innocent. 'She sounds adorable. What colour are her eyes?'

Kolle was startled. 'What?'

'Her eyes, Collie. Your beloved's luminous orbs. What colour are they?'

Kolle thought. 'I haven't the least idea, Charles. Does it matter?' He was not a romantic youth.

'Apparently not,' Charles shrugged, 'provided the lady has relations with a bank.'

'Now, Charles, be serious. If I introduce you to the Beadnells, you must go easy on the jokes and all that.'

'Of course. I know that bankers are not given to immoderate laughter.'

Kolle was relieved that his volatile friend understood the point. 'Exactly. I told the girls you're frightfully clever, and, like all writers, a bit of a dark horse.'

'Girls? Lots of these Beadnell girls on the market, are there?'

'Three. But Margaret, the eldest, is already spoken for, and I've got Anne. That leaves Maria. Plays the harp like an angel.'

In the first-floor double parlour in Lombard Street, Maria was playing the harp like an angel, and so far as Charles was concerned she was one. She was diminutive, just the right size for him, and if her form gave the slightest hint that one day it might become too plump, that in itself was a strong charm. Her dark hair was knotted at the back of her head in Grecian style, and fell in profuse ringlets on either side of her pretty, coquettish face, with its large eyes of a remarkable shade of blue. Many years hence Charles would remember his exact sensations when Kolle had first introduced him to Maria; only he would call her, to his readers, Dora.

All was over in a moment. I had fulfilled my destiny. I was a captive and a slave. I loved Dora Spenlow to distraction!
She was more than human to me. She was a Fairy, a Sylph, I don't know what she was – anything that no one ever saw, and everything that everybody ever wanted.

And here she was, before his love-struck gaze, on this *soirée musicale* in society rather higher than that in which Charles usually moved. There were others in the room, of course – not that they mattered in the least: Kolle's Anne, who played the guitar, Margaret and her fiancé David Lloyd, a young tea merchant, Charles's sister Fanny, who already knew the Beadnells, the dashing Moule brothers, and a young painter, Henry Austin, whose lovelorn looks in Maria's direction were not unnoticed by Charles. In Maria's Album (every young lady kept an Album of choice contributions of verses and sketches by her best friends) there were various pathetic lines by one H.A. 'When first on thine angel form so bright, Entranced, I gazed with ravished eye . . . As Dido art thou painted here? Maria, thou art much too fair . . .' And so forth. When Charles saw them, in due course, he would be violently jealous. At present he was much too intent on his harping and warbling divinity to notice that another young lady's eyes were fixed on himself with something of a quizzical – or was it an acquisitive – look? They were the sharp dark eyes of Mary

Anne Leigh, Maria's best friend.

The cheerful young company in the drawing-room was being observed from a small adjoining snug parlour by the Beadnell parents. They liked to see what their daughters and their respective swains were up to, and they were intrigued by the newcomer in their midst. Mrs Beadnell thought him gentlemanlike – 'what a beautifully made coat, just like Prince Leopold's.' Mr Beadnell, eyeing appreciatively the neat form of Fanny Dickens at the pianoforte, was kind enough to say that young Mr Dickens, if that was his name, looked well set up enough.

'What's he in, my dear?' enquired his lady.

'Bit of a dark horse, according to Kolle, but something to do with the House of Lords, I believe.'

'*Very* interesting.' Mrs Beadnell, a considerable snob, was prepared to overlook the young man's slightly foreign appearance – that big nose and those flashing eyes, the dazzling scarf-pin (*could* that be a diamond?) if he were in some way connected with the House of Lords. And she was displeased to see Mary Anne Leigh making overtures to the young man.

In fact, Charles was doing his best to shake off Mary Anne and approach Maria, who was being sighed over by Henry Austin. Henry was patting Maria's miniature spaniel, Daphne, which Maria had picked up as soon as she had laid aside her harp.

'How nice to see lovely Daphne again, and . . . and lovely *you*, Miss Maria.'

Maria shook her curls and pretended to frown. 'Oh, Mr Austin, you will go to our silly little heads. Not that Daphne is silly. She will eat mutton chops if you cut off the fat.'

Austin gulped. 'I would!' He, like other young men, would willingly have cleaned out Daphne's kennel for one sweet look from Maria. But his tactics were feeble beside those of his approaching rival. Charles's brilliant eyes were fixed on Maria's, he had taken her tiny white hand, and, with a sweeping bow, had kissed it.

'Miss Maria!' he said in thrilling tones. 'I was warned you

played like an angel, but no one told me that it was a simple matter for you to do so, since you are quite clearly nothing less than a divine being yourself.'

Maria was completely taken aback. She was used to the approach shy and the approach sentimental, but this ultra-romantic onslaught was something quite new in her amatory experience. She smiled and dimpled, paled and blushed, and buried her face in Daphne's fur, the ringlets falling round the little dog in a manner calculated to cause any young man not in her favour to go away and shoot himself immediately. Through the cascade of her hair, she could hear her new beau declaring that Charles Dickens was her servant and worshipper for the rest of his life.

In such a soirée it was the custom for all who had talents to display them for the entertainment of others. Charles was no performer on the harp or the pianoforte, his singing experience was largely limited to comic songs, and 'The Cats'-meat Man' might be a little inappropriate. He would, then, recite. He pondered on the advisability of giving the company a little something out of Shakespeare, but hastily abandoned it as he recalled rolling about on a property bed with Dezzie. Instead he decided on a highly romantic and apt set of lines from Mr Alfred Tennyson's newly-published *Poems, Chiefly Lyrical*. It was not a poem of which Tennyson would ever be outstandingly proud, but it enabled him to woo Maria with his voice as well as his eyes.

> O Maiden, fresher than the first green leaf
> With which the fearful springtide flecks the lea . . .

began the poem, going on to assure the lady that she was his 'heart's sun in crystalline', and ending with the sombre reflection that 'They never learned to love who never knew to weep'.

Mr Beadnell, listening, realised with something of a shock that the young man in the drawing-room was spouting poetry. 'He an't one of them poets, I hope,' he said to his wife, who replied, 'Why not ? A poet can be somebody.'

Mary Anne Leigh had recognised the authorship. She

intercepted Charles on his way to Maria. 'So, Mr Dickens. You are an admirer of Mr Tennyson.'

Charles was surprised to meet a literary young woman. 'I think him most promising,' he said with a faint air of condescension towards both poet and critic.

'Indeed he is. I have always thought that if one is unable to compose a good poem oneself, one should at least learn to recite somebody else's well.'

But Charles almost brushed her aside to hear Maria's verdict.

'Oh, Mr Dickens, what a pretty verse that was. Did you make it up yourself?'

Before he could answer, Mary Anne snapped, 'No, Maria dear. Mr Dickens has only borrowed it for the evening.'

Maria decided to ignore her friend's asperity. She caressed the little spaniel. 'Daphne loved it, and . . . and so did I.' She blushed charmingly.

'Perhaps I might dedicate a poem of my own to you some time, Miss Beadnell?' Charles ventured.

She giggled. 'Goodness! What a lark that would be.'

But the elder Beadnells were approaching, and it was time for Charles to exert his fascination on Maria's mama. He made his courtly bow.

'Dear Mrs Beadnell. How fascinating it is to meet the mother of such enchanting and talented daughters.'

Mrs Beadnell graciously acknowledged the fulsome greeting, then whispered to her husband: 'There you are, George. I told you Mr Dickens was somebody of taste.'

Outside, going homeward from the party, Charles was like a man gone suddenly demented. He danced up one side of the street, dashed across it and danced down the other, shouting, 'I'm in love! I'm in love! I'm in love!'

Kolle had watched the evening's proceedings with disapproval. 'You *did* come it a bit strong, Charles!'

Charles slapped him on the back in passing. 'I'm in love, you dust-dry old bank ledger! Amo! J'adore! J'aime!'

'Yes, yes, I get what you mean. But it don't do to come it so strong.'

Charles continued to rave at the top of his voice. 'Divine! Angelic! Angel! Heaven! Love! Love! Love!'

In the house they were passing a bedroom window shot up and a nightcapped head looked out. 'What the devil's going on ?' it shouted. 'I'll have the constable on you! Get home to your beds, damned rake-hells!'

Furiously it watched the madly dancing figure disappear into the distance, followed by a much more diffident one with its coat-collar turned up to conceal its face. Charles was always so embarrassingly conspicuous.

The next day, roaming distractedly in Lombard Street, Charles was seized on by Mary Anne Leigh and borne, purely in a spirit of malice, to the Beadnells', where the three young ladies happened to be at home, discussing the soirée and Mr Dickens's part in it in particular. They stared as Mary Anne almost pushed him into the drawing-room. He, too, was taken aback at finding himself so suddenly restored to the family of his beloved; but barely had he been in the room two minutes before he was holding Maria's hand and gazing into her eyes. At last he pronounced: 'They are!'

She frowned, puzzled, 'What ?'

'Violet. They are the purest, most brilliant violet in the world.'

'Oh, you mean my *eyes*. Yes. People do say they are an unusual colour.'

'Let us have tea immediately,' said Anne, laughing, 'before Mr Dickens swoons – with thirst.'

After that he called as often as he dared. He was privileged to escort Maria and Daphne for walks, though somehow it always seemed that he was escorting Mary Anne Leigh as well. She was by now acutely jealous, for she admired Charles's looks, dash, and obvious brains – all qualities very scarce in the tea-broking world. And that the idiotic Maria should have him – it was too vexing, she would do her utmost to part them. With her cleverness and her sharp tongue it should not be difficult. Mr Dickens would soon see, under her guidance, what a little ninny Maria was, and how unworthy of him.

They were watching Maria frolicking with Daphne on the

grass of the Beadnells' lawn. Charles's face was a study in adoration. Mary Anne looked at him out of the corner of an eye, and said, 'Our dearest Maria is not exactly a brilliant conversationalist, but she has the *greatest* concern for the health of domestic animals.'

The barb went quite unnoticed. He continued to gaze enraptured at the girl and the dog. Mary Anne was stung into going further.

'Strange!' she mused. 'I would have thought, Mr Dickens, that a man of your obvious mental powers would have regarded conversation as an important amenity.'

This time he answered her, witheringly. 'Indeed I do, Miss Leigh. And I get a great deal of it – with my *male* companions.'

And he strode off towards Maria.

She had given him hope. He might call on her. She would not be *too* cruel to him. Of course, there was nothing definite. It was too early even for him to ask if he might speak to her papa. He was, in any case, in no position to do so.

At one of Bellamy's tables he told his father, 'I must earn more money. Much more.'

'What about your stories and squibs?'

'Damp. They don't take off. I need money *now*.'

John Dickens sighed. 'The badge of the tribe of Dickens and other family men. But Charles, is the matter so serious?'

'Father' – Charles's look was as intense as his tone – 'this is my destiny. This lady is my fate. I know it.'

John shook his head. 'My dear boy, I know very well how final these claps of spring thunder may sound – like the end of the world. But natural science teaches us that it's only two clouds meeting in the spring.'

Charles disliked the image, and said so. From the hint of a tiff (so touchy he was these days) he descended to asking the Governor something practical. 'Now you've been intimate with actors all your life, Father . . .'

'And why not? Some of 'em (not many, I must admit) are damned good fellows. A leetle unreliable perhaps, but . . .'

'Did you ever know a rich one, though? Mr Charles Mathews, for a case. What does he earn, would you say? I've heard that on numerous occasions he has earned £100 or more for a night's work.'

'I dare say he has – and well worth it. After all, what does it represent but a few shillings per head of the audience he lifts to a higher plane? But most players die poor, my boy.'

Charles leapt to his feet, his eyes flashing, his arm flung out in a gesture Mr Charles Mathews could hardly have bettered. 'Damn dying, sir! I am planning my life!'

So it was that he found himself back in the bar of the sleazy private theatre, asking the even sleazier manager's advice on how to become a professional player. After a little money had changed hands, and a glass of Old Tom drunk, he was given the name of an actor, who for a small consideration might be prepared to coach him in the Thespian art. Which, indeed he was, having fallen on hard times and possessing an expensive thirst. In the shabby lodgings Charles watched with awe his rendition of Antony's dying speech to Cleopatra. Ponderous, hammy, purple-nosed, and gin-breathing, he yet had power to draw tears to the listener's eyes. The speech ended. Charles was silently murmuring 'I am dying, Egypt, dying.' The old trouper reverted to his usual cheerfully plummy tones.

'Moving, is it not? My Antony, Mr Belville, has brought tears hot as blood and spouting like fountains from the eyes of the dull plebs, often and often.'

'I believe you, sir. Though I never had the good fortune to see your performance myself. Er, might I try the speech?'

'Try the *speech*? I should say not, sir! Can you sit? Can you stand? Can you walk? No, you cannot. And therefore, sir, you may not try the speech.'

By the end of the first lesson Charles had been taught how to sit in the manner approved by the theatre of his time. In the drawing-room it might look a shade ostentatious, but it helped him to practise, in his own room, his address to the elder Beadnells, stating his entirely imaginary income from acting ('two hundred pounds for the night, sir and ma'am.') and his intention to keep Maria in the manner to which she was accustomed.

*

One beautiful summer day, some months later, he was rowing Maria on the river near Richmond. It would have been perfect bliss had they been alone, but as usual they were not. Margaret, Anne, and Margaret's fiancé were disporting themselves on the bank, picking wild flowers and making daisy-chains, and Mary Anne Leigh was strolling by the river-side as near as possible to the rowing-boat. She could not hear – most annoying. In fact, Charles was telling Maria about his prospects as a journalist. She did not seem to follow him too clearly, being preoccupied with Daphne's enjoyment of the river. Charles tried again.

'And now I shall tell you a secret. You mustn't mention it to a soul.'

She pouted. 'Not even Daphne?'

'Of course. Daphne must know everything. The fact is, I've applied to the Lyceum for an audition. Mr Charles Mathews has said that he will see me as soon as they have finished getting up *The Hunchback*.'

Maria looked pained. 'Hunchback? How horrid!'

Charles tried not to let irritation tinge his voice. 'My dearest, *The Hunchback* is a play. Anyway, after they have got it up, they will audition me. And then, of course, I shall have additional income from acting.'

Maria's beautiful, bow-shaped eyebrows shot up. 'Acting? Are you to be an actor, then?'

'Why not? It's an excellent way of earning both fame and money, which I will heap at your adorable feet.'

She gave a tinkling laugh into the dog's ear. 'Oh, Daphne, our silly paws are going to be covered with Charles's fame!'

This time his irritation was plain. 'Please, Maria, you must take me seriously, my dearest dear.'

Again the laugh. 'You are *such* a serious boy, Charles. How could one take you any other way?'

'Boy?' repeated the twenty-year-old with hauteur. 'I am a man, Maria, and you are a woman. An angel, but a woman also.'

She was just a little shocked. 'Woman' was – well, it was not quite a nice word to call one. 'I don't think you should talk to us like that – do you, Daphne?'

It was most unfortunate that on the day of the Lyceum audition Charles should have one of his dreadful colds, caught on a country excursion with Maria. The audition would have to be postponed until next season.

It was even more unfortunate that a certain foppish young gentleman, a dandy and a Member of Parliament, chose to show Mary Anne Leigh round Bellamy's on a day when Sir Giles Watherspoon was being solicited by John Dickens for the odd guinea. On seeing him, Miss Leigh's escort stopped in his tracks.

'I say, there's my wich uncle. I'd best give him good day. Oh lawd, he's with that dwunken old cwony of his – that sycophantic old sot John Dickens.'

Mary Anne pricked up her ears. 'Dickens?' Could it be true?

'Yes, he's some sort of weporter here – always on the tap – absolutely penniless – been in pwison, I believe – disweputable Gwub Stweet hack. Gives the old nuncle the odd puff for the odd dwink, you know.'

'Does he have a son?' she asked thoughtfully.

'Odd question. How the devil should I know?'

At that moment, in their hearing, John was saying, 'Now young Charles and myself would make, I would say, an excellent pair of poll clerks.'

The young M.P. interrupted him. 'Uncle Giles. Allow me to pwesent Miss Mawy Anne Leigh. My uncle, Sir Giles Watherspoon. Just showing Miss Leigh the mystewies of the House, uncle. Good day to you, Mr Dickens.'

John rose and bowed in a stately manner sharply contrasted with Sir Giles's casual nod. 'John Dickens, at your service, ma'am.'

She was all sweetness. 'Too much to hope, I suppose, that you are related to Mr Charles Dickens, sir?'

'I should say I am, ma'am. You know my boy, do you? As promising a shorthand writer as there is in this House. Sir Giles'll bear me out, I'm sure.'

She tended a gloved hand. 'So delighted to have met you, Mr Dickens, truly. Come, Andrew.'

It was at one of the Beadnells' soirées, when Charles had, to the relief of the company, come to the end of reciting a long, bad, and somewhat tasteless poem of his own composition, that Mr and Mrs Beadnell looked meaningly at each other. Charles and Maria were doing the same, for his poem ended, pathetically:

Last here's Charles Dickens, who has now gone forever.
It's clear that he thought himself very clever.
His death wasn't sudden, he had long been ill;
Slowly he languished and got worse until
No mortal means could the poor young fellow save,
And a sweet pair of eyes sent him home to his grave.

The two pairs of brilliant eyes, hers violet, his diamond-bright, held each other. There might have been no one else in the room.

'It's time Maria was finished off,' said Mrs Beadnell.

'How's that, my dear?'

'She shall be finished off, George. Quickly. At school in Paris.'

CHAPTER SIX

He missed her terribly. The occasional note she sent in return for his long letters was brief and cold, he thought. Mary Anne Leigh was hinting that dearest Maria might be enjoying herself too much to write – Paris was, after all, a *ladies'* city . . . He felt he was being driven mad with jealous speculation. At least he had his writing. He threw himself heart and soul into the *Sketches by Boz* (he had taken the pseudonym from his little brother Augustus's pet name, Moses, Boses, or Bos). The *Sketches* were actually getting into print, in the *Monthly Magazine*, though without payment, which John Dickens thought most dangerous and reprehensible. He tried to forget Maria, but it was impossible. She was coming back, and he knew she would be changed.

His fear was confirmed when they met at her home. She was more beautiful than ever, but in a harder, sleeker way. There was a brittle, sophisticated air to the girl whom Henry Austin had once painted as a milkmaid. She was amiable, quite pleased to see Charles, but by no means overwhelmed at their reunion.

He looked sadly down at her, as she sat, elegantly poised, nursing Daphne.

'My very dear,' he said, 'can you ever understand what this separation has meant to me?'

Even her voice had changed, become Frenchified. 'My dear Charles, que voulez-vous? One has to be finished.'

'But my dearest Maria – must one be finished so quietly? I mean I had hardly a note from you, and what you wrote was pitifully brief.'

'Well, some of us are "pitifully brief" writers – unlike yourself. We are not very good on letters, are we, Daffers

67

darling ?'

Charles looked at Daffers darling with dislike. 'One would almost think you missed Daphne more than anything else in London.'

Maria raised her eyebrows. 'Of course I have always realised that you, Charles, are not a true dog-lover.'

'Mary Anne said . . .' he began unwisely. She leapt in.

'Mary Anne said! Of course I know that you and Miss Leigh have found a great deal to talk about, and I've no wish to know what Mary Anne said.'

He was perplexed. What *had* Mary Anne said – to Maria? Had she been making mischief between them? His attempt to question Maria was frustrated by the entrance of Mr Beadnell. It was going to be very hard to get her alone, he realised.

Letters were the answer, his father thought, so he wrote her letters. Meanwhile, Mary Anne made malicious capital out of a letter *she* had had from Charles, in which he had made an unwise remark. She showed it to Maria.

'Note the passage,' she said, 'underlined, in which the ever-gallant Mr Dickens observes that he has borne more from you than he believed any living creature breathing ever bore from a woman before.'

Maria was chagrined. 'He never did!'

'Is that his hand ?'

'It is.'

'Just read the words of your undying devoted swain.'

And so, insidiously, she persuaded Charles that Maria had taken her into her confidence about Charles's shortcomings, and persuaded Maria that Charles had done the same about hers. Charles wrote long, pathetic letters, trying to explain himself and making a thorough hash of it. Everything was finished between them; perhaps it had never really started. She sent back his letters, carelessly wrapped so that anyone might open and read them, and, heart-broken, he sent back hers, in a sad little parcel. His father tried to console him.

'Daresay you have the best of the bargain. Yours'll raise more interest than hers a year or two from now, I warrant.'

'Oh father, I'm too bruised to . . .'

'Your pride is bruised, Charles. It's your old partner Pride.'

It was more than that, Charles knew. It was something far more sensitised than pride, something on which a rejection – his mother's when he was sent to Warren's, Maria's, when she returned his letters – made an indelible impression which would affect his whole life and works.

In a desperate attempt to cheer himself up he went to the private theatre in Gray's-Inn-lane and set out to get very drunk. The manager, glad to be bought a drink but a little afraid of this explosive young man, was trying to read the *Sketch by Boz* which Charles had pressed on him. Charles, leaning on the bar, stared unappreciatively at the stage, where a seedy Harlequin was wooing a somewhat passée Columbine.

'What,' he asked nobody in particular, 'is a single silly little girl against the great magic lantern of London, offering me endless sketches for my delectation? What is one stupid reader lost, I say, against the thousands gained?'

'Quite so,' agreed the manager. 'Can't win them all, can we? But why not use your own name, Mr Belville?'

Charles laid his finger to his nose in a wildly exaggerated gesture of cunning. 'But that's my sublety, don't you see. I create curiosity, and later I shall let the world know. Drink up! Another round, Betsey!'

Turning to hail the barmaid, he saw Dezzie lurking drinkless, wanting to speak to him but alarmed, like the manager, by his demented manner. He beckoned her nearer.

'Desdemona, my darling girl, come over and drink with us. I beg you, little violet-eyed angel, quaff a glass of Old Tom, the drink of the Gods, with us.'

She put her hands on her hips and quizzed him. 'Well, you're in a right old mood tonight, ain't you, Blackie? I don't mind if I do. But take a good look. My eyes ain't violet. They're a lovely dark mysterious hazelnut brown. 'Least, that's what a gentleman told me last week.'

'And he was right, my pretty. Your eternal health! I love brown eyes.' He toasted them in Old Tom.

'And so you may, Blackie,' she said with a smirk, 'for half a crown. I'm a bargain tonight. I'm a bargain every night, come to think of it.'

She watched his rate of drinking with interest. He could put it down all right, but he couldn't carry it, that was for sure. When she saw that he was hardly able to stand she took his arm and, half-supporting his staggering form, led him out into the dark alley at the side of the theatre. He was not only very drunk but also, it seemed, raving mad.

'The world is mine, Desdemona!' he shouted. 'It is the cause, my pretty soul. What a very charming and genteel and thoroughly gentlemanly young lady you are, my dear!'

'And what a thoroughly pickled young gentleman *you* are. Still, rather nice, for all your bad moods. Reg'lar Gas-Light boy, you are.'

'Gas-Light Boy. That's good,' he agreed drunkenly and then began to sob. 'My heart is broken, Desdemona.'

'Well,' she said gently, 'let's see if we can patch it up for you, dearie.' She reached up and kissed him. At once he returned her kiss, clasping her in a fierce embrace. 'Maria!' he whispered into her hair.

'It's Mary, actually,' she whispered back. 'Now how did you find that out? Clever old cock!'

'My angel!' he murmured. She was not used to romantic forms of address. 'Oh, Blackie,' she sighed, 'you do say the most pretty things. Oh, Blackie!' Again and again she kissed him, stopping only when she sensed that he had suddenly half-sobered up – surfaced, at least, from his stupor. He pushed her clinging arms away and stared at her.

'But who are you?' he asked.

'Mary – Dezzie – Maria – what you like, darlin' – only kiss me again.'

He had heard the name that was twisting in his heart like a sword. 'Oh, Maria! You've come to me, haven't you? It's our secret, isn't it?'

Gently but firmly, she took him and led him away through the darkness, to the decaying old tenement house in Clare Market where she lived. His bewildered senses were assailed by unpleasant smells, wild, silly voices, ugly people moving to and fro.

'Nearly home now,' she said. 'Come on.'

'This is not Lombard Street, is it?'

'Almost, dear.'

He stood transfixed at the sight of an ancient crone, filthy and witch-like, sitting on a pile of rags and bones, heating an opium-pipe. The sight of her filled him with horror and revulsion.

Dezzie pulled at him. ''Mornin', Auntie. Oh, come on, Blackie. It's only old Auntie Dreams. She'll give us a puff if you like. Won't you, Auntie?'

Charles's eyes were shut. He was sweating, and muttering. 'This is *not* Lombard Street. It is *not*.'

''Course it is. Or at least it will be soon.' She thrust him into the little cubby-hole she called her room, a grotesque place of shabby finery and grubby drapery, things she had picked up here and there to make the lair more homely and feminine. Under the couch-bed's tattered frill she found a bottle of rum, and waved it triumphantly at Charles, who had already collapsed on the couch, still murmuring that it was not Lombard Street.

'It will be when you've had a slug of this,' she told him. ''Ere, move over.' She lay beside him, looking curiously at him as he groaned and muttered.

'Oh, Maria! I've done it all for you. All my fame is for you. All my work – my fame – my everything – my fame, even . . .'

'Thanks very much, but I'd rather have a big kiss.' She leaned tenderly towards him. 'Tell you the truth, Blackie, I fancy you, truly I do. I always 'as, you and yer snobby ways and yer big eyes. Ooh, Blackie dear!'

To his blurred vision her sentimental, yearning, loose-mouthed face was the young, innocent face of Maria, his at last. He clasped her convulsively. 'Oh, Maria – Maria, Maria!'

The fame of which he had raved to Dezzie was coming his way. The *Sketches* were gaining popularity. One of them even achieved the compliment of being pirated by the playwright-comedian Buckstone, at the Adelphi Theatre. Literary folk were beginning to talk about Boz: ordinary people were

71

beginning to recognise Charles in the street; he was becoming, as Mrs Beadnell would say, Somebody. It was suggested to him by a publisher that the *Sketches* might make a book – perhaps two books – and the artist George Cruickshank was enthusiatic about illustrating them in his inimitably grotesque manner.

And then there was the money – such money! John Dickens was awestruck at the publisher's advance.

'One hundred and fifty pounds!'

'And that's only for the first edition,' Charles said triumphantly.

'First, second, and tenth. And the *Chronicle* pay you a miserable seven guineas a week.'

'Seven guineas isn't too bad a salary for someone of my age. If only . . .' he stopped. John smiled wryly.

'If only you didn't have an indigent parent to support from time to time, eh?'

'Well . . . anyway, Governor, *Sketches by Boz* will make us all a little richer.'

His father sighed. 'I hope so, Charles. Shaw and Maxwell, quondam wine people of Woburn Place, are being very pressing and ungentlemanly at the minute.'

Charles's heart sank slightly. He knew the look in his father's eye.

'And there may be one or two other little affairs of no consequence. We shall have to move again, Charles, but to hell with creditors. One hundred and fifty gold sovereigns, eh? That's a devilish considerable sum of money, my boy. Let's take a good bottle of wine to celebrate it.' He hailed Bellamy's wine waiter. 'Nicholas!'

The Dickens family were to move away from the comfortable house in Bentinck Street, Marylebone. Charles's mother and the younger children would be accommodated in temporary lodgings, and Charles, with his fourteen-year-old brother Fred, was to gain the dignity of bachelor apartments at Furnival's Inn, one of the old Inns of Court in Holborn. He would write of it later as 'a shady, quiet place echoing to the footsteps of the stragglers who have business there, and rather

72

monotonous and gloomy on summer evenings', but the bare, cheerless rooms on the third floor looked well enough to him. He would be independent there, away from his worried, worrying mother, the demands of the small Augustus, the constant appearance of creditors. He enjoyed unpacking his beloved books, arranging his few sticks of furniture, watching Fred, cheerful, indispensable Fred, slapping a lick of paint on the shabby walls. Their father was hovering about, suggesting improvements: a carpet, some curtains, perhaps? Charles shook his head.

'It'll have to do well enough as it is.'

'Tush! Never think small, my boy. Remember, one hundred and fifty gold pieces. Pieces of gold, my boy.'

Charles drew a long breath. 'Governor, a few inconsiderable affairs of your own, thirty-five pounds rent in advance for this palatial residence, a room for you in Hampstead, lodgings for mother and the children . . . I won't go on. The recitation is too depressing, and quite costly.'

His father bowed his balding head in genuine shame. 'I am a great curse to you, Charles. That's what I am, a curse to you and all my poor family. Oh, your unfortunate mother! Those unfortunate children! And you, Charles – brilliant, hard-working . . .'

Charles was embarrassed. 'Please, Governor, do stop.'

'No, Charles, I shall never stop praising you for all you are doing with your life, and blaming your accursed father for the disgusting – yes, I say it again – for the disgusting failure of his own.'

Charles put a hand on the bowed shoulders. 'Come now, sir, one should never allow temporary adversities to crush one's spirit. Haven't you often observed that profound truth to me yourself?'

'I have, I have. But I am brought too low now ever to rise again.'

'You'll manage it, Governor. I know you will.'

John brightened up as though on cue. 'My God, Charles, your confidence is infectious, my boy! I believe I will. Yes. I truly believe I can do it.'

And, after assuring his son that something of quite extra-ordinary interest and profit was certain to come up within the week, and touching him for the three sovereigns which were all that remained to him, John departed, full of cheer.

What turned up, in Charles's chambers on his return from an agreeable evening with his publisher Macrone and a young American publisher, was his sister Fanny, waiting for him in the one shabby chair. She turned as he entered, and he saw bad news in her face.

'Charles, Father has been taken off.'

He started. The phrase usually meant one thing. 'What? Is he ill?'

'Only with his usual complaint – debts. He's been arrested by Shaw and Maxwell.'

'"The quondam wine merchants." Where is he?'

'Where else but in the sponging-house?'

Charles sighed. 'Well, here we go. One more chorus of the same old song.'

Fanny looked at him with exasperation. Still smiling, still cheerful, after all he had had to bear, still, no doubt, willing to help the author of their misfortunes out of yet another hole. She dearly loved her brother, but sometimes she wished he were not so good-natured. 'What will you do?' she asked.

'Why, raise the wind, of course. What else does a Dickens do in such "temporary circumstances"?'

'Oh, Charles. I hope you're not becoming as bad as he is.'

'Why, I only hope I may prove as good at it.'

His first move was to ask the editor of the *Morning Chronicle* for half his month's salary in advance, which was granted. He then betook himself, by means of a long walk at a brisk pace, to Brompton, in which respectable suburb there lived George Hogarth, Editor of the sister paper, the *Evening Chronicle*. Mr Hogarth was a Scotsman, intellectual, a well-known musicologist, and had been friend and legal adviser to one of Charles's literary idols, the late Sir Walter Scott. It was not, however, to talk of Sir Walter that Dharles was calling on Mr Hogarth: there was a little matter of money involved.

74

18 York Place. He looked up with approval at the bland front of the well-kept dwelling, and gave a smart rat-tat to the knocker. The girl who opened the door was cast somewhat in the style of a Mohammedan houri, or one of those Eastern young ladies beloved, in every sense, by Lord Byron's heroes. Nearly as tall as Charles, she was plump but, he noted with approval, slender-waisted. Her dark glossy hair, shining like a blackbird's wing, fell in graceful twines on to the collar of her pretty rose-striped dress. Rather too fine for a maid, Charles thought. The Hogarths *must* be well off. He was particularly taken by her large, luminous eyes, of a clear blue, and by the look of good-nature which played about her full red lips. She did not remind him at all of Maria.

'Yes?' she said.

'This is the house of Mr George Hogarth?'

'It is.' He noted that she had a very slight Scots accent. The Hogarths must recruit their servants from home ground.

'The office informs me that Mr Hogarth is working at home today.'

'He is.'

'In that case, my dear, would you tell your master that Mr Charles Dickens is calling on him?'

She dimpled. A girl of few words, but likeable, very.

'I shall, sir.'

'And may I come in, my dear?'

'You may, sir.'

He followed her into the handsome, conventional hall, and glimpsed, through the door that she opened, a large parlour which was obviously used as Mr Hogarth's study – for there he sat at a paper-littered desk – and as living-room for his family, of whom two young girls could be seen playing at some parlour-game. Charles was surprised to hear the maid announce:

'Mr Charles Pickins to see Mr Hogarth.' He touched her shoulder in mild correction.

'Dickens, if you please.'

She choked back a laugh. 'Sorry, sir. Mr Dharles Chickens.' Then she exploded into laughter in which the younger girls

75

joined her. The taller one said, 'Oh, Kate, don't be awful! Those puns!'

Mr Hogarth looked up vaguely from his papers. 'Oh, Dickens – is it you?'

'Mr Hogarth, sir. Forgive me for disturbing you at home, but . . .'

'Glad to see you. Girls, please – get out of here.'

The girl who had spoken before, a pretty creature of about fifteen, pleaded with him. 'Oh, do let's stay!' and, to the girl who had let Charles in, '*Who* is he?'

'I don't know,' replied that facetious young lady. 'We must leave Mr Dockins to talk over his terribly important business with Father.'

Charles stared from one to another, the small girl at the table, the taller one beside her, the supposed maid. 'I'm Georgina,' said the child, and 'I'm Mary,' smiled her sister.

'And I'm Catherine – sir,' said the other girl. Charles stared at her with frank admiration which brought a warm blush to her cheeks. It made her, he thought, more attractive than ever. He stared after her retreating back as she shooed her younger sisters out.

Mr Hogarth was waving him to a chair. 'Mr Dickens, I am delighted to see you. But what brings you here, sir?'

Charles detached his mind from his host's daughter.

'I have a request to make, sir.'

'My dear fellow, anything – so long as it isn't money.'

Charles's face fell. 'Oh. Well, actually . . .'

'Say no more,' said the perceptive Scot. 'I see it is money. I know the appearance of a young author looking for funds extremely well.'

His tone was encouraging. 'Well, since you mention it, Mr Hogarth, an advance against my small contributions to the *Evening Chronicle* would be of immense value to me at the present time.'

'I know exactly how you feel, my dear fellow, but financial matters are not really within my province.'

'Of course, sir. I simply wanted the benefit of your great experience – your advice.'

76

Mr Hogarth swept an expansive gesture. 'Advice is free, my boy. You may have any amount of advice.'

Charles settled himself back. 'Well, then, say I was to deliver you several contributions in advance of copy-date, I wonder would you feel inclined to use your influence to encourage an advance? The smallest advance would be more than welcome.'

The editor looked dubious. 'It would be most unusual. I mean, why, Mr Dickens, should we require to hold so many of your contributions ahead of copy-dates?'

'Ah – well, sir, there you see is the precise point, and it's most like your experience to have brought you to it at once. The point is that I am under great pressure from other papers and magazines to supply them with sketches, and while I myself would prefer to remain in my present close relationship to both the *Chronicles*, I have, as I explained, this present emergency to meet.'

'Are you saying, Mr Dickens, that the *Evening Chronicle* may lose your contributions if such an advance is not forthcoming?'

Charles looked radiantly innocent. 'My dear Mr Hogarth, such a thought had not entered my mind. But now that you have formed it, well, I may indeed be forced to reduce my . . .'

'Say no more, my boy, you have made your point extremely well, and I think you may assume that any influence I have will be used to effect you the advance you require.'

Charles beamed. 'Thank you a thousand times, Mr Hogarth, sir.'

'Not so many thanks,' said the editor with a canny smile. 'The advance will, I assure you, be too small to justify them.' He was looking keenly at the bright young face, the brilliant eyes and fine brow. 'Your work and determination indicate to me that you have the makings of a true professional author.'

'Indeed I hope so, sir. I would take as my model the great Sir Walter Scott, your own fabled intimate.'

'Sir Walter would never have thanked you for such an honour. He always saw himself as a gentleman who happened to write.'

Charles smiled. 'Well, in that case, let me say that I propose to be a writer who happens to be a gentleman.'

It had been the right thing to say, he could see. 'Very good, sir! Now, since it's too early to take anything more interesting, perhaps you'll stay for tea.'

'I should very much like to take tea with you, sir, some other time. But at the moment I'm afraid I am committed elsewhere.'

He was saying goodbye when Catherine entered with a laden tea-tray. Her cheerful face clouded when she saw him preparing to go.

'Are you leaving already?'

'I regret that I must,' he said. 'But I will return, very soon.'

For the second time that afternoon she blushed. 'I hope you will, Mr Dickens.'

He smiled. 'Ah! You have my name right at last.'

'I had it right at first,' she confessed, 'but I am sometimes overwhelmed by an irresistible compulsion to make puns.'

Charles joined in her laugh. 'I suffer from the same disorder myself. We must make puns together soon.'

'I would like that,' she said frankly.

Pausing at the door with a serious air, he asked, 'You don't entertain, I hope, a pet dog?'

She laughed. 'A dog? I detest the wretched smelly little objects.'

'Perfect!' He threw her a dazzling smile, and bowed over her hand gallantly. Mary joined her, as she watched him go down the garden path.

'Oh, has he gone so soon?'

'He will be back before long.'

Mary clapped her hands. 'Oh, how nice that will be!'

Catherine turned a quizzical look on her. She had no intention that Mr Dharles Chickens should be nice for anyone but her, even her dear sister.

And he, striding about on his wind-raising mission, was glowing with pleasure at the memory of the girl like a full-blown rose. He had not noticed her sisters in the least.

The wind was raised. A shower of gold sovereigns had been flung on to the table in the sponging-house, and John Dickens was once more restored to the bosom of his family, this time in lodgings off the Strand, conveniently distant from Bentinck Street.

The Hogarth family were, as usual, sitting about in the airy cluttered parlour looking on to the garden. Mr Hogarth was reading in a magazine a new series of *Scenes and Characters*. He shook his head in wonderment. 'So he's writing for them as well,' he mused. 'The *Morning Chronicle*, the *Evening Chronicle*, the *Monthly Magazine*, and now this! The devil drives that young fellow.'

Catherine looked up sharply from her needlework. 'Is it Mr Dickens you're talking of, Papa?'

'Ay. He works like a daemon, does that Dickens.'

Suddenly Mary screamed. 'There's a terrible face at the window, look!'

They looked. In at the french windows a frightful face was peering. It appeared to be that of a heavily bearded sailor, judging by the round hat. A moment later, amid the screams and exclamations of the company, a figure clad in the full costume of an Able Seaman in His Majesty's Navy bounded in, saluted the company, and broke into a lively hornpipe, which he danced to his own whistled accompaniment. They watched him, hardly believing their eyes. At the end of his performance he bowed gracefully and vanished back into the garden.

George Hogarth turned to his petrified family. 'Well – what the devil was that all about?' he asked them.

Catherine was fanning herself. 'I feel faint.'

'What a funny person,' said Mary pensively. 'Probably wounded in the Battle of Trafalgar.'

'Still, what impudence!'

The knocker of the front door was boldly wielded. Mary went to answer it. They heard her saying 'Mr Dickens! What a surprise!'

'A pleasant one, I hope, Miss Mary.'

'Oh, very pleasant.' He followed her into the room. 'You just missed the most extraordinary thing, though.'

'Oh? What was that?'

'A strange old sailor jumped into the room, did a hornpipe

and then jumped out again.'

'We think he was wounded at the Battle of Trafalgar,' added Catherine.

Charles greeted them all. 'How sorry I am to have missed your strange visitor.'

Catherine was looking at him keenly. 'Yes, it is a pity. But if you should run into the old chap, give him back this bit of his beard he seems to have forgotten.' And she yanked off his chin, with a painful pull, a piece of crepe hair which had been left behind when he dragged off the false beard. He yelped, and everybody burst out laughing, except Mr Hogarth, who had once more become absorbed in his notes and had not heard a word of Charles's conversation with the girls. He looked up.

'Just had a sailor in here, Dickens. Strange fellow. Good subject for one of your sketches in the *Morning Chronicle* – or the *Evening Chronicle*, or the *Monthly Magazine*, or even *Bell's*.'

Charles looked faintly embarrassed. 'Yes . . . Well, did someone mention tea ?'

Mr Hogarth sniffed. 'Surprised you have time for tea and social engagements.'

'Time, Mr Hogarth ? I have all the time in the world.' He looked ardently at Catherine, who blushed. She always seemed to be blushing these days.

In fact, time was what Charles lacked. As well as his tremendous literary output, he was travelling here and there on his Parliamentary reporting jobs. On the way to Bristol by post-chaise, accompanied by his old friend and co-reporter Tom Beard, he was impatient and incensed by the cartoonist Cruikshank's failure to meet a deadline for the new *Sketches by Boz*. *He* always kept his deadlines – was ahead of them, even. Why couldn't other people be as industrious and efficient ? All his efficiency and dynamic energy was needed for this present assignment, for the *Morning Chronicle* was out to beat *The Times* in reporting Lord John Russell's speech at Bristol. He gave Beard his orders.

'As soon as he finishes speaking you will dash to Marlborough in the chaise, transcribing your notes as you go.'

Beard looked dubious. 'I hope I can move so fast.'

'You will, Tom, you will. At Marlborough a horse express will be waiting to rush the report to London.'

'Is that necessary?'

'Absolutely essential. *The Times* have only thought of having a chaise and four all the way. A rider on horseback will beat them hollow. I'm certain of it. We shall beat *The Times*, Tom! We shall be the fastest reporters in the game.' He settled down in the corner of the chaise, securely confident, and fell asleep. Beard stared at him in admiring wonder.

CHAPTER SEVEN

They were not quite engaged, but there was an Understanding. Catherine was in a state of confusion; Charles was so ardent, so pressing, so flattering, that she felt she was being swept off her feet. Surely he was going to propose? They were long past Christian-name terms – she was Katie, Tatie, Pig, Wig, Tit-mouse, anything that sprang to his lips. They talked lovers' baby-talk. Yet, though Charles had started all this and babbled away happily enough, there would come a point in the conversation when Catherine knew that she had suddenly begun to irritate him, that he wanted her to say something different. What, for heaven's sake, did he expect of her? She had no idea.

They were walking in the Hogarths' garden, strolling, arm-in-arm. Now, surely, he would declare himself. It couldn't be that he was taking the whole thing for granted? Was she not going to get a proposal, a little romance? She knew that Mary and Georgina were watching them from a window. Oh dear, Charles *would* go on so about money . . .

'Not only,' he was almost shouting, 'do I have one hundred pounds due from publishers, and numerous commitments from magazines, but I have my salaries from both Chronicles . . .'

She broke in. 'Really, Charles, I am quite bad at book-keeping.'

He stopped and glared at her. 'Book-keeping? What has book-keeping to do with it, my dearest Tit-mouse?'

'Well, I don't understand commissions and things, although if it means you're doing well, I'm very glad.'

'*Well?*' (Now he was quite furious, she could see.) 'Of course I'm doing well. Very, very well indeed. As well as any bachelor in London.'

'Then – that's very nice.' Her heart sank lower as she saw his indignant face.

'Nice? Is that all you can say? Really, *nice* seems a most inadequate response to my question.'

Even Catherine's patience could snap. '*Question*? What question?'

He looked surprised. 'I've already spoken to your father. He seemed quite delighted.'

'How nice for Papa!' She pulled her arm from his and walked away, Charles following her and catching her up in a few steps.

'Well, dear little Mouse, what do you have to say to me?'

She turned on him. 'What do I have to say? I have to say that if this is your idea of a proposal, Mr Dickens, I'm – well – I'm not – *oh*!'

Bursting into tears, she ran away and flung herself on to a garden seat, where she sat with hidden face and heaving shoulders. Charles comprehended her as little as she him, but it did just drift across his mind that he might not have been quite so abrupt. Girls did expect a bit of gallantry, sometimes. He tried to remember the sort of things he had said to Maria in his silliest days. They had seemed to come naturally then, but now they rather stuck in his throat. He approached the heaving form.

'Dearest Tit-mouse, how can you ever forgive your stupid Tarlesie?'

Her 'Go away!' was almost inaudible.

He sat down beside her and put an arm round her, turning her tear-wet face on to his shoulder. 'Never. I will never go away from my darlingest angel.'

Her voice was weak, but he was relieved to hear that it trembled on the edge of a giggle. 'Go away, Mr Pickins!' she said, and suddenly laughed. He joined in, and they sat rocking together.

'Dear little Mouse.' For once he was not shouting. 'Please marry me, dear little mouse, or I shall be terribly unhappy.'

She gave him her most beaming smile, and they fell into one another's arms, to the infinite gratification of the two-girl audience at the window.

Now that they were really engaged, Charles was working harder than ever, if it were possible. His ambitions had been given a double set of wings. In the bare parlour at Furnival's Inn he sat scribbling, scribbling, out of place and time, lost in the impetus of his brain and his pen. Young Fred eyed him quizzically, sitting by the low fire, waiting for the kettle to boil and toasting bread. A flicker of flame against his hand drew from him an involuntary 'Ouch!'

Charles continued to scribble. 'Mmm? What?'

'I just said "ouch".'

His brother raised his head, eyes clouded with concentration. 'Thank you. I will.'

'Will what?'

'Hmm?'

'Oh, nothing. Would you like a piece of hot buttered toast in your ear?'

'Thanks,' replied Charles with a vague smile. 'This really is coming along very well.'

'So is my hand. It'll be delicious with a little butter on it.'

Rising and stretching, Charles perceived for the first time what was going on. 'Tea – and toast. What an excellent fellow you are, Fred.'

'Yes, I am, amn't I,' said Fred complacently, brewing the tea and buttering the toast. He poured tea into their two cracked, random cups. 'You'll have to get a few more cups when you're married.'

'Yes.' Charles was obviously uninterested in cups. 'I think I shall press on regardless tonight, Fred.'

'O lor! Not tonight again.'

Charles rubbed his hands in front of the fire. 'Best strike while the pen is hot and the ink bubbling with ideas. Do it now, Fred. Don't delay.'

Fred was serious for once. He might be younger than Charles, but he knew, he suspected, a lot more about some sides of life. 'All very well, Charles, if a fellow doesn't have the responsibilities of an engaged person on his hands.'

His gentle warning made no impression. Eating toast, Charles mumbled, 'Kate won't mind. She knows it's all for our good. It's for her future I'm working, Fred, as well as my own. Well, for the good of all our futures, you might say.'

Fred persevered. 'I mean, you've only been engaged three weeks.'

'Work must go on, Fred. I've explained it all very carefully to Kate.'

'I know you've explained it. Haven't I carried the letters to her and seen her get sulkier and sulkier?'

Charles took another piece of toast with a demoniac smile.

'Never fear. I shall send her a real corker tonight. I will *not* be dictated to by a capricious girl, Fred. I've seen which way that folly leads, and I'm resolved never to allow my heart to rule my head in that again.'

'Again?' Fred looked a question.

'Never you mind. Make some more toast. And afterwards you shall take a note to Miss Catherine Hogarth.'

Sighing resignedly, Fred picked up the toasting-fork, which was patently too short. 'I shall use this hand this time. The other one's quite cooked.'

Catherine read Charles's 'note' in her bedroom, and cried. It was, in fact, quite a long letter, couched in strong, reproachful terms.

My dear Catherine: it is with the greatest pain that I sit down, before I go to bed tonight, to say one word which can bear the appearance of unkindness or reproach; but I owe a duty to myself as well as to you, and as I was wild enough to think that an engagement of even three weeks might pass without any such display as you have favoured me with twice already. I am the more strongly induced to discharge it.

The charges went on and on. Her sudden and unlooked-for coldness had surprised and deeply hurt him. He could not have believed that such sullen and inflexible obstinacy could exist in the breast of any girl in whose heart love had found a place. If three weeks of his society had wearied her, she was not to trifle with him as though he were a toy. Oh dear! What was this? 'I shall not forget you lightly, but you will need no second warning.'

Mary, roused by her sister's sobs, crept into the bedroom. She took in the scene at once. 'Is it another – from him?'

Catherine turned a desperate face to her. 'What have I done? Oh, what have I *done*?' The letter ended with a line she could hardly make out through the blur of her tears; something about her more readily understanding the extent of the pain so easily inflicted, but so difficult to be forgotten.

'Oh Charles!' she sobbed. 'Forgive me.' Mary drew her gently down to a chair.

'But what has happened, Kate?'

'Charles is not coming tonight and it's all my fault.'

Mary sat silent beside her weeping sister. It did not occur to either of them that the Catherine of tonight was quite unknown to her family. The former Catherine had been always good-humoured, jokey, even-tempered to a fault. What had made her like this, always on edge or crying? Mary was very young. To her Charles was always charm itself. She never received broadsides or commands or threats from him. It was all quite incomprehensible. Mary wondered if one would ever truly understand anybody in this world.

Unaware of Catherine's reaction to the 'note', Charles was working away, happy and fulfilled, laughing at his own jokes, mentally patting himself on the back. He was dimly conscious of Fred's entry.

'Oh, Fred, I shall read this to you later on. You'll love it. Where have you been?'

'To the Hogarths', an't I? And Miss Catherine was *not* delighted.'

'Never mind, never mind. Make some grog, or maybe we'll go out and get a bit of supper.'

'There's a gentleman come.' Fred ushered in the short, neat, brisk man who had been hovering in the passage. Charles startled him with a dramatic reception, leaping up, hand clasped to brow, taking the two traditional steps back, his eyes registering amazement. 'My God!' he cried, 'it's you!'

Mr Hall, Junior Partner in the publishing house of Chapman and Hall, hoped he had not inadvertently dropped in at an asylum for lunatics. 'Sir?' he quavered. Charles fixed him with a glittering eye.

'Of course it is – it's you!'

'Well, if you say so – that is . . .'

'I do, I do. Oh, Fred, what an amazing omen.'

Fred seemed speechless, and Mr Hall nervously eyed the space between himself and the open door. He thought of bridging it with one leap, as this apparently demented author advanced on him, addressing him as Genie – or was it Jeannie? 'Perhaps,' he ventured, 'I had better come back at some more convenient time.' He had not the slightest intention of doing so.

Charles continued to rave. 'You it was who presided over my first success, blessed spirit!'

The man was certainly quite, quite mad. 'I really don't know what you are talking about, Mr Dickens. I am Hall, William Hall of the firm of Chapman and Hall.'

'And you have been or had been or were principal or assistant to a stationer and bookseller?'

Hall was surprised at this rational note. 'I was, sir.'

'And on a certain occasion, an unforgettable day, a moment of historic immensity, you, Mr Hall, sold to me, Charles Dickens, a copy of the *Monthly Magazine* containing the first sketch by the Inimitable Boz? I bless you for that for ever, sir! Grog for all, Fred. Sit down, Mr Hall. You are for me eternally an omen of good will, and whatever proposition you bear . . . You *do* bear a proposition, I take it?'

'Well,' said the by now considerably relieved Hall, 'an idea has occured to Mr Chapman and myself —'

'I accept!' cried Charles.

On the following evening he was regaling the Hogarth family with a spirited impersonation of Mr Hall telling him, 'We have concluded an arrangement with the popular comic artist Robert Seymour for a series of plates depicting the mishaps of a Nimrod Club of Cockney sportsmen.'

George Hogarth nodded sagely. 'Seymour's been planning that for a long time. But there's been difficulty in getting a writer to it.'

Charles was annoyed. '*If* I may continue?'

'They tried,' mused Mr Hogarth, 'both Theodore Hook and Henry Mayhew but both of them were far too busy, of course.'

Catherine saw Charles's angry face, and nervously plucked her father's elbow, whispering, 'Please let Charles go on, Papa.'

But he was still rambling gently. 'Of course, Seymour is a difficult fellow, very melancholic. Well, well, carry on, Charles.'

Charles threw him a curt nod. 'Thank you. So, says Mr Hall, "This firm has the greatest interest in *your* work, Mr Dickens. We are delighted you have agreed to contribute to our *Monthly Library of Fiction* your extraordinary comic sketch *The Tuggses at Ramsgate*."'

Mary clasped her hands. 'Oh, that is a funny one!'

Triumphantly, Charles turned to his future father-in-law.

'So you see, sir, I was not entirely unknown to Messrs Chapman and Hall in my own right. "Mr Chapman and I have been much impressed by your sketches in the *Monthly Magazine*", says little Mr Hall. Well – I made it quite clear to Mr Hall that in my opinion sporting adventures are dreadfully overplayed, that I had something in mind that was very much better, and that Seymour would do very well to vary his manner a little, and surprise his public by taking a few pointers from my writing.'

They cheered, but it took him some time to get into their heads what had actually happened. Mr Hall had commissioned him to write twenty monthly parts of 12,000 words each, which after the serial publication would subsequently be reissued in covers.

'But Charles,' said Mr Hogarth, 'I'm not quite clear yet on one point. What exactly is your thought for this Chapman and Hall project?'

Charles put on a bland aloof air, as though the answer were really too obvious to be stated. 'My thought? Very simple. I thought of Mr Pickwick.'

But alas, Robert Seymour's visual idea of Mr Pickwick was not Charles's. Indeed, Charles vetoed the picture of a thin, miserable-looking man as absolutely and impossibly wrong.

He raved at Chapman and Hall.

'Here I have launched Pickwick in all his might and glory. I have him with his friends on the coach to Rochester. I have brought in Alfred Jingle – a palpable hit, if I may say so, in all modesty.'

Chapman and Hall looked uncomfortable. Chapman said 'Yes . . . well, I agree that Mr Seymour is holding to his own lines. Though I have expressed my own opinion that Pickwick must be fat. I have already described to Mr Seymour a friend of my own at Richmond – a fat old beau who always wears drab tights and black gaiters. Good humour and flesh have gone together since the days of Falstaff.'

'Bravo, Mr Chapman! But how to communicate this eternal verity to the lugubrious Mr Seymour?'

Hall, meanwhile, had been leafing through a book on fishing, muttering that he had seen something, somewhere. Suddenly he found it, and waved the illustration at them. 'I think I have the answer here.'

The line-drawing showed the figure who was to become familiar to countless millions of the reading public so long as reading continued: short, rotund, bald of head, beaming through small spectacles, Mr Pickwick was tenderly holding an umbrella over some ducks in a thunder-storm.

Charles's eyes liquefied with tears. 'It is he,' he said emotionally. 'We have him. It is Pickwick.'

Because Charles was now too busy for such matters, it was Mary, Catherine and sometimes Fred who undertook the cleaning and sprucing of the chambers at Furnival's Inn which were to be the young Dickens's first married home; not the old bachelor chambers, but another set of three good large rooms with a kitchen in the basement. They were certainly more presentable than the others, but far from splendid. Catherine, smudgy-faced in a pinafore, flung down her duster in a temper.

'Oh, why do we have to stay in this dusty, dark old Furnival's Inn?'

Mary soothed her, seeing that she was almost crying. 'It'll be lovely, Kate, you'll see.' Catherine clung to her.

'And you *will* be here, won't you? You will stay with us?'

'Of course I will, dear. If you're sure Charles has no objection.'

'Charles adores you.' She choked, flinging herself into her sister's arms. 'Oh, Mary!' Mary heard her whisper something she could not catch.

'What, dear?'

Catherine repeated, very softly, 'I'm so frightened of being married.'

'Come now. Charles is very kind.'

'Yes. But he's so determined.'

'Is that bad in a man?' Mary asked.

Catherine didn't know. She had no views on men, or their determination. She had no idea, even, what it was that Charles was determined about, except for a feeling that it concerned something other than herself, and that it might one day crush her into dust thicker than any that lay on the floors and shelves of Furnival's Inn.

The empty rooms soon acquired possessions, if not anything that might be called furniture. Charles and Fred jubilantly pushed a handcart along Holborn. It bore, among other items, a pair of quart decanters and another of pints, a crystal jug and three humbler brown ones, a pair of glass lustres, in Catherine's favourite pink, and two china jars. At home there was a sofa already established, which Mrs Dickens's servant Sally was going to cover for them, a handsome sideboard and a small table. The goods on the handcart had been a bargain at three pounds seven shillings, and Charles reflected with pleasure that twenty-four pounds were left over from the advance on the first two numbers of *Pickwick*. 'Enough to furnish a mansion, my boy.'

His happy face changed as he caught sight of the familiar jaunty, shabby figure approaching them, swinging a cane. Charles hurriedly jabbed Fred with his elbow.

'Silent as the grave about the *Pickwick* money, Fred.'

'Say no more, brother Boz.'

They pushed the barrow until it came level with their father, who swept them a salute. 'The Inimitable Boz and Fearless

Fred, his devoted Figaro!'

They greeted him. He appeared to dash an unseen tear from one eye.

'My dear, dear boys. How it warms this ageing heart which has, not to put too fine a point on it, recently been somewhat buffeted by outrageous fortune. Yet, giving to the ungrateful world two such fine young fellows, among other blessed children which, I must say, seem from time to time, and times are desperately hard at the present – almost too numerous to mention – where was I?'

Charles hardly dared to glance at Fred. 'I think you were about to say that though you are hourly expecting something to turn up, you find yourself at the moment temporarily financially indisposed. Is that it, Fred?'

'I think it may well be, brother Boz.'

John Dickens was incapable of seeing a joke against himself. He beamed.

'My dear, dear boys. How understanding, and how very movingly *simpatico*. I was telling a good friend just now about my trip to Naples in the old days for the powers-that-be in the Naval Division. What's that I see? A convenient port of call? A well-earned leave, my hearties.'

It was the old, old scene. They were sitting at a public-house table with their father on the other side of it, downing a foaming pot of porter. Charles kept a careful eye on the handcart, which they had been allowed to bring in with them as it was a quiet time of day.

'Ah!' John smacked his lips. 'A draught of porter at the end of a hard day sets a man up for an evening of domestic happiness, as you will learn yourself very soon, Charles my boy. Marriage is a solemn affair, my boy. A heavy bond. An unending responsibility. A dreadful expense.' His eye strayed towards the handcart. Fred nudged Charles.

Charles shifted uneasily. 'Ah well. They say that two can live as cheaply as one, and certainly Fred and I have managed well enough. Haven't we, Fred?'

'So we have.'

'Of course you have, my merry boys. And why should you

not? Bachelors is one thing, but husbands is quite another. Take myself, for example. As a bachelor, a young gentleman about town, my wants were small. Even with a little carelessness here and there, things, as you might say, swung along very well. Then I was blessed by domesticity. Result? Permanent exhaustion of the financial organ. I think I might put down another blast of this excellent porter.'

Charles ordered one.

'Thank you, my dear, dear boy. Where was I?'

'Blessed and bankrupt?' suggested Fred.

John made a face. 'That word! Suffer it not to issue from the lips of a Dickens. Still, sufferance is the badge of all our tribe in such matter. All except your distinguished self, that is, Charles.'

Fred administered another nudge to Charles, who half-rose, saying, 'Yes – well, we'd better be getting our things back home.'

'Spending money like water, eh, Charles? Say no more, my boy. If you've got it, show it, says I.' He laid his finger to his nose. 'I hear on the Rialto that your efforts have been quite rightly rewarded with a commission of considerable value.'

'Just work, Governor, just work.'

'Not *just* work, Charles. For one of our ilk work is a blessing. We embrace work. We worship and adore work. You should be grateful to lie in the azure arms of beautiful work.'

'Well, I shall have a wife to provide for very soon.'

John clapped his hands in theatrical glee. 'Yes, indeed! You are blessed in all particulars. Whereas I . . .' he bowed his head. 'But no more of that.' As he buried his face in the second pot of porter Charles and Fred exchanged glances, and a silent message passed between them. The inevitable moment had come. John was quite patently waiting for Charles to make an offer. He emerged from the porter with a slightly ruffled expression. Some people couldn't take a hint, it seemed.

'Ah, yes,' he grumbled, wiping away froth. 'For myself I ask very little, and I trust that you yourself will discover that to be a family man is to be Destiny's beggar. Not to put too fine a point on it, my boy, I am in serious need of funds.'

Charles, looking at him, felt a tide of hatred welling up into his throat. If he allowed it to overwhelm him he would say or do something he would be sorry for. The hatred was drowning all the love he had once felt for his father. The little boy and the bluff handsome man who had looked down on Gad's Hill Place, they were gone, killed by endless nagging appeals for money. I have kept my promise, Charles thought. I have been persevering and worked hard, as he told me I should – God knows how hard! But I have no fine house, only three ugly rooms and a few sticks of second-hand furniture, thanks to this blood-sucking parasite. He choked the hatred down; violence was in his nature, a great stored-up hoard of violence, but this was not the way to expend it. He made his voice calm, expressionless.

'How much this time?'

John's face brightened. 'Fifteen pounds would resolve it.' He saw the coldness in his son's eyes, and did another sum. 'Er, ten pounds would keep the demons at bay.'

'Five pounds, Father. And that is the last contribution I expect to make for a very, very long time.'

John reeled back dramatically. 'Impossible! An insult to my creditors, and a very paltry gesture indeed to one whom, if I might say so, has . . .'

Charles stopped him with a raised hand. 'You might say so as often as you will, Father. I have paid out for rent, furnishings and never mind what else, and I am about to be married on a couple of hardly enormous publishers' advances. I am a man about to commit himself to the support of a woman. I put it to you, Father, that I'm no longer to be regarded as the provider of an annuity.'

Fred stared at Charles, the ever-patient, actually resisting their father. John's face fell into sulky lines. For once he spoke without fine phrases or blandishments.

'I refuse. You may keep your miserable charity for those who have no pride.'

But he was watching eagerly as Charles methodically counted out five sovereigns and laid them in front of him. 'Of course,' he added hastily, 'I realise that you intend no derogation of my paternal status. Er, shall we say seven ?'

Charles rose and reached for the coins. 'Come on, Fred.' But his father had scooped them up and pocketed them.

'You're a capital fellow, Charles. We shall never fall out – never, never, never. A glass of wine with your foolish ageing parent before you leave ?'

'We must go on. And you should, too, Father.'

'Pity. Carry on, my lads, then. I think I see a friend in the corner there. Bye, bye.'

Fred stole a look at his brother's stern face as they continued along Holborn. He knew that there was no remorse in Charles's spirit, only anger; and this Fred felt to be quite justified, for Charles couldn't put his nose round the door at George Street without one of them trying him for a touch, either Papa or Mamma. Mamma was almost worse, really, for she wasn't even amusing with it. She just rattled on in a sort of whine about how hard times were and how Letitia and Augustus could die of under-feeding for all Charles cared. Fred knew that Charles hated Mamma; and now it was Papa as well. He sighed. At least it would be jolly at Furnival's Inn.

Their laughter rang round the room, still under-furnished but far more habitable than when Charles had first taken over the chambers. The new treasures were laid out to be admired on the only table, a gaily patterned cover disguised the short-comings of the sofa. The fire was lit, for it was a cold March evening. Its glow and the light of several candles threw a warm radiance on four young faces. Charles, his temper quite restored, was trickling wine into the new decanter, while Fred cooked his speciality, mutton chops, over the fire. Fred laughed at Mary over his shoulder.

'I'll teach you to cook mutton chops,' he said.

'And I'll teach *you* how to wash up. There was piles of it.'

Charles held up the wine to the light, then poured it into four glasses.

'Beautiful decanter. Beautiful wine. First glass for a beautiful mouse.'

Catherine snatched the glass with a pout, saying 'Fanks' in a cold, small voice. Charles bent over her solicitously.

'There, there. Is my little mouse coss?'

'Ess.'

'Why is oo coss, dearest, darling Pig?'

She shrugged. 'I don't know. I dust is.'

His patience was beginning to wear thin. 'Well, *why* is oo?'

'I dust said, I don't know, didn't I?'

He stood up, angry. 'Well, oo *sood* damn well know.'

Catherine burst into ready tears. 'Oh! Oo swore at little mouse.'

He shook his head. 'Catherine, a saint would swear at some of your inexplicable turns of mood.'

Mary leapt into the breach. 'Kate has been a little off-colour all day, haven't you, Kate?'

He was not to be placated. 'Well, it's becoming a little bit too much of a habit. Help yourselves to wine. I was about to propose a toast, but my mood had been completely upset.'

Catherine sniffed. 'I'm sowwy, Tarles. Weely I am.'

'Oh, do stop that silly childish talk,' he snapped at her. 'It's time you behaved like a grown woman, Catherine. Must I remind you that you are to be married in three weeks' time?'

The tears returned. 'You don't have to remind me of that,' she sobbed. Mary threw him a reproachful look.

'Oh, I see!' he said. 'You don't want to think about your marriage, is that it?'

Weeping, her hands to her eyes, she ran out of the room, into what would be their bedroom, where she subsided into a chair and sat rocking to and fro in distraction. She was only twenty. Mamma had said quite clearly that gentlemen expected a little capriciousness from an engaged girl. One should not always be too easy. It seemed quite otherwise with Charles. It was he, not she, who had invented the baby language, and treated her as a little girl. Yet she had only to be 'coss' and he would fly into a fantod and make her cry. And now to ask her to behave like a grown woman, after all! It was too bad. Why could he not have got himself engaged to Mary, placid Mary, so good-humoured, without her own tendency to give way to tears that provoked tantrums?

The chair was rickety and very uncomfortable. But she

would not go back to them in the parlour. She would stay in the bedroom and suffer.

It was just as well. Standing, feet apart, in front of the fire, the master of the house was informing Mary and Fred, in authoritative tones, 'I will not accept ill-temper and capriciousness from any woman. And that is absolutely and irrevocably final.'

He was in much the same mood next morning, at Chapman and Hall's, as he surveyed without pleasure the cover of the first part of the *Pickwick Papers*, showing Mr Pickwick in a punt, dozing over a fishing-line.

'Mr Pickwick does *not* go fishing,' declared his creator emphatically. It is most unlikely that he will *ever* go fishing. I believe, indeed, that he absolutely *detests* fishing.'

By now Chapman and Hall were thoroughly intimidated by their fiery young protégé. They exchanged a nervous glance before Hall ventured, 'I suppose he *might* go fishing – sometime – under protest. Might he not, Mr Dickens?'

'Out of the question, Mr Hall.'

Chapman cleared his throat. 'Look here, Dickens. I doubt if the readers will take Mr Pickwick up as a sort of religious matter, you know. They will be content enough to see him fishing in a good drawing on the cover and read of him doing something else in the text within.'

Hall backed him up. 'I daresay Mr Chapman is right, you know.'

Charles gave them an acid smile. 'I have no doubt that Mr Chapman is right. The point at issue, though, it seems to me, is something different. I believe *my* readers will expect *my* characters to have a consistency and a truth which will justify them in following their adventures with devoted application.'

A furtive exchange of glances. 'Well, it's certainly to be hoped that *The Papers* takes on,' said Chapman. 'It's a considerable speculation, an innovation . . .'

'I believe that they *will* take on, but only if I keep honestly to my compact with my readers and give them, in paper after paper, the true world of Mr Pickwick. The *true* world, I say, not the world of that excellent but cross-grained artist gentleman Robert Seymour.'

'I see.' Chapman sighed. 'It's a question, then, of whether the artist is to follow the writer, or the writer the artist.'

'The text comes first, Mr Chapman.'

'In this case the plates came first. The initial idea was Mr Seymour's, you know.'

'Pickwick is *mine*!' Charles cried passionately. 'I will not allow him to be misrepresented by anyone.'

Dear me, said Chapman's eye to Hall's, this fellow is a confounded maniac. Aloud Chapman said, 'I suppose sooner or later you gentlemen will have to meet and have this matter out. What do you say, Mr Hall?'

'I say later rather than sooner, Mr Chapman,' replied Hall hurriedly, with visions of a violent confrontation. 'When shall we have the next number, Mr Dickens?'

'Soon, very soon. I am a little disarranged at the moment with the imminence of a wedding, but I shall not allow it to disturb my work.'

'A relative, Mr Dickens?'

'No. Myself, Mr Hall.'

But for all his coolness about it, the wedding day was a happy one. The early April morning was fine, blossoms adorned the orchards and neat gardens of Chelsea. A fresh wind blew from the river to greet the newly-wed couple as they came out of St Luke's. Catherine was blushing and beautiful, hanging adoringly on the arm of her slight young husband. He looked at her with possessive pride, and beamed happily at the immense crowd of relations he had acquired. Not only were all the Dickenses gathered there, but a bewildering array of Hogarths thronged the porch: Georgina was at home with the twins, Edward and Helen, but four brothers were there and dearest Mary stood at her sister's side as bridesmaid. Catherine's gown and veil were simple; her father was not in a position to splash out on wedding finery, but she looked all the better for that, thought Charles, his eye dwelling fondly on the voluptuous curves, the glossy ringlets, the deep blue eyes that so fondly met his.

Mingling with Hogarths were Dickenses. John and Elizabeth,

both by now slightly maudlin, in best clothes reclaimed temporarily from the pawnbroker. The bright face of Fred, the loving face of Fanny, here with her fiancé Henry Burnett, little Letitia, and the baby of the family, Augustus or 'Boz', nine years old. Charles assumed a patriarchal stance. They were all his; relations, dependants, pensioners, worshippers. He was a married man.

The honeymoon was to be spent at the village of Chalk, near Rochester. It was part of Charles's childhood, and he felt a need to go back into those scenes as he now was, perhaps to reassure the ghost of the little boy of Chatham that there was something brighter beyond the shades of the prison-house. Catherine lay beside him in the bed which took up most of the tiny bedroom. Charles was already peacefully asleep, but she was awake, crying very quietly, so as not to disturb him. She loved him so much. Her mother had tried to warn her, but she had not expected him to be quite so brisk and matter-of-fact about it, as though it were just part of his routine and her feelings were not important at all.

Yet he loved her too. She was quite sure he loved her.

CHAPTER EIGHT

For all the pleasure of striding out nine or ten miles a day from Chalk through the surrounding countryside, working off his energy and leaving Catherine resting at Mrs Nash's cottage, Charles was relieved to get back to town after a week's honeymoon. There was only one unpleasant factor in his welcome back: Chapman and Hall were not happy about the sales of *Pickwick*. The sales still lagged far behind the printing, the public were not buying, and the reviewers were lukewarm or baffled. The publishers were chagrined, but still, they told him, hopeful of something to retrieve the situation. 'You have created a magnificent English Don Quixote, Mr Dickens, but some essential ingredient is missing.'

Fresh from the publishers' office, his brow dark with gloom, Charles returned to Furnival's Inn. His young family, Catherine, Mary, and Fred, were playing word-association games in front of the fire, in fits of laughter because Catherine had said 'Sausage' and Fred had followed it up with 'Jam'. Charles ignored them as far as possible, refused his lovingly-cooked supper, and instructed Fred to prepare grog.

'I've asked the horrible Robert Seymour to come over for a glass. You girls, take your suppers into Mary's room and leave us to prepare for the bilious Seymour.'

Catherine was inclined to be rebellious, but Mary silenced her, and they stole away for a picnic on the floor. Charles waited for his visitor, impatiently muttering over the passages in which Mr Pickwick reaches the White Hart in the Borough. 'A great, rambling, queer old inn, with corridors and passages and staircases wide enough and antiquated enough to furnish material for a hundred ghost stories.' No more ghosts. There had been plenty already. A familiar, perhaps ? A Genie, out of the *Arabian Nights*, the *Tales of the Genie*? A Mr Hall? A servant?'

He was biting his pen when Fred darted in to announce Mr Seymour. The shabby, cadaverous figure hovered in the doorway as if it would prefer not to come in. Charles leapt up, pretending a spirit of welcome he was far from feeling.

'My dear Mr Seymour! What an honour for me to meet you, sir. It's taken too long, but then, you know, publishers, like Caesar, believe in divide and rule. Fred, make the grog, dear boy. Fred makes the best grog in town. Unless you prefer some other tipple?'

Seymour, exuding disapproval, waved the offer aside. On being invited to take a seat he dusted off the corner of the sofa and lowered himself on to it. Charles assumed an expansive attitude opposite him.

'You can have no idea how much I have enjoyed your work in the past, sir.'

Seymour looked sour. 'More than you have in the recent present, it would seem.'

Charles appeared not to understand him, then laughed. 'Oh, I see. My dear Seymour, you mustn't think I'm critical. No, sir, I thought the sketch you did for *The Stroller's Tale* excellent, in parts. The furniture of the room was depicted admirably. The alterations I wanted were simply for the woman to be younger, the dismal man less miserable, and the sick man emaciated, but not repulsive. That was all, sir. Otherwise I considered the sketch quite perfect.'

Seymour's smile was bitter. 'Good. Apart from the fact that I am unable to draw personages, I am glad you regard me as a competent craftsman. May I quote you as a testimonial when I apply for my next commission?'

The interview was not going well, in spite of the charm Charles was throwing into it. He motioned to Fred. 'Hurry it along. Come, Mr Seymour, a good blast of Fred's special.'

Fred ladled out a steaming, fragrant tankard of grog and handed it to Seymour, who sniffed it with disgust.

'I detest spice,' he said.

Undaunted, Fred withdrew the tankard. 'One coming up

without spice, sir.' Charles undertook some more placatory tactics. He was not used to resistance when he set out to please someone.

'Really, Seymour, you must not take my comments in bad part. I've your success in mind, as well as my own.'

Seymour sprang to his feet. 'My success, sir! My success has been established these many years past, sir. I daresay that when you were still polishing the cradle-marks off your back-side, my reputation was well grown.'

Charles waved towards the sofa. 'Entirely so, my dear sir. Yours is a fame undoubted, acknowledged, and long established, I agree. And like all very long established reputations, it can benefit occasionally from a little fresh spice.'

The reference was unfortunate. Seymour glowered at him.

'I hate spice, sir! Damn it, I hate it!'

Fred proffered another, spiceless tankard, which he refused. He glared malevolently at Charles.

'I have come, Mr Dickens, not to get your puerile advice on my career, but to give you a little about your own. It is this: a shorthand-writer may become a first-class hack, but the best hack in the world will never, never be an artist.'

He made towards the door, but Charles was there first, blocking it.

'Let me pass, sir!' Seymour fumed. Charles met his gaze unflinchingly.

'You may pass out of my house, sir, and out of my life, as quickly as you wish. But let me tell you this, Mr Seymour: whether I am a shorthand-writer, a hack or an artist, I care not. I tell tales for money. But if you are to draw my tales, sir, you will draw them as *I* write them. Good night to you, sir.'

Seymour had gone, the door slammed behind him. Timidly the girls crept back into the room, to find Charles white and shaking with anger, hardly able to speak. Catherine put her hand on his arm. 'Poor Tarles.' He shook it off.

'I'm going out.'

'Oh, but it's so late. I want Tarlesie to stay with Tittle-mouse.'

He was scrambling into his coat, reaching for his hat. She

followed him to the door. 'Please, dearest. I shall be fwightened.'

He burst out at her, 'Don't you see ? A fire is burning in me. I must walk it off.'

Fred, worried, went after him. 'Shall I come with you, old Boz ?'

Even in his rage, Charles had a kindness for his young squire. He touched Fred's shoulder gently. 'My dear young Sancho Panza,' he said with a smile, and was gone.

'Sancho Panza,' said Fred. 'Who's he when he's at home, I wonder ?'

'Don Quixote's man,' replied the well-read Mary.

Fred had no time to enquire further, for the door had opened again and a great tornado had blown into the room, yelling 'Sancho Panza!'

The coat was thrown to Catherine, the hat tossed to Fred. The pale furious Charles of a moment ago had given way to a luminous-eyed angel, glowing with inspiration, holy fire sparked off by a chance remark of his own.

'My Genie Fred!' he addressed his brother. Fred bowed.

'My gracious Boz.'

'Wittles, Fred.'

'Sausage and jam, Boz.'

'Exactly, Fred.'

Catherine looked from one to the other of them with a frown of worry. 'What *is* it, dearest ?'

'My Pickwick, my divinity! The missing ingredient. Sancho Panza. Sancho. San. Sam . . . that's it!' He threw himself down at the table and began to scribble furiously. At the White Hart Inn, Southwark, 'a man was busily employed in brushing the dirt off a pair of boots . . . he was habited in a coarse-striped waistcoat, with black calico sleeves, and blue glass buttons, drab breeches and leggings. A bright red handkerchief was wound in a very loose and unstudied style round his neck, and an old white hat was carelessly thrown on one side of his head . . .

'A loud ringing of one of the bells was followed by the appearance of a smart chambermaid in the upper sleeping gallery, who, after tapping at one of the doors, and receiving a request from within, called over the balustrades: "Sam!"

'"Hullo," replied the man with the white hat.

'"Number twenty-two wants his boots."

'"Ask number twenty-two whether he'll have 'em now, or wait till he gets 'em," was the reply.'

Sam Weller, second of the Immortals, had been born.

It came as no small shock to the self-dazzled Charles, still infatuated with his brain-child, to hear that on the night Seymour finished the new plate for *The Dying Clown* he had gone into the garden and blown his brains out. Alone at Furnival's Inn, Charles wrote and wrote, Seymour's face ever before him, and the words of the letter left by the suicide. 'I have never done a crime my country's laws punish with death. Yet I die, my life it ends. I hope my Creator will grant me peace, which I have prayed for in vain whilst living.'

'It was his destiny,' said Charles. 'He had his. I have mine. Nothing can change it.'

Fred had crept from his truckle-bed behind a curtain and was anxiously hovering. Charles gave him a weary smile.

'The work continues, Fred. The work is always in progress, Fred. The work is never-ending, Fred.'

'Of course.' Fred was trying to be comforting. 'It wasn't your fault. I mean, you couldn't know he was ill . . .'

'He was ill!' Charles shouted. '*I* am ill. Every artist, every writer is ill, Fred. The illness is loneliness, the impossibility of communicating with people other than those who live in our minds.'

He bent over the table again, while Fred, worried, busied himself making grog.

Out of Seymour's tragedy came success. Young Hablôt Knight Browne's drawings had all the humour and point that Charles had envisaged; Charles persuaded him to call himself 'Phiz' as a fizzy complement to 'Boz'. *Pickwick* now swept the reading public off its feet. As the story came out in numbers eager crowds waited for it at the bookstalls. The *Pickwick* characters were household names. Doctors read *Pickwick* between seeing patients, patients read it in the waiting-room.

Strolling through the streets, the proud author heard Sam Weller's sayings on the lips of streetsweepers and cab-drivers. The critics, who had not known what to make of the earlier numbers, became ecstatic after the triumphal entry of Sam. 'There is not a place,' they proclaimed, 'where English is spoken to which Boz will not penetrate. Meanwhile, take whatever means you must to borrow, steal, or preferably buy *The Pickwick Papers* by the Inimitable Boz.'

Charles had arrived, and in proof of it the publisher Richard Bentley offered him the unheard-of sum of five hundred pounds for a new three-volume novel. Macrone, publisher of the *Sketches*, was not pleased to be losing the option on the new work, and as a generous gesture Charles allowed him to buy, for a mere hundred pounds, all rights in the *Sketches*, a work from which he had already coined ten times as much as its author had. Charles was wildly elated with his new wealth, and with the idea for the new book, which was brightly clear in his mind. It was to be the tale of a lost child born in a workhouse, a poor motherless boy. He was playing with the notion of calling it *The Parish-boy's Progress*.

His energy seemed literally boundless. At the St James's Theatre a company was performing his farce, *The Strange Gentleman*. Even after it had been running for sixty nights he was unable to keep away from it, listening rapturously to the applause, joining in with it himself, only being persuaded with difficulty not to go on stage and take a bow with the actors. His spirits were unquenchable. Meeting the journalist and critic John Forster at dinner, he refused to be downed by that ponderous gentleman's condemnation of his literary style, and even drew from him a reluctant compliment. Neither man knew that Forster was to become his close friend and adviser, and eventually his biographer.

A brownish fog rolled along the length of Holborn, darkening the room where Catherine and Mary sat straining their eyes over their sewing. Catherine's bridal bloom had vanished. Almost nine months pregnant, she was pale and puffy of face and heavy of body, never very well and usually complaining. Suddenly she bent over sharply, causing Mary to look up.

'I think I feel something,' she said nervously.

'Oh, Kate! You *keep* feeling something.'

'I can't help it, can I? It's not entirely my fault. Your wonderful Charles Dickens has something to do with it.'

Mary looked startled. 'I don't understand, Kate.' Mary was aware of her own girlish admiration for Charles, and even a certain envy of Kate for having captured such a brilliant, handsome and altogether wonderful husband. It was only natural for her to dream sometimes, to speculate how life would be if *she* were Charles's wife; she thought she might possibly appreciate him rather more than Kate did, or perhaps show it in a different way. She knew Charles's great affection for her, but it would have been wickedly disloyal to have set out to charm him away from Kate, even had she the chance. She had no illusions about her own looks, which added up to a certain girlish attractiveness, but no more. Her nose was too big, her brow too high, her neck too long, her front teeth inclined ever so slightly to be rabbity. Catherine was quite lovely when she was in her best looks, and she and Charles made a most handsome couple. Mary looked pityingly at Kate, on the other side of the fire, holding her sewing away from her swollen body. Charles really should be at home more just now.

Charles, at that moment, was not very far away. In a narrow, fog-filled Dockland street off the Ratcliff Highway he was walking with a very stout, formidable-looking man who carried an equally formidable-looking stick. Though he wore plain clothes, he was an Inspector of the Metropolitan Police. He was showing Charles some of the realities of the background to his next novel, the story of the parish-boy. Charles was looking about him, from slimy cobbles to half-seen roofs, bright eyes piercing the fog, bright brain recording every noteworthy detail.

'What concerns me, Inspector,' he said, 'is simply where such a boy would find himself?'

'In the stone jug, I daresay. Prison, sir. A poor orphan thrown upon this town must become a thief.'

'A pickpocket?' Charles recalled seeing one of those nimble youths deftly swipe a silk handkerchief out of the back-pocket of an old gentleman absorbed in *Pickwick*.

'A prig, anyway, sir, a thief. There are gangs of them, you know, they work together. One distracts the victim, another bumps into him, a third makes off with his wallet or watch.'

'I see. A boy would take up with other boys, a gang of them. Living where?'

The Inspector smiled pityingly. 'Bless you, sir, where do a million rats live in London town? In what dark holes, high or low, they can find.'

'A rat-pack of boys, with a little rat-leader, I suppose.'

'Sometimes not so little, sir. Look at Ikey Solomons, the Jew fence. Brought up at the Old Bailey before Mr Serjeant Arabin in 1830, arrested on eight indictments, found guilty on two. Copped seven years' transportation, deserved a life-sentence. Had kids of his own and used others too.'

Charles was fascinated by Ikey Solomons. 'To pick pockets for him?'

'Anything. Looked after the little devils, though. Kept 'em well fed and warm.'

Charles saw the den in his mind's eye, the cunning-faced old man, the sharp wizened boys. 'Like a father-rat.'

The Inspector grunted disparagingly at this flight of literary fancy.

'A big father-rat, and a warm rats'-nest,' Charles mused. Suddenly the door of a small tavern they were passing flew open, and a shrieking woman rushed out, chased by a burly man carrying a stick. He was shouting.

'You lousy, poxy, stinking, rotten dirty thieving cow! Where's my money?'

She spun round, defending her head with her arms. 'I ain't got no bloody money!'

He raised the stick. 'Lying bitch!'

But arm and stick were arrested in mid-air as the Inspector stepped forward. 'I'd just put that up, if I was you, Tom,' he said. The other peered at him through the fog.

'Who the hell are you? Oh, it's yourself, Inspector. Just a bit of a rag between a cove and his dear lady, guv. Nothing serious.'

'He hit me, the bastard, he hit me!' screamed the woman, who was quite clearly an ordinary prostitute. The Inspector gave her a not unfriendly shove.

'You be off, Nancy. And you, Tom. I'll have you if you don't watch out.' The two figures slunk away, the woman into the fog, the man, swearing, back into the tavern from which came an alluring glow and a smell of hot spirits. By common consent, the Inspector and Charles turned into it.

Charles and Mary were panting up the stairs to the chambers in Furnival's Inn, a small but heavy side-table carried between them. Despite their breathlessness they were talking nineteen to the dozen, as they always did.

'Oh, what a gang my Twist people are!' he was saying. 'They seem to have taken me over entirely, the Jew especially.'

'Did you ever meet a Jew?' she asked.

'Well, not exactly. There used to be some in Chatham in the market, and of course some of them are fences in the East End.'

'Fences?'

'Receivers of stolen goods. Only my Fagin has a whole gang of young boys, like a pack of little rats, and the great old grey father-rat teaching and looking after them.'

'You sound as if you rather liked him.'

'Well, I suppose I do, in a way, as one likes all the people one writes.'

'Is Fagin a Jew sort of name?'

His face changed. 'I don't think it is, really – more Irish. It was the name of a boy I knew once, a very kind boy, Bob Fagin. He was a sort of father to me at that time.'

'What time was that, Charles?'

They had stopped on the landing outside their front door. Charles's eyes were seeing memories as he felt for his keys, too abstracted to look for them.

'A long time ago,' he said, 'in a different world, another age.'

'Do you think the man we bought the table from was a Jewman?'

'Sure to be. They always sell tables. Oh Lord, I hope Kate likes it. She's so difficult and up and down lately. Fred! Where *is* the boy? Now you put the table down, Mary. Fred will carry it.'

'I can manage it.'

He was alarmed. 'You'll strain yourself.'

She laughed. 'Charles, I'm not a china doll.'

'Yes, you are. A pretty little china angel doll for the top of a Christmas tree.'

She made a face. 'Ugh! I'm actually quite strong.'

'Nevertheless I can manage for myself. Fred!'

But it was Catherine's voice they heard from the bedroom. 'Oh, come, Charles, please . . .'

'At once, my love. Now, Mary, you open the door ceremoniously, and I'll bring in the ark of the covenant.' Carrying the table before him, he began to intone, 'Here is the best side-table in the woor-ld. It is for the most beautiful pig in the woor-ld.'

Catherine was not in any state to be amused. She was pale, sweating, and very frightened. 'It's started,' she told them. 'Fred's gone for the doctor. Oh, Mary!'

Charles peered over Mary's shoulder at his wife. 'Oh God! what is it?

'It's started,' Mary said quietly. Charles was by now as pale as Catherine.

'Oh, no! We must do something. What must we do? Oh, God, what have I done?'

Mary was wiping Catherine's face with a damp towel. Catherine was moaning, but with a touch of temper.

'Charles, why are you never here?'

He knelt beside her. 'I'm here, my beloved. I'm here, my heart. Forgive me. Forgive me, my little tittlemouse.' She tried to laugh, then winced as another pain caught her.

'Don't speak,' he urged her. 'Say nothing. Don't strain yourself. We must give her something, Mary, we must.'

Mary, with comparatively fresh memories of the birth of the twins to her mother, was perfectly calm and gently competent. 'It's perfectly normal, Charles, really. Now do go away.'

'How can it be normal? It's terrible. Oh – I feel quite faint . . .'

Mary was pushing him out. 'Please go away, Charles. Go and write.'

Catherine faintly seconded her. 'Yes, go away, Charles.'

He took her hand and kissed it. 'I will if you want me to. Whatever you want, my dearest, I shall do, and I shall always do.'

'Kiss me first.'

He kissed her brow, then her lips, murmuring, 'My poor little soul.'

An hour later he was sitting in the living-room, hunched miserably in a chair, his hands over his ears. The doctor was with Catherine, who was making a great deal of noise. Fred, who like Mary was used to the advent of babies, sauntered in.

'Well, well,' he said, 'this is a fine 'ow-do-you-do.'

'What, what?' Charles shouted distractedly.

'I just said this is a fine 'ow-do-you-do. That's all.'

Charles scowled. 'Oh, don't be so fatuous, Fred.'

'Yes. Well. Quite so. Sorry, I'm sure.'

Charles glared at him. 'Sorry? What help is it to be sorry now?'

'Why, what have *I* done?'

'That poor girl going through the agonies of the damned, because of us, Fred.'

'*Us?*'

'Man, Fred. Man.'

Fred patted his shoulder in a fatherly manner. 'Don't let on so, Boz old boy. Women expect it, you know.'

Catherine's cries became more and more heart-rending. Charles stood up, looking pale and sick, and almost ran out of the room.

'That's right,' Fred called after him, 'you take a nice walk.'

Mary put her head round the bedroom door. 'Where's Charles?'

'Gone for a walk.'

'Thank God.'

It was early evening, already quite dark, when Charles came home, having tired himself out walking frantically through miles of streets, muttering passages from *Oliver Twist* aloud, to the concern and dismay of passers-by. At the foot of the stairs he hesitated, about to fly again should the same dreadful sounds assail his ears. But instead, he was startled by another voice than Catherine's; the loud, lusty bawling of a baby. For a split second he was uncomprehending, then, with a joyful face, he ran up the stairs two at a time.

Peace and calm reigned in the bedroom as he entered it. Baby Charles had dropped off into a sudden sleep, Catherine, smiling and restored to flushed, dishevelled beauty, was nursing him, while Mary, with her smooth hair for once coming down, sat proudly beside them on the bed and Fred tidied up the room.

'Hurrah!' Fred greeted his brother. 'It's a boy!'

'I know, I know,' said Charles, pushing past him to Catherine's side. Tenderly he looked down at her, as she uncovered the tiny crumpled face of Charles Dickens Junior for his inspection.

'My very dearest, most beloved, quite remarkable and utterly sweet wife,' he said. 'Thank you, thank you.'

CHAPTER NINE

It seemed to Charles that the cottage at Chalk had shrunk alarmingly since he and Catherine had spent their honeymoon there. In fact, it had, not surprisingly, retained its old dimensions; the difference was that nearly two years had passed, and that it was now expected to accommodate not only themselves but young Charley and his wet-nurse and Mary, not to mention the coming-and-going presence of Mrs Nash, their landlady, who was tucked into a corner of it somewhere. Charles wondered whether she shared the small stable at the rear with the horses.

Diligently, even violently, he was polishing his boots in the kitchen. Next door Charley was crying lustily. Charles peered ruefully at the distorted reflection of his face in the leather.

'Where there's blacking, there's tears,' he remarked to himself.

The cries went on, mingling with calls for him from Catherine. With a sigh he abandoned the boots and went into the sitting-room, where Charley, purple-faced, lay screaming in his crib, fussed over by the women.

'D'ye think I should feed him again, ma'am?' asked the amiable, heavy-breasted young Scots nurse.

'You've just fed him,' Catherine snapped. 'He isn't a baby pig that needs feeding the whole time, you know. Oh, Charles, he cries far too much, and it's all my fault!'

Oh, not more tears, he thought. Must it rain inside as well as out, perpetually, implacably, even in an English February? 'There you are – a born writer,' he said to Charley. 'Always complaining. Whatever are you worried about, Kate?'

She was standing holding the baby with a sort of hopeless, wooden awkwardness.

'Shall I take him back, ma'am?' proffered the nurse.

'Oh, take him, take him. He seems not to want his natural mother, so take him.' She thrust the squalling bundle back into the nurse's arms. At once he calmed down and began to coo and gurgle as he was borne upstairs. Charles patted Catherine's shoulder.

'There you are, you see. No trouble at all, my mouse. You really must let nature take its course, my love.'

She spun angrily round. 'How *can* I let nature take its course? That's exactly what's wrong. That's why he cries so much. Oh, I know he's going to hate me for ever because I can't feed him myself.'

'Oh, not that old song again. Many ladies do not feed their babies. Good lord – ladies have always used wet-nurses, and why not? Why should you be so concerned about it, my dear Kate?'

She jerked herself away from him. 'Oh, you don't understand anything. Everybody says you're so clever and how much you understand, but you don't understand anything that really matters.' She ran out, slamming the door. Charles and Mary exchanged weary glances.

'She really is getting worse,' he said quietly.

'She's just very upset.'

'Aren't we all upset?'

'I'm sure she'll get over it in time,' Mary said.

'But how much time? Anyway, I've got to go to London and deprive myself of this wonderful little holiday we're all having together, in order to look at hundreds of expensive houses suitable for a successful but soon to be impoverished writer with, no doubt, a soon to be immensely increased family to keep.'

Mary's eyes were reproachful. 'Oh, Charles, think of poor Kate.'

'Yes, yes, yes. Poor Kate, and poor Charley, and poor me . . .' He was looking at her fondly. Always good-tempered, always loyal to Kate, always cheerful, his little girl, his dear Mary. 'And you, poor, poor, lovely, adorable, angelic you!'

She blushed. 'You shouldn't talk to me like that.'

'I should, and I shall, and I must. Mary, do you imagine that there is any pleasure in my family life at the present time other than your blessed presence?'

She was still protesting, and he babbling self-pityingly on, as they walked to the stables.

'Who has time to listen to the problems of my work? Who gives me unending sympathy? To whom do I turn in the utter boredom of this place for comfort?'

The utter boredom, Mary reflected, had been considerably alleviated for him by immense daily walks, twenty-mile marathons in the winter countryside: to Chatham, where the hulks of old ships lay and life seethed as busily as it had done in his boyhood; to Rochester, where he could laugh over the Pickwickians' adventures at the Bull; through the marshes to Gravesend; to Little Cobham and the tiny picturesque Leather Bottle, the inn to which he would send the heartbroken Mr Tupman. Then, flushed with exercise, health, and good Kentish ale, he would return singing to his 'petticoats', the two baby-ridden girls in the stuffy cottage. Whoever had been bored, it was not Charles.

For once Mary's tone was sharp. 'You should not speak so of the place where you spent your honeymoon.'

'Oh, no. Let us not speak of that at all. My very dear Mary, you are too divinely young to be spoken to of anything but the most perfect . . . love.'

Mary frowned. 'I shall go in immediately if you speak so, Charles.'

'But why should I not speak of it? What harm is there in an affection as perfect as ours – an emotion untarnished by the mundane, tedious commerce of life?'

Her smile had faint annoyance in it. '*I* am alive, as well you know.'

'Alive? Ah, of course you are! Magnificently alive and quite, quite perfect.'

'Oh, well. I suppose if it makes you happy then there is no harm. Now let us talk sensibly. Will you see Mr Braham about a new burletta?'

'Yes, and skin him,' Charles promised.

The Green Room of the St James's Theatre was a babel of loud theatrical voices. The curtain had come down on another performance of *The Village Coquettes* and the usual animated post-mortem was in progress. Charles pushed his way through the throng towards John Hullah, the young composer who had supplied the music to Charles's libretto. Hullah, talking to a pretty actress who was removing her make-up, saw him and waved.

'My dear Boz! What a stranger. Had enough of the country, have you?'

Charles was inhaling deeply. 'Ah, the smell of it, the delicious stale air of the theatre. That's what the country doesn't have, John.'

Hullah was searching a sideboard. 'There was a bottle of good brandy hereabouts recently, I remember.'

Charles laughed. 'I don't need it. I shall just drink in the atmosphere.'

There was certainly plenty of it to drink in, composed of heavy smoke from the gentlemen's pipes and cigars, with an occasional wisp from a daring lady's cigarette, and the smell of gin and porter mingled with that of grease-paint and scent, the whole blended by that ineffable breath which blows from stages, and is more like wood-shavings than anything else. Charles loved it and raffish people, mimes, wits, whores, who drove the blue devils away.

A pretty face was smiling at him through the smoke. It was the charming, bold Miss Allison, at present only sustaining the part of one of the dancing, singing villagers, but hoping for better things, and not particular how she achieved them. 'Beautiful Boz!' she said, patting his cheek, 'are you back?'

He kissed her hand. 'Adorable and accomplished Miss Allison, I am, and starving for supper. Are you?'

'Indeed I am, and have a gentleman waiting for an hour to feed it to me.'

Charles struck an attitude, still holding her hand. 'Let him wait all night.'

'Ah, Boz,' she sighed, 'I would sooner keep him waiting than you, were it not for one small unconsidered trifle.'

114

'Which is, lovely lady?'

'That he, dearest Boz, is in management. Nighty-night, old flower.'

She stood up on tip-toe to bestow a kiss on his cheek, and was gone, in a flutter of lace and a whiff of patchouli. Charles looked after her with a certain wistfulness; what an agreeable change she would have made . . . Hullah was leading him over to where a fragile-looking girl was having her hand held by Pritt Harley, the spectrally thin, middle-aged comic man who was playing Farmer Stokes in the present piece. Harley beckoned to him and introduced the young lady as a promising ingenue. 'And this, my dear, is Mr Boz, a very excellent writer.' She gave Charles a smile and her small hand, which Harley seized and patted.

'You must always be kind to writers, my dear, for they're useful fellows. But you must keep your finer feelings for leading actors. Now, Boz, do you have something for me? I need a Pickwick with something singular to it.'

'My dear Harley, that's exactly what I have planned for you – precisely.'

'Have you, have you? Give me a sample, just a touch. What's the story, eh?'

'The story is, dear Harley, that Braham doesn't pay.' He turned to Hullah. 'Does he, John? How behind is he on what's due on the last opus?'

Hullah shrugged. 'My dear fellow, I never stop pursuing him.'

'Damn and blast it!' Harley burst out. 'I shall speak to him myself. If he wishes to retain the services of distinguished artists, he must provide them with adequate material and compensate the word-mongers commensurately. Fear not, Boz, I shall deal with Master Braham. And you'll let me have a new piece soon, eh?'

'Dear Harley, your favoured scribe waits on you.'

Charles and Hullah moved on through the chattering mob, Hullah scooping up the errant brandy bottle. He paused to pour a glass each.

'Come on, let's eat, drink, and if we get the opportunity, be merry. For tomorrow we return to being husbands, fathers and dolts who write for money we don't even get paid promptly.'

Charles drank his brandy, still brooding on money. John Braham, who had certainly started life off as Abraham, had been immensely successful in his time as a tenor singer. According to himself he had been 'discovered' in Naples as a street-urchin with a divine voice either by Nelson or Sir William Hamilton; the details varied. Later he had been a friend of the Hamiltons and a frequent performer at Emma's musical evenings. He it was who had drawn tears from every eye after the Battle of Trafalgar with his pathetic rendering of *The Death of Nelson*. He had had a notorious and prolonged amour with the singer Nancy Storace, and after her retirement had married the ambitious Fanny Bolton, who had persuaded him to launch himself into theatre ownership and management. Undeterred by his failure with the Colosseum a few years earlier, he had built the St James's at a cost of £26,000. Most of the very good money he had earned on the concert-platform had gone into the building of what was already known as 'Braham's Folly', and elaborate Jewish jokes were told about him, usually by those he was slow to pay.

As if on cue, the Green Room door opened and Braham himself entered. In his sixties now, he was an impressive figure, big-chested, showily-dressed, the once raven curls thinning and grey, the expressive eyebrows still black in an olive face. Charles jerked Hullah's arm and made purposefully towards the manager, on whom other people were converging. Cutting off their approach, he sailed into the attack.

'My dear Braham!'

The eyebrows rose dramatically, the full-lipped Oriental mouth expanded in a smile that was not, perhaps, wholly enthusiastic.

'Ah, Boz. I had heard you were in the country.'

'So I was, but, you know, country prices are going up.'

'Are they indeed?' said Braham, vaguely, his eyes searching the crowd for an escape route. 'Now, where is the person I was looking for?'

Charles buttonholed him affectionately. 'Here I am, dear

old chap, and telling you how desperately expensive life is, so that one really has to be paid sums owing for value given.'

'Of course, of course. But this is hardly the time to . . .'

'Perfect time, I would think,' Charles interrupted remorselessly, 'since John tells me you are eager to get a new burletta.'

'Ah, well.' Braham sighed. 'That's so.'

'And by a strange coincidence I happen to have completed only yesterday the most rib-tickling, funny piece you ever did read.'

'Indeed? Good part for Harley?'

'The greatest part for Harley ever written, I would say. Wouldn't you, John?'

'I would.' Hullah looked with admiration at his friend, only to be tackled directly by the manager.

'Why haven't you mentioned this piece of Boz before, dammit?'

'Well,' said Hullah shiftily, 'I would have done, only Boz does these things so much better himself.'

Braham consulted his large, ornate watch. 'I had an engagement, but you may as well join us. Let's go to supper and talk about it, Boz.'

They supped, and talked about it, in a private room above Rule's Restaurant in Maiden Lane. Braham's previous engagement proved to be none other than the comely Miss Allison, who, deprived of a possible proposition from Braham, flirted delicately with Charles on the off-chance of being escorted home. The supper conference resulted in an agreement for another burletta, to be known as *Is she his wife? or, Something Singular*. Charles went home rejoicing. He was never happier than in this, the Other World, as he called it to himself, the world of the theatre which he might have inhabited altogether but for Fate's bestowal of a bad cold on the day of Mathews's auditions.

Furnival's Inn was not to be home for much longer. The intelligent Fred, sent to scout round the agents and the noticeboards, had found his brother a house. It was No. 48 Doughty Street, in Bloomsbury, a substantial terrace house in a private thoroughfare near Gray's Inn, with a porter in livery and a porter's lodge at the entrance to the street to ward off undesirable visitors to the street. The house had twelve rooms, a substantial basement, and a pleasant garden, even a stable. It was expensive, but what of that? *Is she his wife?* had brought in another hundred pounds from Braham, which would account for the eighty pounds the first year's rent would cost.

He had taken it. He looked forward to telling Catherine when he got back to Chalk, to banishing the look of discomfort on her face, to assuring her that the lack of room they had suffered from at Furnival's Inn would be more than supplied in Doughty Street. But she was asleep when he tiptoed into their bedroom. His stumble over a chair-leg woke her, and she murmured sleepily. His attempted news-breaking was lost in embraces, in the small tender words she could say to him when she was not harassed by the baby or provoked by his admiration for Mary. There would be yet another Dickens on the way before the moon went down.

Out in the country next morning, riding or walking their horses, Charles and Mary were talking about the grand new house, the visitors it was to have, the occasions it was to see.

'I hope you'll tell Kate about all this,' she said. 'If she's to be queen of this great salon, she ought at least to know.'

He removed a tuft of grass from a stirrup. 'I told her last night,' he said casually.

'Oh? Was she pleased? Of course she was.'

'Naturally. In fact, she didn't seem to take it in. Oh, Kate doesn't bother about these things.'

Mary frowned. 'Of course Kate bothers. You do have some extraordinary ideas about women, Charles. It's exactly the kind of thing a woman bothers about most, a grand house, and grand people visiting, and a family, and – oh, everything.'

Charles patted her shoulder. 'Well, it needn't bother you then, little angel girl.'

Really cross now, Mary snapped 'And I suppose that puts *me* in my place.'

He looked enquiring. Coldly she said, 'I am a woman, Charles. A grown woman. You yourself have told me of women no older than me with children. I am not a – a doll, or a toy, or something.'

'Dearest angel child . . .'

'I am *not* an angel child!' she said furiously, and, running over to her horse, mounted it and galloped off. Baffled, he mounted his and pursued her, catching up with her wild galloping only after a long stretch in which she rode like a Maenad, her hat blown off, her ringlets streaming behind her. Riding hard himself, he was sure her horse had bolted. By a supreme effort and a sharp detour across a field he managed to draw level with her, catch her bridle, and pull her horse to a walk. She was laughing, excited.

'Oh, that was wonderful, Charles. Wasn't it wonderful?'

Frightened, angry, he said sternly, 'How dare you?'

She pulled away from him and rode on, her shoulders squared, her laughter quenched. He dismounted and ran to catch her up, walking beside her flowing skirts, glancing up anxiously at her set profile.

'Get out of my way, Charles. Or apologise.'

'Apologise? Whatever for? For saving you from being thrown by a bolting horse?'

'He didn't bolt. I was in complete control. Now stand aside and let me ride on my own way, or apologise.'

Baffled (for he had really established in his mind the image of her as a china doll, a simpering angel, a beautiful boneless creature from the Book of Beauty) he trailed along beside her. 'Of course I'll apologise,' he said, in a voice very different from his usual assertive tone, 'if you can show me that I've been wrong in any way . . .'

'How will you apologise?'

'How? I shall just . . .'

'Yes, you'll just say you're sorry, and the next time you feel like it, we shall all be your toys as before.'

He shook his head, dazed. 'I cannot begin to understand what has happened to you. How *should* I apologise to my little Mary?'

Very cold and grown-up, his little Mary said, 'You may kiss my boot.'

Charles stared at the small foot she held out to him, in the highly-polished black boot. At close quarters, he could see his face in it. The smell of Warren's blacking was in his nostrils. His feelings in turmoil, he put his lips to the shining leather.

At the St James's, some days later, he and Hablôt Browne were coming away from a rehearsal of *Is she his wife?* Miss Allison, playing Mrs Lovetown, had looked singularly beguiling as she uttered speeches that had started life with Catherine. 'I could bear anything but this neglect. He evidently does not care for me. I declare that if I hadn't known you to be such an exquisite, good-tempered, attentive husband, I should have mistaken you for a very great brute.'

Browne was smiling, shaking his head. 'No doubt about it at all, Boz. Miss Allison is yours for the taking.'

'Or yours, or Braham's, or Hullah's, or anybody's.'

'Well, of course. Yes, possibly. Sooner or later. Why not, indeed? But for the moment definitely reserved for Boz. But you had better strike while she's hot.'

Charles gave a short laugh. 'I hear she's always hot.'

'Seems to me you're off our virginal leading lady.'

His friend was frowning, abstracted. 'Tell me, Phiz, what do you make of them? I mean, generally.'

'Actresses?'

'No, no, women. Actresses are not women.'

'Some of them give a damned good imitation, though. Far better performance than most of the originals give.'

'Why are they so complicated?'

'Are they?'

'All right, then. Why are they so simple?'

'See what you mean, of course,' said Browne, who did not. 'Still, they do have their complications.'

'Angels and devils, both at the same time.'

'Quite so. Wonderful, ain't it.'

'No. An angel should be an angel, a devil should be a devil, a woman should be a woman, Phiz. A nice, pretty dollish sort of a person. Oh, why can't they be like that? I mean, those who aren't frumpish spinsters, or sisters, or old hags, or something equally ridiculous.'

Browne studied the intent face, trying to read sense from it. 'I haven't the least idea of what you're talking about, Boz old boy. Have you?'

They exchanged stares. Charles had, in truth, no more idea than Browne. His views on women were drawn from a hopelessly tangled muddle of individuals. His mother, once beloved, now a betrayer and a cadger, cordially hated. His sister, once his best friend and childhood sweetheart, lost to him through marriage to another. Maria, his one-time Angel . . . he could not even let his mind dwell on her. Catherine, once so voluptuous, laughing, good-tempered, quite changed. Or was it he that had changed both himself and her? His wonderful mind had met a challenge he could not face. The nearest he could get to answering the riddle was to seize upon the case of Catherine. What had transformed her to somebody he still loved at times but in the main rather disliked? It could only be marriage. Perhaps, then, the answer had to do with a loss of innocence. That was why he loved Mary, or thought he did. He shut the thought of the episode in the meadow near Chalk, when she had seemed to tantalise him deliberately, out of his memory. Mary must always remain innocent; then he would always love her.

'Vimmen!' he said to Browne in his Tony Weller voice. 'Vimmen, Sam, vimmen!'

In order to move into Doughty Street, with new furniture and extra staff it was necessary to get some money from somewhere. The obvious source was Richard Bentley, the somewhat curmudgeonly publisher who had bought the rights in *Oliver Twist* with the proviso that Charles should edit his magazine, *Bentley's Miscellany*, and contribute sixteen original pages a month to it. Grudgingly enough, Bentley obliged with an advance of a hundred pounds and agreed to act as a reference for the lease of Doughty Street. At the same time, Charles persuaded him that the time had come to acknowledge a hidden truth to the world. 'The famous and wealthy Boz is none other than your humble servant, Charles Dickens!'

The removal was over. In that state of felicity which follows such upheavals the Dickens family and Browne were celebrating in the new parlour, a spacious, handsome one indeed compared with Furnival's Inn. Round the fire which was driving off the chill of an early April night and warming up the newly-papered room the five young people were sitting, toasting the founder of the feast in champagne.

'Charles Dickens!' they cried, raising glasses to him, and Fred added 'Coupled with the name of the unforgettable Mr Pickwick. Happy birthday, Pickwick old fellow!'

Charles stood up, thumbs beneath lapels, for all the world like a very pompous personage answering a very pompous speech.

'My lords, ladies, gentlemen, Mr Pickwick and any dogs who may be present . . .' He himself joined in the laughter that surrounded him. 'Thank you, thank you, my dearest, most beloved family. Oh, we shall be so happy here, shall we not? You, my dearest Catherine, and you, our very dear Mary, and you, old Fred, and you, young Phiz, and little Charley Culliford Boz Dickens, blessedly sleeping somewhere up there in one of our twelve elegant rooms . . .'

'With private garden in the rear,' put in Fred.

'On a very genteel private estate,' added Browne.

They all laughed. Charles looked round the circle, misty-eyed. 'Bless you, bless you all,' he said tearfully. The champagne was going down very fast. He produced a piece of paper from his pocket. 'There are no creatures in the world,' he proclaimed, 'with whom I would rather share my life and fortunes. Feast your eyes, my dearest creatures, on that!'

Fred was the first to handle the cheque. His eyes widened as he saw the amount. 'Five hundred pounds!' he gasped. The others exclaimed in joyful amazement.

'Wherever does that come from, Charles?' Kate asked.

'Grand birthday present for Pickwick from Messrs Chapman and Hall. Pass it round the audience, Fred. My young assistant will pass the hobject haround for your hinspection, ladies and gentlemen. There are to be dinners, special advertisements, and general national celebrations which I hope no one will confuse with the forthcoming Coronation of our divine young queen, with whom I confess myself to be totally in love. No, no, friends, all this celebration is devoted to none other than your own, your very own, your very own humble servant, Charles Dickens!'

They chorused the name with him, and Fred dashed round refilling everybody's glass. The girls flung themselves back in a state of pleasurable collapse on the sofa, their faces close to each other. Mary looked at Catherine.

'Are you feeling quite well?'

'Of course I am.'

'Only I thought you looked a little pale.'

'I'm perfectly all right. Come to that, *you* look more than a little red.'

Mary put her hands to her cheeks. 'Yes. I do feel hot . . . oh, it's all so exciting.'

Charles and Browne were talking seriously. 'An official statement really must be issued soon, making it quite clear that Boz is Charles Dickens.'

Browne smiled. 'Get a statement made from the throne after the Coronation ceremony, perhaps.'

A few days later Mary was laughing over a copy of *Bentley's Miscellany*. Trust Charles to break the news with a pun.

> Who the dickens 'Boz' can be
>   Puzzled many a learned elf,
> Till Time unveiled the mystery,
>   And Boz appeared as Dickens's self.

She cut out the verse and pasted it into her scrap-book of cuttings, all about her famous brother-in-law. Catherine's voice floated up the stairs.

'Mary, do come and have tea. You've been up there for hours.'

As Mary half-rose to call a reply, a wave of faintness or giddiness struck her, knocking the breath out of her body like a wave of the sea. She slumped into her chair, head in hands, breathing stertorously, until the feeling passed and she was able to call that she would be down in a moment.

On Saturday, May 6, there was a gala night at the St James's. The management presented a triple bill consisting of *The Village Coquettes*, extracts from *Mr Pickwick*, and *The Strange Gentleman*. A typical Saturday night audience had received all three with wild applause, and the appearance of the author with his cast at the final curtain drew prolonged cheers. A happy party arrived back at Doughty Street, for Catherine and Mary had been in the best box in their best finery. They were all laughing and chattering as Charles turned the key. Fred met them in the hall.

'Well? How did it go?'

'Magnificent!' cried Mary.

'Very well, really,' added Catherine. Charles was suddenly serious.

'What's troubling you, brother Boz?' Fred asked.

'I was just thinking what a pity it was that you missed such an occasion; quite unforgettable.' Little did he know the truth he was uttering.

'Well,' said Fred, 'how about a good old Furnival's Inn grog to celebrate it?'

Charles agreed eagerly, but Catherine was yawning. 'I'm tired, Tarles,' she complained moving to lean on him. Her cloak caught a small flower-vase on the table, and it fell over, spilling water and flowers on the floor. She saw Charles's look of exasperation and said defensively, 'Well, it isn't my fault. I'm tired.'

'We will not stop you from going to bed, Kate,' he said coldly.

'Then I'll go.' She flounced past him and up the stairs.

'Perhaps we had all better go to bed, Charles,' Mary said. 'It has been lovely, but it's so late.'

He was sulking. 'Oh, as you like. The mood's broken now, anyway.'

She came close to him, looking up into his face, her hand on his arm.

'All parties come to an end, Charles,' she said gently.

Suddenly he smiled. 'I suppose they do. Goodnight, my . . .'

'Mary. Your Mary.'

Tenderly Charles said, 'My Mary,' and kissed the hi smooth forehead. For a moment he looked down at her, fixing her in his mind's eye; the white shoulders revealed by the low dress, the long slender neck, the small hand pale against his dark blue coat, the little ring sparkling on it. Then she was gone, smiling back at him from the stairs.

Fred was surprised to find the ladies vanished when he brought the grog into the parlour, but was only too happy to help Charles drink the lot. Charles had launched into a vivid description of the evening's entertainment when a sound from upstairs halted him.

'What was that?' said Fred. They listened, and it came again, a choking cry. Little Charley in the nursery, or what? Charles leapt to his feet and rushed upstairs, Fred after him.

The sound was coming from Mary's room, not a cry now but a dreadful harsh breathing. She was standing, one hand to her breast, the other clutching the back of a chair. Her face was distorted with agony, her eyes staring. She reached out to Charles, trying to gasp out his name.

'Oh, God! What is it, what is it?' he cried. 'Oh, Mary! My God, my God!' He half-carried her to the bed and laid her on it, as Catherine came in, saying sleepily, 'Whatever is it? What's all the noise?'

'Go for the doctor,' Charles snapped at Fred, who sped off. They heard the front door slam and his footsteps running down the street, as they stared, appalled, at each other across the bed.

'What is it? What can we do?' Charles asked helplessly.

Catherine was twisting her hands. 'I told her not to get so excited. She should never drink. I told her again and again . . .'

'But what is it, what is it?'

'One of her awful turns. She's had them once or twice. But we all thought they'd passed over. Wait, I'll get my drops, they'll quieten her. You cover her up so she doesn't take cold.'

As he bent over her he heard her trying to speak.

'Is it still so bad, my dearest?' he asked, and she managed to answer 'It feels . . . like . . . a hand of ice on . . . my heart.'

He was in tears of distress for her distress.

'Oh, my dear, my poor dear.'

She tried to smile. 'It's not so painful . . . now . . . I can breathe . . . better.'

'Thank God, thank God.' He sat on the bed beside her, his arm round her, her head resting against his shoulder. The scent of the camellia in her hair came up to him, exotically sweet and strong. He laid his cheek against the glossy wing of hair.

'That's better, isn't it?'

With the terrible clarity of crisis, he realised now how much he loved her.

She was murmuring. 'Charles . . . God won't let me die, will He?'

'No, no, of course not.'

'It wouldn't be fair, would it?'

He stroked her brow. 'No, dearest, it wouldn't be fair.'

'But He might.'

'What, dearest?'

'You know.'

'Don't even think of it. It's just one of your turns, Kate says. I didn't even know you had turns, although I should have guessed that one so beautiful and accomplished would have everything.' It wasn't a very good joke, but it made her smile a little.

'But He might,' she said again. 'He often does unfair things.'

'Oh, no, my darling girl, no. Please, rest, my love . . . sleep.'

'I will. If you say it again.'

'Sleep.'

'No. All of it.'

'Rest – my love.'

'I will – my love.'

She closed her eyes and lay back against him. He looked down at her, rapt with the new feeling that had come to him. For minutes they were thus, still and peaceful, until Catherine returned with the drops.

All that night they stayed with her in turns. The doctor came, pronounced the condition not to be serious, and went away, angry at having been called out so late. They summoned him again next day, early in the afternoon, when Mary's colour became livid and the dreadful breathing began again. On the doctor's instructions Charles fed her with a few drops of brandy from a spoon, and she slipped into a sleep from which she never wakened.

CHAPTER TEN

The heavy mourning he wore seemed to quench the light that normally shone from his face. He was pale, aged, defeated, as he stood alone at the side of Grave 977 in the new, smart cemetery of Kensal Green. It was a pretty, feminine headstone they had made for her, with two little fans flanking the oval curve about the epitaph he had composed himself.

MARY SCOTT HOGARTH
Died 7th May 1837
Young Beautiful and Good
God in His Mercy
Numbered her with His Angels
at the early age of
seventeen.

One day he would lie there beside her, he swore; their dust, as the polite euphemism was, would mingle. He hoped the day would soon come. He had no interest in life, no spur to write. The monthly instalments of *Pickwick* and *Oliver Twist* had been temporarily suspended. After Mary's death Kate had suffered an early miscarriage through shock, and Charles had removed her and himself to Collins's Farm, a pleasant, sequestered old house on Hampstead Heath, near the dark twisty lane that led to the hamlet of Golders Green. There he could weep without being seen, and walk and walk over the Heath, as far as Hendon, over Finchley Common, north-east to Enfield and Edmonton, anywhere he could be alone with the grief that was eating him.

He looked round at the lines of tidy, clean new graves. The cemetery had only been open four years. It was exactly the opposite of the horrible overcrowded boneyards of the City which he would castigate in *Bleak House*. If there must be death, it should be like this, orderly and respectable. (One day, in another century, pilgrims would come here to read headstones that bore the names of legions of his friends and colleagues: Braham and Harley, Forster and Harrison Ainsworth, John Leech and George Cruickshank among them. It would be a post-mortem gathering of the Dickens Circle.)

He twisted round on his finger the ring he had taken from her dead hand. It would always be with him, he promised her, until he and it returned here together, and once again it would lie near the delicate bones . . .

A voice behind him startled him out of his morbid fancies.

'My dear fellow!' his father was mellifluously booming. 'Forgive this intrusion upon your grief. I had an overwhelming desire to look upon the grave of our dear little child, and Fred was kind enough to humour an old man and keep me company.' He saw the marks of undried tears on Charles's face, and his own creased with pity. 'But since I find you unexpectedly here I shall not stay, but leave you to your reflections. Forgive the intrusion, my dear, dear boy.'

Charles turned, touched and surprised. The Governor had never seemed particularly fond of Mary. He began to stammer some kind of thanks, while Fred tried to signal a warning. An ulterior motive was as usual at the bottom of John Dickens's action, and it unerringly guided him to steer his son away from the graveside for a good brisk walk which ended in the garden of the Spaniards Inn, a pleasant tavern on the lane that ran above the woods where Collins's Farm nestled. The grey afternoon had turned brighter, birds pecked at the cherries ripening on the high red wall bordering the garden. John flicked away a wasp hovering above the rim of his tankard, and beamed upwards at the rift in the clouds.

'Ah, the sun, the sun, the blessed sun. Happy days!'

Charles had sunk back into despondency. 'Oh, Fred, how I weary now for our rooms, our three little rooms in Furnival's Inn.'

Fred shifted uncomfortably. 'Ah, yes.' he said, 'happy days.' It might equally have been a toast or a reminiscence.

'The joy of it all,' said Charles, 'when *she* was there. And now . . .'

John patted his son's shoulder briskly. 'We take these knocks in our time, dear boy. I can hardly remember how many beloved babes your mother has borne me, only to have them snatched away by the cold hand of the Grim Reaper.'

Charles was not listening. 'Such a guileless heart and affectionate nature.'

'Just so. Drink up, my boy.' His father's tone carried a shade of impatience. 'Ah yes, she was indeed a worthy object for the sympathy and compassion of the world. But life must go on, my son.'

Normally Charles and Fred would have exchanged meaningful looks at this, one of the Governor's obvious gambits. But Charles was impervious to hints just now. His large, mournful eyes were fixed on his father with a far-away gaze.

'I dream of her every night,' he said.

'Of course of course, my boy. We all think of her constantly. She is ever in our thoughts. Nevertheless . . .'

'No, no. I dream of her, of Mary, every night, I tell you. Every night exactly the same.'

'That's rum, ain't it?' was Fred's comment.

John shook his head. 'Very strange, my boy. But we Dickenses have always been strongly tuned to the netherworld. The Celtic blood in our veins, the apprehensions and intuitions of the ancient bards, it makes us dreadfully sensitive to the tremulations and tintinnabulations of forces that – that ordinary mortals do not see, nor sense, nor hear.' It was a good effort, considering that he had just made it up, Celtic blood and all.

Fred said gently, 'It's a dream, Charles, that comes from grieving so much.'

'No, Fred. It's more than that. It's her, Mary herself . . . she comes to bring me a message, but I am unable to understand it, to hear her words. Oh, Fred, she looks at me with such a look of appeal – a look to break my heart.'

He was almost weeping again. Abruptly he stood up.

'Forgive me. I must go,' he said. He strode away from them,

not seeing the other drinkers, the full-blown roses whose petals were brushed off by the sweep of his cloak, the sparrows pecking on the grass. His father looked after him with resignation.

'Poor dear boy. Well, well, we shall have to look elsewhere. Hey ho. I think one more to drown the sadness of it all, eh, Fred?'

Charles was back at work. Writing like a demon, he had murdered Nancy bloodily at the hands of Bill Sikes, hanged the murderer from a chimney as he fled from the Law, and trapped Fagin, the old grey father-rat, in the condemned cell. Some of the agony of Mary's death had been written out in the near-fatal illness of Rose Maylie, the insipid heroine in whom he had tried to mirror Mary's innocence and beauty. He felt a good deal better, and he had a new book in mind. He discussed it with John Forster, that peppery didactic man who was fast becoming his best friend and the intelligent recipient of his ideas. Long ago, in his childhood, he had heard of a young boy who had died as a result of ill-treatment in one of the notorious Yorkshire boarding-schools to which unwanted boys, usually illegitimate, were sent to be out of the way. The memory had lurked in his retentive mind, and an advertisement in a newspaper had revived it. Here was a plot, and more than a plot, a Cause, something to absorb his energies.

'I shall expose the whole rotten business,' he told Forster over supper, waving his fork. 'The neglected ill-fed boys, the beatings, the food crawling with maggots ... five in a flea-infested bed ...'

Forster shook his leonine head in kindly moderation. 'It won't help the artistry to exaggerate.'

'Damn the artistry! And there's no exaggeration.'

'Have you looked into these schools, then?'

'Not yet, but I intend to. It will be the most damning exposure of them ever written. I will finish them off, John. I will, I swear!'

He applied himself ravenously to his dish of grilled chops, while Forster studied him with admiration and a certain puzzlement. Suddenly Charles looked up, his face intent.

'What does it signify if one dreams something again and again?'

'Too many hot mutton chops, too late at night,' suggested Forster. 'I give no great significance to dreams.'

Charles asked Browne the same question, as they sat on the Heath, Browne absorbed in a sketch.

'What do you make of a dream that comes to you every night, Phiz?'

'I don't know.' Browne put in a detail, and held the paper away to admire it. 'A jolly good drawing, I would say.'

'I'll describe it to you. See if you can draw it.'

'Bit busy at the moment, old boy.'

'Never mind that. Try. Listen, now: in a small bed surmounted by a pale blue and white painting of a Madonna lies a young girl, flowers on her breast, a book in her hand. Her face is pale and calm, free of any trace of pain, so fair to look upon, so beautiful . . . and dead.'

Browne looked at him with compassion. 'Really, my dear old Boz, it isn't good for you to dwell on it so.'

'What? Dwell on what?' Charles gave a sudden manic laugh. 'Not at all – not what you think at all. A character in a story. I shall write it and you shall do the drawings for it.'

Scribbling feverishly in his study, he was finishing off Fagin. He muttered aloud as he wrote, pulling faces, turning himself from the impassive warder to the terrified, half-demented old prisoner.

'"Here's somebody wants to see you, to ask you some questions, I suppose. Fagin, Fagin, are you a man?"

'"I shan't be one long," he replied, looking up with a face retaining no human expression but rage and terror. "Strike them all dead! What right have they to butcher me?"'

Triumphantly he flung down his pen, sending a sputter of ink across the desk. 'Got you at last, you swine!' he said. 'I've got you for ever!' He was half-joyful, half-sorry. Catherine, peeping round the door in her nightgown, was alarmed by his look. She was so often alarmed by him nowadays.

'Why don't you come to bed, Charles?' Her voice reached him through the noisy whirl of his own words, echoing round his head. The horrible picture of the cowering Fagin became a transparency, fading to show him her prettily flushed face and tender look. She seemed very young, very like Mary. He swivelled his chair round and waved the sheet of paper at her.

'I've got him at last, Kate. He's finished for ever!'

'Come to bed, Charley dear, please,' she said gently. 'Piggy's lonely.'

'Piggy shouldn't be up. Bless me.' His eyes roamed appreciatively over her plump shapeliness. 'You're so strong and healthy and indestructible, my dear, dear indestructible Katie-mouse.'

'Do you think so?' She was smiling. He jumped up from his writing-chair.

'Let's make some punch and sit by the fire, and have fun like we used to. Shall we do that, Kate?'

'Why not?'

'Good. Who was that lady I saw you with last night?' he said, leering at her.

Straight-faced, she answered. 'That was no lady. That was your wife.'

He pulled her to him and kissed her. Fagin was dead, the evil spirit who had been part of him for so long; some kind of weight had been lifted from his creator's heart.

It seemed as though Fortune had decided to bestow her warmest smiles on him. 1838 was a year of success. Charles's *Memoirs of Grimaldi* sold in gratifying quantities, and the monthly instalments of *Nicholas Nickleby* were eagerly awaited, as the story of the intrepid young usher and villainous Yorkshire schoolmaster Squeers unfolded itself. The wretched orphan Smike had the same appeal as poor Oliver Twist. People clamoured to meet young Mr Dickens, women fell in love with his romantic long hair and vivid face, artists requested permission to draw and paint him. At twenty-six, he was a celebrity. Fashionable hostesses vied with each other to entertain him, and he maintained the same debonair ease at the table of the terrifying aristocrat Lady Holland as at that of the beautiful Countess of Blessington, queen of the demi-monde society at Gore House. The actor in him came out strong on these occasions, enabling him to conceal his lack of formal education and social background. He knew nothing of art or literature in the widest sense. He had never had a lesson on which forks and knives to use at a banquet, but he was learning fast, and it would have been a sharp eye indeed that detected him making a mistake. Almost incredibly, he was elected a member of the exclusive sought-after Athenaeum Club, on the grounds of being an Eminent Person.

Doughty Street was acquiring a growing domestic staff. There were maids, a cook, a groom called Henry, who also acted as Charles's manservant, and a nursemaid for the babies. Little Charley's sister, Mary, was born in March, a sedate, good-tempered child. Because it was not quite bearable yet to say Mary's name without pain, the 'instalment of posterity in the shape of a daughter' was known as Mamie, though Charles insisted on bestowing on her the nickname of Popem Jee. Little Charley was The Snodgering Blee; all the children to come would be labelled with such whimsical grotesqueries. As for Charles himself, he was beginning to assume, facetiously, the title of Inimitable, given to him long ago by his Chatham schoolmaster.

A new luxury had come into the lives of the Dickens family; they were able to take holidays. Charles rented a summer cottage at Twickenham, Surrey, in pleasant country by the Thames, and when that had to be given up he transported his family to Ventnor, in the Isle of Wight. The dusty, malodorous London summer was not for them to endure, whoever else might suffer in it.

Only one shadow clouded the bright prospect. John Dickens lurked in his shabby lodgings, spider-like, ready to creep out at any fortuitous moment to snatch a few guineas from his son's pockets. Those pockets were comfortably filled, certainly, now that Forster was Charles's mentor and literary manager, but the demands of a family, a house, a staff, and a style had to be met. There was no additional pocket for the support of scheming pensioners. Stories were coming to Charles's ears which he wished not to believe; stories of scraps of his own writing filched from his desk, odd pages of manuscript, notes rescued from the waste-paper basket, all sold by his father to collectors on the strength of his growing reputation. The stories, unfortunately, were all too true.

Once again, John had brought it off. For a few pieces of paper in his son's striking handwriting, guaranteed to be worth a fortune in a few years, he had taken three pounds off a collector. Home again, he peeped playfully round the door. His wife was sitting by the fire, her eyes glazed with dreams and alcohol. She was thin, faded, shabby; pathetic bits of finery proclaiming her still a desirable woman in her husband's estimation. The glass from which she was sipping had not been very well washed; the room was untidy. Her untidiness was one of the things which most irritated her eldest son.

She started from her reverie as her husband, singing joyfully, burst into the room.

'I am here, my heart!' he declared with a flourish. She was awake at once, sharp-eyed and sharp-eared.

'Did you see Charles?'

'I did not.'

She sniffed. 'Has he become too high and mighty to give an interview to his own father?'

'Not at all, not at all, my dear. Charles is astoundingly busy, amazingly successful, increasingly sought-after, as popular and requested as I was myself at his age . . . almost. Ah, you remember, my dear, what days they were, what happy, happy days!' He subsided into the chair opposite hers with his feet on the fender. His wife was in no mood for sentimental reminiscence.

'So then, what of our present affairs? What are we to say to the tradesmen?'

He waved a careless hand. 'Tut, tut, my love, I will not have you worrying about such things. I've never allowed it and I will not now, as we float side by side into the glorious sunset of our lives . . .'

'We're not so old as all *that*, John,' she bridled. Fifty was not too old to put one's hair in curlpapers every night, certainly.

'Of course we're not. We never shall be.'

She jumped up and ran over to him, perching girlishly on his knee. 'Oh, John, John, did you raise the wind, my dearest sailing-ship?'

'I did, I did, my little bum-boat.' He fished some coins from his pocket. 'Four whole pounds, from Messrs Chapman and Hall. Little Mr Hall said, "It isn't business, you know," but Mr Chapman replied, "We can't refuse Mr Dickens's father so small a sum."'

'I should think not, too.'

He mused. 'More than fifteen thousand, I calculate Messrs Chapman and Hall have made out of our *Pickwick* alone . . .'

'Why only *four* pounds, then, John?'

'Ah. Yes. Why? That's all we're being pressed for, is it not, my chuck?'

She sighed. He was at it again. Hopelessly improvident, romantic John, whom she always ended up by forgiving. She watched him searching his pockets.

'But I sold that bunch of bits and pieces in Charles's hand for a pound,' he was saying happily, 'and thus I bring you gifts galore.' Out came one little package after another: a sticky clump of sugar plums, bright black-and-white striped peppermints, two marzipan mice with sugar eyes and thread tails; and, from a capacious back pocket, a bottle of the best Madeira.

'I spread my argosy before you, Queen of my Soul. The marzipan mice are for Augustus. The sugar plums . . .' popping one into her mouth '. . . are for your own rich ruby lips.'

Mouth full, she was saying, 'Oh, John, John!'

Since Messrs Chapman and Hall had proved such an easy touch, he felt he could not do better than return to them with a scheme so ingenious that he smiled, laying finger to nose, as he walked briskly along the Strand in the direction of No. 186. Mr Hall, hearing him announced, groaned; but already the unwelcome visitor was bouncing into his office, tall hat cocked to one side, double chin comfortably tucked into a rather dirty stock. He swept Mr Hall a courtly bow.

'I have come, sir,' he announced, 'to repay you a trifling

amount due.'

Hall sat up with surprise. 'Repay, Mr Dickens?'

'Indeed, indeed. Plus interest, of course.'

Hall felt inclined to pinch himself. Surely he could not be fully awake. 'Oh, my goodness,' he stammered, 'that will not be required.'

'I insist, sir, I insist. John Dickens always returns with interest, Mr Hall. And in this case, as between friends, as between those related by the bond of Genius, interest *shall* be paid, sir.'

Hall gave up. 'Well, as you please.' John Dickens extracted from his pocket, with stagey slowness, a majestic document of legal appearance, decorated with seals, and laid it on Hall's desk.

'I ask you to study this, sir.'

Hall donned his spectacles and perused it. He looked up, baffled.

'But this is a promissory note.'

'Indeed it is, sir. Correct. Oh, the eagle eye of a true gentleman of commerce . . .'

'But . . . for twenty pounds?'

'For twenty pounds exactly, sir. Precisely, Mr Hall, you have it in a nutshell. Twenty pounds.'

'Made out to Chapman and Hall.'

'Who else, sir? Who are the benevolent deities of the Dickens tribe, sir?'

'And signed by your good self, Mr Dickens.'

'Precisely so. I would trust my signature to none others than to Messrs Chapman and Hall. No, sir, you shall have the word only of one who may lay his hand upon his heart and say he has never – never, sir – broken a promise, nor gone back upon his undertaking, nor forsworn himself, nor . . .'

Hall had pushed his spectacles up to his forehead. He was very much wishing his partner were present to deal with this illogical, worrying person. Patiently he said, 'But the sum you owe us is a mere four pounds, with interest if you insist. Why, then, a promissory note for twenty pounds?'

'Ah, you perceive the discrepancy, Mr Hall, and again I

congratulate you upon the clarity of vision of the true *homme d'affaires*. But do not concern yourself, dear sir. You may make up the difference in cash.'

'The difference in *cash*?'

The tall hat nodded vigorously. 'If you insist, sir, thank you, cash will be perfectly acceptable. Some fourteen or fifteen pounds or thereabouts.' He laughed heartily. 'We won't fall out over a few shillings, one way or the other. No, I shall give you the benefit of it, sir. Fourteen pounds, sir, and we shall call it quits.'

Though baffled, Hall rang the bell for his clerk. 'That's very generous of you, Mr Dickens,' he said doubtfully. 'Isn't it?'

It was, of course, only a matter of time before Charles found out. Chapman and Hall had received yet another document from John Dickens.

'It is marked confidential,' Hall said, apologetic. 'In it he points out that he owes Messrs Chapman and Hall fifty-five pounds five shillings.'

Charles, pacing the office, wheeled round, showing Hall a pale furious face. 'Does he, by God!'

'He regretfully informs us that perdition will claim him unless he finds a further fifty pounds immediately. Although hourly expecting a matter of financial advantage to mature, he religiously believes that Messrs Chapman and Hall will extend their relationship with his distinguished son to cover his miserable and unfortunate self.' Seeing his author's angry, shamed face, he added gently, 'I assure you, Mr Dickens, we would never have brought this to your attention, were it not that . . .'

'Please continue. I have not the patience to read it myself.'

'"I am embarrassed that people might accuse me of obtaining money, as it were, under false pretences, but I observe that when a man is placed in the situation in which I find myself, he will snatch at a straw to save himself from drowning."'

Charles banged his fist on the desk. 'Oh, the literary twists and turns of my dear father! A family talent, you know. Well, then, to the point.'

'The point is that Mr John proposes insuring his life in our favour for one hundred pounds for three years.'

'God! So that's why he seemed to interested in the details of *my* insurance arrangements with the Sun. So much for his anxiety on behalf of my growing family.'

Hall, embarrassed, drew shapes on the corner of an envelope.

'A most ingenious suggestion, I admit,' he said, 'but then Mr John *is* ingenious in these matters.'

'He is, he is. And has been. But I swear he will continue to be no longer. You will ignore this absurd and impertinent proposition, Mr Hall. You will kindly deduct fifty-five pounds and five shillings plus any interest due . . .'

'Oh, there's no need for that.'

'I insist. You will deduct it from my own account and forget the entire matter. Good day, Mr Hall.'

As Charles sped through the streets, his feet winged by fury, his father was seated at a paper-strewn table in the parlour at his lodgings. He was engaged in his favourite occupation of drafting a letter couched in fulsome phrases. Frequently it was a begging letter, but in this case it was one of thanks to Messrs Chapman and Hall for their financial assistance. He was rounding it off in his beautiful clerkly copper-plate.

'". . . by one o'clock tomorrow, to avoid the most awful consequences." That's very good. "I am sure it will reflect no disgrace on you that you have to this extent assisted the father of one with whom it has been your fortunate lot most successfully and consistently to do business." Thousands they're making out of my Charles, thousands,' he reflected to himself. '"I must thank you furthermore for not telling my son about these matters, for I am sure it could have led to a breach of a most distressing nature."' He laid down his pen with a smile of satisfaction, and called.

'My dear! Come in. I shall read you my latest composition.'

But his wife, in the hall, was speaking to someone, saying that the visit brought her an unexpected pleasure. Her tone was sarcastic, but John was unprepared for the identity of the visitor she showed into the parlour. It was his eldest son, with a grim, set face that boded no good. John had been saying 'Let me read this to you, my dear,' as the door opened. Hastily he pushed the draft letter aside and snatched up the current number of *Nickleby*.

'Ah, Charles! My dear boy, what a rare and unexpected pleasure. I was about to give your mother a little reading of the latest. Dotheboys Hall, ha ha! There are the remains of a bottle of excellent Madeira in the cupboard, my dear. Kindly set it before us, with two glasses.'

Charles did not look like a man about to enjoy a glass of excellent Madeira. 'Don't disturb yourself, Mother,' he said in a tone ferocious enough to dampen his father's spirits. This time, John knew, there was going to be trouble. He turned to his wife, who was hovering, reproaches to Charles on her lips.

'I think perhaps you had better leave us for a moment, my dear, while you adjust your hair.'

'I don't require to adjust my hair simply because my famous son has found time to . . .'

He cut in on her. 'Kindly go and adjust your hair, my dear.'

Sulkily, she went. Father and son looked at each other, son standing over the older man who smiled and smiled, marshalling all his resources.

'Father,' Charles barked, 'affairs have come to my notice . . .'

'Charles, Charles, my very dear boy, my dearest son, before you say anything . . .'

Charles raised his voice. 'Father, I *will* be heard!'

'Of course you will, the whole world over, my boy. And what a sound it is, as of an orchestra playing great music to the delight of the heavenly spheres. My boy, I am the merest insect in the sun of your . . .'

His choice of phrase was unfortunate. '"Sun" indeed!' Charles roared at him. 'The Sun Assurance Company, sir! The company with whom I have insured my life, to your great satisfaction. I might have known my family's welfare was not foremost in your mind.'

John was cowering behind the table, trying to muster his defence.

'What can I say, my dear boy? It seemed a goodish idea at the time.'

He had said such things so often, parrying anger with a pathetic childish frankness, softening Charles's heart with his utter capitulation. Now all his old appeal was useless. Charles's face was, as someone had said, like steel, as hard and as inflexible. He spoke without warmth.

'Father, the time has come when I can no longer allow my career, upon the success of which the fortunes of our entire family depend – I cannot allow it to be threatened, my reputation to be damaged, my pride and that of the public in the name of Dickens to be tarnished by these miserable little devices of yours to extract money without regard.'

John bowed his head. 'I agree, I agree, my boy. It's disgusting. I loathe myself, and furthermore, it's becoming more difficult all the time.'

Charles stood looking coldly down on him. 'It is the end of the road, Father.'

As though these were words of hope, John surged up from behind the table, all eagerness. 'It is, is it, my boy. What now? Eh? What now, I wonder?'

'What now' was something John and Elizabeth Dickens had never anticipated in all their conferences about their expectations from Charles. They were not to receive a lump sum, or a guarantee of debts up to a certain amount, as John had pleasantly speculated might be the case. Their sentence was banishment.

Charles was not hard-hearted, but when his mind was made up he could be utterly ruthless. While his parents were in London, on his doorstep, he could never breathe freely. He was too conscious of family responsibilities to abandon them; therefore he must provide for them, accommodate them at a safe distance where they could be comfortable, live within their means, and spare him and his business associates the embarrassment of their presence. Remembering his reporting travels, he dashed off in the direction of Devon; quiet, pleasing, healthy, and a long way from London. In the village of Alphington, near Exeter, he found Mile End Cottage, on the road to Plymouth, 'a jewel of a place', with a highly respectable landlady living next door. He wrote enthusiastically to Catherine from the Exeter inn.

'I cannot tell you what spirits I have been put into by the cottage . . . It is in the most beautiful, cheerful, delicious rural neighbourhood I was ever in. There is an excellent parlour with an open beaufet in the wall and a capital closet, a beautiful little drawing-room above that – a kitchen and a little room adjacent . . . a noble garden, and cellars and safes and coal-holes everywhere.'

To Forster he wrote on similar lines. 'The discovery of the cottage I seriously look upon as a blessing (not to speak it profanely) upon your efforts in this I hope no longer sad, cause.' When he set off back to London on a bright cold morning his heart was light with the consciousness of duty done. It would be, no doubt, a wrench for his parents to leave London, but after the first pang they would see how much their circumstances would be improved. At Alphington even they could not fail to be happy.

But John Dickens's face, as he came to survey his new home, reflected the very reverse of happiness. Through the shining little windows in the upstairs drawing-room there was visible a charming prospect of meadows in front, and adjoining the hedge of the neat small garden a glimpse of orchard. To the left, Exeter Cathedral reared its towers on a distant hill. Strolling across to the back window (the room was just as commodious as Charles had said) he stared gloomily at the view. A range of hills whose trees were breaking into the soft green of spring; a field of sheep with young lambs. Not a living soul was in sight. Their landlady, Mrs Pannell, in the adjoining cottage, was fat, elderly, suffered from a vague affliction known as Nerves, and quite patently wouldn't be good for the loan of even a penny. John's spirits were lower than they had ever been in the worst depths of financial despair.

Elizabeth was looking round with something like pleasure. She had known comfort, even something of luxury in her youth, and after years of being hounded from one dreary, shabby lodging to another, this little house with its spotless paint and pretty wallpaper seemed very agreeable. Charles had not exaggerated its charms, whatever else might be laid to his charge.

'It's really very charming, John,' she said. 'Almost elegant – for a cottage.'

'Oh, charming. Very charming indeed, my dear. Delightfully rural. But so far from London.'

'Those who offend the great Boz must suffer exile,' she said bitterly. Then, to comfort him, 'Augustus will improve in health here. And Letitia and Henry could come to stay with us, and Fanny, after her confinement, poor girl. And Charles says we are to have Dash to bark at the tramps.'

John did not appear to find the company of Dash, a sharp-tempered terrier whom they had left behind with their London landlady, a highly elevating prospect. But his spirits were incapable of remaining at zero for long. A shaft of sunlight broke suddenly from the dull skies, illuminating the twelve-year-old Augustus chasing hens in the orchard. His face spread into a beam.

'But what is exile to a soul as free as a bird?' he enquired of the china-cupboard. 'Say rather that Alphington is Eden, for I have in it a man's dearest companion, and little Cain out there to keep us company.'

They hugged each other, and Elizabeth smiled up at him. 'At least all bills are paid in Eden.' It was a pleasant thought! Augustus's schooling, the rent and rates, all furniture and fittings provided, the odd fowl or side of pork free from Mrs Pannell's brother at the farm down the road. It was no more than Charles owed them for the upbringing they had given him.

John, embracing her, gazed over her thin shoulder at the distant prospect of Exeter Cathedral. Where there was a town there was life, hope, bars, and coffee-rooms. Even more cheeringly, there was a coach-office from which the 'Defiance' started for London.

Charles had persuaded the Sun Life Assurance Society to insure his life for the sum of a thousand pounds without much difficulty, having been able to inform them truthfully that he had never had gout, asthma, rupture, or fits, and was not afflicted with consumption of the lungs, though he regretfully admitted to having had the cowpox as a child. What he kept quiet from them was the suffering he still endured from the violent spasms in his left side which had attacked him since the days of the blacking factory, and earlier. Mr Pickthorn, his regular medical attendant, made light of them, prescribing for them doses of calomel so stringent as to force him to cancel all immediate public engagements, and soothing draughts of henbane.

But Charles felt himself in need of reassurance about them. A busy, famous man could not afford to be ill. He had, besides, another painful, nagging complaint; a fistula caused by the long periods of sitting at his desk. He took both complaints to the distinguished Dr John Elliotson, who had been until the previous year professor of the practice of medicine to London University, but had been compelled to resign the post because of his advocacy of mesmerism, a science then associated with witch-doctors rather than respectable practitioners.

Elliotson gave Charles a thorough examination, shook his head over the henbane prescription, and was interested in the spasms.

'It sounds to me like renal colic. The kidneys may well be the cause. I'd like to investigate it further, Mr Dickens. As to the fistula, I don't like that at all. I'm sure it will require surgery before long.'

Charles shuddered. 'Perish the thought.'

'A fistula *in ano* can hardly be ignored.'

'I agree with you, sir. But for the moment I shall try to do so.'

Elliotson understood the reluctance of anyone to undergo the agonising operation, which would have to be conducted with the patient fully conscious; but he was puzzled by this young man.

'Well, then, it's a pleasure to give you my advice, Mr Dickens, for I'm an immense admirer of your work. But why, may I ask, sir, since you apparently don't propose taking it, have you come to me?'

Charles laughed, settling back in his chair. 'To tell you the truth, Dr Elliotson, I'm encouraged by your kindness to reveal a professional motive I have in making your acquaintance. I have heard of your experiments in the less orthodox realms of medicine – in mesmerism, phrenology and magnetism – and my interest has been greatly engaged.'

Elliotson frowned. 'I do hope, Mr Dickens, that you are not thinking of bringing your great influence and facility to the support of those who scorn all except the most trodden ways of science and medicine.'

'I ? Not at all. I am a committed wanderer along the least-used and strangest paths myself. I wondered . . . if you would be my guide ?'

The doctor's face brightened. He had suffered much humiliation at the loss of his London University chair, and it was a ray of hope in darkness to find this superbly intelligent person on his side. 'I should be very glad to tell you and show you what little I know.' he said. 'But I must warn you, the orthodoxy is much against our work in these fields.'

Charles's eyes sparkled; they were, thought Elliotson, quite remarkable eyes. 'That seems perfectly suitable, for I am much against the orthodoxy.'

A friendship rapidly grew up between the two men. Elliotson received a signed copy of *Nickleby* 'as a very feeble mark of my lasting esteem and admiration'. Dinner invitations were issued on both sides. One October evening, in the parlour at Doughty Street, the Dickens family, with their guests Forster and Browne, watched with amazement a demonstration of mesmerism performed by Elliotson on a young Belgian student, who, in deep trance, allowed a long steel pin to be driven into his cheek, uttering no sound as it went in, and telling Elliotson, in a far-away sleep-voice, that he felt no pain. Catherine looked away; she was near the birth of her third child. Forster was frankly incredulous, accusing the doctor of trickery. Calmly, Elliotson borrowed Catherine's watch, held it to the brow of the entranced youth, and asked him to name the watch's maker. His subject did so, correctly.

'You see, Forster,' said Charles, 'you miscreant disbeliever and upholder of orthodoxy!'

But Forster still muttered. Elliotson handed him the watch, requested him to note the number inside, then applied it to his subject's brow, as before, and again was given the answer which Forster, and only Forster, knew. He blustered no more, and Charles crowed in triumph.

It was not long before he offered himself to Elliotson as a hypnotic subject. The doctor was happy to accept, but less happy with his long struggle to subdue the patient's consciousness. Patiently he counted, patiently he directed a light into the persistently open eyes, until at last the familiar signs appeared. With a sigh of relief, Elliotson asked, 'Well? Are you asleep now, Mr Dickens? Answer yes or no.'

The sleepy murmur came. 'Yes.'

'Finally, so, you're in a deep sleep – very deep.'

Charles was completely relaxed, limp-muscled, lying back in the chair.

'But you can still hear my voice?'

'Yes.'

Elliotson studied him with interest. 'You were extremely difficult to mesmerise, Mr Dickens. Were you resisting the magnetism?'

'Yes.'

'Why? Were you afraid to succumb to it?'

'Yes.'

'What did you fear would happen if you succumbed to it?'

'Dreams.'

'What dreams?'

'Mary.'

'Mary?'

'Dead.'

Elliotson leant forward intently. 'Mr Dickens, you will continue in your sleep, but less deeply. You are now sleeping less deeply. Now: who is Mary?'

'Mary Hogarth.'

'A relative?'

'Sister-in-law.'

'Of course. I remember now hearing you had suffered a sad loss quite recently.'

'Dreams,' Charles murmured.

'Of Mary?'

'Yes.'

'You fear them?'

'No.'

'What do you feel about them?'

There was a hesitation. Then, 'Love. Love. Love.'

It was not the sort of revelation the doctor liked receiving from patients he knew in private life. 'Oh, Lord!' he said to himself, and to his subject, 'Do you want me to stop these dreams?'

'No.'

'Do you want to forget them, after you dream them?'

'No.'

'What would you wish, then, Mr Dickens?'

'Love Mary.'

Embarrassed, Elliotson said, 'Well, I think that's enough for the moment. I will count five, Mr Dickens, and you will awake. You won't remember this discussion. You won't remember anything except that you have been in a deep and restful sleep. One . . . two . . . three . . . four . . . five.'

His patient's eyes opened, and he smiled. 'Well. That was a very good sleep. Did I do well?'

Elliotson laughed. 'When you finally decided to accept the magnetism, you did very well. I think you could be a very good subject.'

'Did I say anything of interest, by the way?'

'Routine answers to routine questions.'

'Strange, I have a vague impression of something else. Ah, well, I won't say that to take such a rest every so often wouldn't be acceptable, but my intention is to learn how to mesmerise others, and this exercise has been extremely interesting, Dr Elliotson. I really feel I understand a little of the process.'

'The essence,' the doctor said, 'is to gain the confidence of the subject sufficiently for him totally to relax any opposition to the suggestions you make to him, and, above all, to ensure that these suggestions are not out of key with his character. The subject cannot be made to do anything against his own will, or which may be damaging to him.'

They talked of mesmerism, Charles intent on and memorising

the doctor's every word, until the question was poised which was in his mind, conscious or unconscious, day and night.

'Tell me, what significance do you attribute to that very common phenomenon, the recurring dream?'

Mary. Mary galloping beside him, laughing, mock-angry, holding out her small shining boot for him to kiss in token subjection to her. Mary by the fire at Furnival's Inn, Mary at Doughty Street, pouring wine for Forster and Browne, her cheeks as rosy as the wine. Mary at the door of St Luke's, Chelsea, in a pink dress with a little rose-wreath in her hair. Mary lying dead, her hands crossed on her breast. Mary a smiling spirit comforting him, folding him in airy embrace or hovering above him, pleading, some unspoken message on her lips. Mary for ever virgin, for ever sainted.

He tried to hypnotise Catherine, but she merely went to sleep and snored gently. She was, after all, very near to being confined again. He turned away from her, disgusted.

CHAPTER ELEVEN

Charles strode through Lincoln's Inn Fields like a man pursued by Furies. As he strode, he muttered, causing heads to turn, and thrashed the air with a bundle of papers. He was not afraid of being thought eccentric, and a raging grievance possessed him. Arriving at No. 58, a noble Georgian mansion let off in suites of rooms, he swept through Soane's elegant porch and up the staircase to John Forster's chambers. The clerks in the outer office looked up as he passed. They knew better than to ask him his business or hint that Mr Forster might, just possibly, be engaged. He burst into the inner office without knocking.

Forster raised his head from his writing. 'My dear Charles. I had hoped . . .'

His friend, the very model for Henry II suborning the murderous knights, flung down his bundle of documents on the floor.

'Will no one rid me of this pestilential bestial bandit Bentley?' he roared. Forster raised a placatory hand.

'It is being done, my dear fellow. Just as you came in I was about to . . .'

'"Being done"! For nine months, damned near, it has been "being done", damn the tedious, prolix, idiotic, process of your law. For nine months I have carried this growing suppurating monster in my vitals like a dead infant . . .'

'If it is dead,' said Forster with the glimmer of a smile, 'it cannot be growing or suppurating. But . . .'

'But me no buts!' The inkstand rattled as Charles banged his first on the desk. 'Read me no academic lectures on the use of prosody. I know how to spell bastard – it's identical with bandit and Bentley. The swine is using my name again in his advertisements announcing *Barnaby Rudge* as if it were his own. I will not tolerate it. I will *not*!'

Forster knew his Dickens, but this behaviour was extraordinary and somewhat alarming, even for him. Getting up, he indicated a chair.

'Please, my dear fellow, sit down and possess yourself for a moment. Take a glass of something.' A decanter and glasses stood on a table nearby, for the refreshment of clients. Charles waved it violently away.

'Drink. You think the solution to everything is vinous. I tell you, *Barnaby Rudge* is not Bentley's.'

'It is not anyone's yet, Charles, for in the said nine months you haven't written it. However, you agreed a contract with Bentley . . .'

'I agree nothing.'

'You mean you reserve the right to disagree, reject a contract, when it no longer suits you. But the fact is, Charles, Bentley agreed to pay two thousand pounds outright with a further one thousand when the sales exceed ten thousand copies, and still another thousand pounds after fifteen thousand copies. A possible total of four thousand pounds for the entire copyright of a book which, two years before, you agreed to write for a mere five hundred pounds. Not bad, I should say.'

Charles's face had been growing steadily more mutinous. 'Lies!' he burst out.

'It is not lies, Charles. It is so.'

'I don't care. You must get me out of it.'

Forster wondered in passing how he himself had ever acquired a reputation for irascibility. He felt himself to be an angel of patience beside his difficult client. 'I *have* got you out of it,' he said, 'as I've been trying to tell you since you stormed in unannounced. I have agreed a settlement with Mr Bentley.'

Charles stared. 'You have?'

'I have. You shall pay him fifteen hundred pounds . . .'

'Fifteen hundred? *I* pay Bentley? What the devil for?'

Forster took a deep breath. 'For the assignment to you of his interest in *Oliver Twist*, and the relinquishing of all further claims upon your writings, either produced or promised.'

Charles sat down, deflated and sulky. 'Oh. Well, I suppose that's all right. Though I didn't expect to have to pay the bandit myself.'

'It's more than all right. It's perfectly fair and an excellent bargain for you. Furthermore, you will purchase the Cruikshank plates for *Oliver Twist* and the copies of that novel still in stock, for seven hundred and fifty pounds.'

Forster's temper was rising, and when Charles began to ask plaintively where he was to get all the necessary money, he was quelled in a rising growl.

'Don't interrupt me! or I'll turn down the offer on your behalf and withdraw from your business entirely.' He slumped sulkily back in his chair, heavy eyebrows knit, spectacles snatched off and held menacingly close to his breast-pocket. When he lost his temper there was nothing Charles's theatrical friends could learn from him. Charles stared at him, shocked.

'Well, my dear fellow. I don't know why you're so put out. Please continue.'

Forster did so, in a growl. 'I have further arranged that the finance for this arrangement will be forthcoming from Messrs Chapman and Hall. They will deduct it from three thousand pounds which they will give you for a six-month copyright of *Barnaby Rudge*. So you will have money in hand after the entire transaction is completed. Now, if you can improve on this, I suggest you do so, and leave me to contend with simpler affairs, like protecting the India Company from a flux induced by too much heat and curry, or persuading Her Majesty the Queen not to marry a German prince . . .'

His friend's crestfallen face arrested him in mid-sarcasm. 'What is it, Charles? The arrangement with Bentley upsets you?'

Charles shook his head. 'No, no, no. I think you've done marvellously well for me, and I'm deeply grateful. No. The . . . other matter.'

'The arrangement with Chapman and Hall? But the three thousand pounds is only for a six-month copyright, and on the past showing you will earn . . .'

The head-shaking continued. 'No, no, no, my dear,

dear friend. I mean the awful betrayal by those idiots who surround Her divine little Majesty. That such a perfect child should go to a bewhiskered German princeling, an alien word-gargling foreigner, is horrifying to me.'

Forster would have sworn before a court of fellow-barristers that nothing Charles Dickens did or said would surprise him, but he was beginning to feel himself beaten. Certainly the twenty-year-old Queen Victoria had betrothed herself to her cousin Albert of Saxburg-Gotha, against the advice of some and the anti-German prejudice of others. She was, he supposed from the prints and an occasional processional glimpse, a pretty enough, petite creature, four feet nine in her slippers with a pink and white face and a beak of a nose, but . . . a perfect child! His own impression was that Her divine little Majesty was quite capable of taking care of herself, a German princeling, and an entire dynasty, if need be; in which he was in time proved perfectly right. He wondered, aghast, whether Charles had in some fit of dementia pinned Mary Hogarth's image on to that of his Queen. Aghast, he heard his friend saying, 'I shall tell you the truth, John. I am deeply in love with the Queen.' Breaking into the melody of 'My Heart's in the Highlands' he sang:

> 'My heart is at Windsor,
> My heart is not here,
> My heart is at Windsor,
> A-following my dear.'

'I don't think I quite understand you,' Forster said, his eye on the bell by which he summoned his clerk. Charles fixed him with a semi-mesmeric gaze.

'I have wandered about the grounds of Windsor Castle all day. I feel so heart-broken when I look up at the windows of the royal bedchamber that I cast myself down in the mud of the Long Walk and refuse all comfort but mud, mud, mud!' He gave a loud, insane laugh.

To Forster's horror and embarrassment, the pose (if pose it was) was continued even in public. Together they visited Gore House, Kensington, where the enchantingly beautiful Marguerite, Countess of Blessington, reigned over London's artistic society in company with the king of dandies, Count d'Orsay, nominal husband to her stepdaughter. In the crimson and gold drawing-room, surrounded by wits and notabilities, Forster's appalled ears heard Charles declaiming 'I am lost in misery. My wife aggravates me. I loathe my parents. I detest my magnificent new house. I think of the Serpentine . . . of the canal . . . of the razor . . . of poison . . . of hanging myself from a pear-tree, or starving to death.'

Forster tried not to look at the fair, puzzled face of their hostess, the raised eyebrows of the Count, or the delighted grin of the wit Sydney Smith. Under his breath he muttered 'Charles, the joke's wearing thin, don't you think?'

Charles rounded on him melodramatically. '*I* shall wear thin, nay, I shall wear to a shadow. I shall murder Chapman and Hall. I'll turn Chartist and lead a bloody assault upon Windsor Castle and save Her single-handed. I love the Queen, I swear it!'

Ever a smoother of troubled waters, Lady Blessington was at his side in a rustle of silken skirts, her kind smile and soft Irish voice calculated to soothe the wildest ravings. She laid a white hand on his sleeve.

'Mr Dickens, come and meet my talking crow. He's heard you have a talking raven, and is longing to discuss him with you.'

Forster could not help hearing one of the attendant wits muttering something about his friend being raven mad. He tried not to hear Charles telling Lady Blessington that after the Queen's marriage he proposed to be embalmed and kept on top of the Triumphal Arch at Buckingham Palace whenever Her Majesty was in town, and on the north-east turret of the Round Tower when she was in residence at Windsor.

It was an immense relief to Forster when the Royal Wedding was over, and he found himself in an atmosphere of comparative sanity in the chambers of Chapman and Hall. Charles seemed to be himself again, but for a certain look in the eye; Forster wondered how much of his recent wild talk had been an elaborate form of joke, and how much founded on real emotion. There had been a great deal about marriage being the end of love, and the Queen being sacrificed to a German ogre; Forster hoped there was nothing wrong in the Dickens marriage. He could see nothing wrong with it himself; Mrs Dickens blooming and beautiful, if rather more inclined to embonpoint than formerly, the three children well-grown and apparently thriving. Mamie was plump and calm, Charley's lofty brow beamed intelligence, while Katey, the latest-born, was already showing signs of taking after her father in mercurial temperament, thereby earning herself the nickname of Lucifer Box. It was better, thought the bachelor Forster with a shudder, than Popem Jee.

They had called in Chapman and Hall to discuss Charles's new project about which he seemed to be highly enthusiastic, if mysterious. He was still unbalanced in manner, Forster noticed, holding up the proceedings to thank his publishers effusively for their tremendous confidence in him. They looked embarrassed, as they often did in their most profitable author's presence.

'Not at all,' Hall said, coughing.

'I'm sure it will be justified,' said Chapman.

Charles's eyes glistened with emotion. 'Of course, of course. But I do wish to assure you of my conviction that our relationship is to be a lifelong affair . . . rather than a marriage, which, as we all know, is tedious in the extreme.' He gave his sudden, loud laugh, and Forster glared at him warningly. But the Queen was not under discussion on this occasion, it seemed. 'No, no, gentlemen,' Charles went on, 'Forster and Dickens are in love with Chapman and Hall, and the whole world may know it.'

'Well, good enough,' was the stolid comment of Chapman. 'And now may we, the happy recipients of your passion, hear what you are to deliver?'

Forster sensed a ridiculous answer on his friend's lips, and broke in. 'Well, gentlemen, perhaps I may say that the new project is a weekly periodical to be sold for three pence a copy.'

'Another weekly?' Chapman enquired.

'Not *another* weekly, but a unique and amazing weekly flight nto the Arabian Nights on a carpet of many-coloured words.'

Chapman looked puzzled. 'An Oriental excursion?'

'A set of Arabian Nights tales and others, and much else, after the plan of Washington Irving's *Alhambra*.'

'Together with satirical and observational pieces,' put in Forster.

'And some travel writings, perhaps?' suggested Hall. 'Travel's going down very well these days.'

Charles waved expansively. 'Of course. I may even commit myself to go to foreign places and write a series of descriptive sketches. America, for instance, or Ireland ... I've scarcely had time to work out the details yet, gentlemen, but think of a magic carpet woven by Charles Dickens and painted by such great artists as my own Phiz ... by George Cattermole ... by – I don't know. The best, the very best there is.'

Chapman and Hall were exchanging alarmed glances. Chapman cleared his throat. 'It will be a costly business.'

'We have the figures here,' said Forster, passing them over to Chapman, whose horrified face Charles was quick to note. Chapman tossed the estimate over to Hall, who looked equally shocked as he read them. Charles maundered airily on about the Magic Carpet, in an attempt to fire their enthusiasm, but Chapman was not to be distracted from his grievance.

'We pay all expenses of advertising, printing, illustrating ...' he protested.

'Of course,' Forster said calmly.

'We pay Mr Dickens fifty pounds a week for his work on this ... carpet!'

'Thirty-eight pounds a week for *assistance*!' chimed in Hall.

Forster was unmoved. 'You will hardly expect Mr Dickens to do all the ordinary business of the paper himself.'

Chapman agitatedly snatched the paper back and studied it. 'But just look at the rest of it, Mr Hall. We pay Dickens half the realised profit on each number, while *we* bear all the loss of any individual number on which a loss is incurred. Is that fair?'

Charles bestowed on him a patient smile. 'Gentlemen: Bradbury and Evans, whom you know from your returns and profits on *Pickwick* and *Nickleby* – profits which touch the thirty thousand pound mark, I am assured – these gentlemen insist that the new paper will sell fifty thousand copies and more per week, within no time.'

Chapman was not placated. 'Even no time is a very long time indeed to support losses, Mr Dickens.'

Hall was still perusing the estimate. 'Chapman and Hall begin getting half profits after the first twenty thousand copies. But this means *your* profits would be between ten or eleven thousand pounds, Mr Dickens, while ours would only be five thousand.'

'Exactly,' Charles said happily. 'You will have the satisfaction of knowing that you have compounded the fairest arrangement ever made with a writer in the history of our exploited down-trodden breed.' He called for sherry, which Forster produced and poured.

Chapman's brow was still furrowed. 'We must study these figures. They seem impossible to me, although you appear to have checked even the printer's estimates.'

Charles handed round the sherry. 'Everything has been checked, but study them by all means. They will seem more possible the longer you do so, I'm sure.'

Hall sighed. 'It's a hard, hard bargain, Mr Dickens.'

Charles's smile was brightly uncompromising. 'Slavery to fill the pockets of others is even harder, dear Mr Hall. Oh, by the way, gentlemen, I feel you should know since we are to be even more intimately associated – I have given up the Queen.'

September, that year of 1840, saw the Dickens family at Broadstairs, a small, pretty resort on the Kent coast, climbing over a crescent-shaped cliff surrounding the bay. It had golden sands instead of the usual East Coast shingle, and delightful rocks with dimpling pools between them, rich in crabs, cockles, and mussels. The family was lodging at Lawn House in Albion Street, a pleasant place looking across a cornfield to the sea, which Charles fancied was winking at him like a sleepy lion, as he worked in a small front room. They had stayed at Broadstairs before, and it was to his personal taste; otherwise, whatever the family's views, they would not have been there.

Fortunately, they liked it, too. Mamie and Charley romped and screamed on the sands with hordes of other children, while Catherine nursed baby Katey. She was almost five months pregnant with her fourth child. Languidly she watched Charles, Fred, Browne, and Forster larking about on the beach. She was not included in such romps, nor did she wish to be. She was getting very heavy, even allowing for her pregnancy, the prettiness of her face disappearing in fat, her bosom billowy, bracelets of flesh forming round her wrists. She knew Charles disliked it, but what could she do? Doctors made one eat for two when one was carrying; and then, there was really nothing to do but sit about at home, now that they had so many servants, she herself with a personal maid.

She thought with pleasure of their new home. With Katey's birth the Doughty Street house had become too small for them. Charles had rented a new one, this time in Devonshire Terrace, Marylebone, in the New Road and opposite the recently-opened Regent's Park. The first house in the terrace, it was a fine, commodious one. Catherine particularly liked the graceful curving staircase, with niches for statues, and the garden, big enough for Charles to play bowls in with his friends, and hidden from the street by a high wall. It was sumptuously furnished, compared with Doughty Street and its poor little pieces bought mostly second-hand. White window-blinds and satin curtains, pile carpets and new mahogany doors, all any woman could want. And yet ... very little of Catherine herself had gone into the choice of furniture or fittings. Much had been Forster's choice, Forster who had such splendid taste and would settle for nothing but the best. She thought that if she had been consulted, there would have been a lot less white about the place, and more upholstery and wallpaper that didn't show every fingermark. It was a little trying to the nerves, if one liked a peaceful life, listening to Charles continually dinning into the elder children that they must never touch the sides of the staircase with their hands, never run in from the garden in outdoor shoes, always keep their toys and personal possessions neatly arranged, always shut doors and drawers. All quite right, of course, but so different from her old home, Papa's nice cluttered study-parlour, Mary's and Georgina's toys spilling out of their cupboard. And *they* had grown up all right, she and the other Hogarth children; or perhaps Charles didn't think so, except for Mary. Mary would always be perfect, because she was dead.

On the beach, the four men were strolling by the edge of the incoming tide, Forster the only sedate one. Charles, Fred, and Browne were shouting ridiculous quasi-nautical phrases at each other.

'Sheep-shank your mizzen!'

'Haul up your main t'gallant sprit boom!'

'Broil up your capstan bar!'

At each exchange they shrieked with laughter, and Fred and Browne, their boots tied round their necks, leapt in and out of the lapping foam. Forster, oblivious, was brooding.

'I'm not certain of the title,' he mused.

'It's a wonderful title,' protested Charles.

'Mm. One should call a weekly paper something less out of the way, I think.'

'Perhaps, but one should call *my* weekly paper something very much out of the way. No more arguments, John. It is to be *Master Humphrey's Clock*. A raven, based on my own dear Grip, keeps a hoard of assorted manuscripts in an old clock, and Master Humphrey shall read them to us, or something of the sort.' He broke off to shout at Fred, 'Fold in your tucker bags!'

'Shove up your bollingers!' Fred retorted.

Charles yelled with laughter. 'What the devil are bollingers?'

Hardly able to speak for laughing, Fred retorted, 'Why, don't you know . . . bollingers are bottle-shaped snarling ferkins!'

Two old gentlemen, passing by, stopped to gaze in astonishment on the shrieking pair. 'Ah, how sad,' said one to the other. 'You see, it's quite true what they say. Poor Boz!' Someone, somewhere, had started the rumour that Charles was mad. Like all derogatory rumours it had spread quickly, and here was confirmation of it. Charles had heard it, and delighted in playing up. With a face suddenly serious, he approached the old men and addressed one of them. 'Pray, sir.'

'Yes, sir?'

'May I ask you, sir, are you gentlemen natives of this place?'

'No, sir. Why do you ask?' The old man seemed inclined to retreat behind his broader companion.

'Because . . .' and Charles's face was graver than ever, 'because I fancied I detected Broad Stares on your faces!'

In a renewed gale of laughter from the three young men, the two old ones hurriedly walked on. It was certainly true what people were saying about Mr Dickens.

As ever, Charles summoned friends to join him. Except when writing, he liked to be the centre of a jovial throng. His solicitor friend Charles Smithson was staying in Broadstairs with his family, who frequently joined the Dickenses for meals and beach frolics. With the Smithsons were two young ladies, Milly Thompson and Emma Picken, on whom Charles loved to exercise his demonic fascination, while they, in turn, enjoyed being deliciously frightened by his daring, dashing mock-courtship of them and of his extravagant language. The younger and prettier girl, Emma, was the principal target for his wild attentions. Catherine was not jealous; she had met this kind of thing many times before, and she had no doubt she would meet it many times again. So long as Charles stayed lunatic-silly there was no need to worry. It was when he got moony-silly, sentimental, that she began to watch him. She was watching him now, but with mild amusement, as he chased Emma along the old jetty towards the sea. The sun was setting; Emma's pink dress glowed and her fair ringlets streamed out behind her as she ran. It was really a pretty, idyllic scene, only marred by Emma's loud screams. Charles, his eyes 'like danger lamps' as the girls said, had almost caught her up, roaring 'The Dicken shall have Miss Picken!'

'Help, help!' shrieked Emma as he caught her round the waist and bore her rapidly towards the water. 'My dress, oh, Mr Dickens, my very best dress!'

'To the Dicken with your dress!'

'But it's the only silk dress I have! it'll be ruined!'

He held her in a savage grip, declaiming. 'Better you should be protected, and your silk dress ruined, than a darker fate, my dearest maiden of the amber-dropping hair. Your beauty makes me drunk . . . I am seized with the divine afflatus!'

'Oh, Charles, you are *so* silly,' observed Catherine to the air, removing a blob of sand from Mamie's mouth. The new nurse-maid should have stopped the child putting it there, but she was too busy staring at her master's goings-on. Why, he'd got the poor young lady into the water now . . . was he going to drown her? She was making a terrible noise, poor thing.

Really frightened now, past pretence, Emma was screaming like a train-whistle. 'Oh, oh, it's up to my knees. It's above my knees now!'

Her captor whispered lasciviously in her ear. 'It's moving in the right direction, then.'

Catherine called out, 'Charles, don't – you'll spoil the poor girl's dress.'

'Dress?' he roared back. 'Talk not to me of dress. Am I not immolating a brand-new pair of patent leathers still unpaid for? Come, Queen of my Heart, fair enslaver, beloved of my soul – let us drown together!'

'Oh, Mr Dickens, I'm wet to the skin!' sobbed his victim.

'Oh, that I might be a wet silk stocking to touch that cold wet pearly skin. In this hour of abandonment to the shafts of destiny shall we be held back by silken raiment? No! Neither leather nor prunella, whatever that may be, shall protect us from the massive bolt of Fate!'

At last, with a violent struggle, she broke free of him and ran back down the jetty, dripping and crying, towards Milly, who looked shocked. Standing in the sea, Charles was laughing like a maniac.

Of course, there were days when it rained, even at Broad-stairs, so that the young Dickenses had to stay within doors. Not for Catherine, however, the torment of finding continual occupation for them, or, alternatively, listening to them fight-ing. A ready-made entertainer existed in the person of their father. In the large, comfortable parlour at Lawn House they were assembled with their nursemaid, Fred, their mother, Emma Picken, Milly Thompson, and Browne, passing the time with the consumption of an enormous tea. Even Grip the raven was in attendance, being fed with a cucumber sandwich and watching, with a beady eye, the curtains drawn over an alcove from which mysterious whispers and an occasional curse were proceeding. At last the moment came. Muffins and sandwiches half-way to their mouths, the company watched, awestruck, as the curtains parted.

The figure who stepped forward was easily recognisable as Forster, though clad in a curious costume which made him appear like a cross between Mr Pickwick and a circus ring-master. In an affable bellow he demanded the attention of those in his audience who were still eating.

'Ladies and gentlemen – and you too, little Snodgering Blee, Popem Jee, and Lucifer Box . . .'

Squeals of excitement interrupted him. He held up a large hand for silence.

'I wish to introduce you to, in England for the first time, Unparalleled Arabian Necromancer, the marvel of the age and magician par excellence: entertainer-extraordinary to the crowned heads of Europe, including His Highness the Tartrate of Magnesia, and His Whiskers Prince Addleburt the Viskery – for the first time, says I, on any stage in England, the great seer . . .'

A shout from Fred urged him to get on with it.

'I will, sir, at once. The one and only – your own – Rhia Rhama Rhoos!'

Gasps of 'Ooh!' and 'Aah!' greeted the strange apparition who bounded on to the stage beside him. A dwarfish, sinister hunchback salaamed and grinned at them, mopping, mowing, and bowing in all directions. His bulbous nose was almost as blue as his beard, his robe was covered with cabalistic signs, his turban surmounted by a huge imitation emerald and an aigrette of black feathers. As he moved, puffs of smoke came from his ears, his hump, and his wide sleeves. Baby Katey began to cry and Mamie got behind her mother, while Emma and Milly clung together. Amid much shushing, the Being addressed them in a thick accent reminiscent of no particular part of the globe, but very striking in its effect.

'Lovely ladies – and delicious children – and whiskering addleberts – and jumpellmen! I am here this day before you one and hall for to doing a ver' special perfromance of my magicky. First it comes to you the Leaping Card Wonder. This wonder is the result of nine year seclusion on mine own with gobblings and gernowmys in the mines of Russia. Watch careful or I bite off your nose!'

Little Charley squealed, in terror only half pretended. Grip, stimulated by his master's voice, however disguised, put his head so far on one side that he all but fell over, and remarked 'Hello, old girl!' It got him a laugh but caused the magician to bend a tremendous frown on him.

'Silence, bird! or I use your *tail* to write my *tale*. And now – the Leaping Card Wonder.'

Watching the deft hands, Browne whispered to Fred, 'When does he do it? When?'

'Shush.'

There followed the Pyramid Wonder and the Conflagration Wonder (with blue flames and screams from the ladies). Again Browne whispered, 'Where did he learn to do that?'

Fred shrugged. 'In der Horient, I suppose.'

'But *where*?'

'I don't know, old boy. He never sleeps, probably does it at night with the aid of an imp out of a bottle.' His eyes followed his brother, now among the audience producing presents for all from their ears, hair, and clothing, amid shrieks of delight. When he reached Emma Picken Fred saw him move in very close to her, but was unable to hear the hoarse whisper.

'For the lovely little darling lady with the delicious sweet skin . . . I give her these.' And, with a flourish of his beringed hand, he produced from her bosom yard after yard of the most delicate silk, until she was almost covered in it, and gasping with surprise.

'For to make a new silk dress!' he hissed in her ear, before returning to the stage for his final trick.

'And now in the end from mine magicky, I am giving you Travelling Doll Wonder, where you are seeing the smallest little lovely girlie Queen in the whole world, God bless her.'

He held out to them a little wooden effigy of Queen Victoria, wrapped in a shawl from which only the crowned head emerged.

'You can all see my little Queen? Werry vell. Now, my Queen. You are a naughty little lady and to Rhia Rhama Rhoos not werry nice, so he send you off to swim in de viskers of horrible Addleburn von Toofree.' With a quill from the black aigrette on his turban he tapped the figure on the head. In a flash it was gone, leaving only its shawl behind. He scooped up the tiny shawl on the end of the black feather and waved it about.

'De Queen is dead – long liff de Queen!'

Nobody, least of all Charles, would ever be able to say how Quilp came to be born. The mysteries of creation are unfathomable, even to the author. Perhaps the name came, obscurely, from the feather he had used in the Travelling Doll Wonder. Quill. Quill pen. Quilp. The character, Daniel Quilp, the evil, lecherous, savage dwarf of Tower Hill, who dominates *The Old Curiosity Shop*, lay deep within Charles himself; was, indeed, himself, in those moments when some wicked spirit led him to practise diableries on people who would be baffled and frightened by them. Outwardly Charles must conform (and would have to do so increasingly the more famous he grew) to his image as a devoted family man, the apostle of home joys and innocent fun. It was too much to sustain. All the suffering, anger, frustration Charles had ever felt in his twenty-eight years went into the making of Quilp: dirty, deformed, almost a monkey, delighting in tricks, deceptions, and the suffering of others, his horrid career was the escape-valve for Charles's pent-up savagery. As he wrote he chuckled, grimaced, laughed, and raved, wolfed food in the dog-like manner of Quilp, leapt on the furniture, and rolled on the floor. His family kept well away from him.

The Old Curiosity Shop was part of that curious muddle, *Master Humphrey's Clock*. The exotic magic carpet for which Chapman and Hall had been asked to pay so dearly had never been woven. What emerged as the new weekly was a somewhat tame collection of stories, legends of old England, a fantasy spun round Gog and Magog, the giants of the Guild-hall, a pallid resurrection of Mr Pickwick and Sam Weller. Chapman and Hall might well have ground their teeth in disappointment had not two highly successful novels wound their way in serial form through the *Clock*. They were *Barnaby Rudge*, a rattling story of the Gordon Riots in the previous century, with a lovable idiot boy as hero, the owner, like the Dickenses, of a talking raven; and *The Old Curiosity Shop*.

It was a novel with two strong threads. One was the plot in which Quilp reigned as Demon King, in league with a villainous lawyer and his repulsive sister. The other, and the one which Charles's reading public avidly fell upon, was the saga of Little Nell, the child who led her grandfather, a compulsive gambler, far away from London and the temptation of the gaming-tables. The public loved Nell, idolised her as Charles did. And this in spite of the fact that she was like no mortal child – or adolescent girl, for her age was never stated. For all the humanity she showed, she might have been a plaster angel, or the china fairy doll at the top of the Christmas tree to whom Charles had likened Mary. She seldom laughed, never joked, was never seen to be out of temper. Endlessly patient in all her trials, put upon yet sweetly uncomplaining, she journeyed on through England, breathlessly followed by legions of readers.

As 1840 ended, *The Old Curiosity Shop* was also coming to its close.

'I'm afraid,' said Charles to Forster, 'I'm going to have to kill her off soon.'

'What ? *Kate* ?' They had been talking of her imminent lying-in.

'No, no, no, that's of no public interest. No, I mean poor Little Nell.'

Forster gave a deep sigh. 'I know. And so does your public. There have been many imploring letters recommending the poor child to mercy. Do you not think you could devise some reprieve ?'

Charles shook his long locks impatiently. 'Do you think I care less for her than the wretched readers do ? I'd do anything to keep her alive, but Destiny, John, Destiny – the logical and inevitable and irresistible end to all stories.'

George Cattermole was briefed to draw the scene in which Nell lay dead.

'It is winter time, so there are no flowers; but upon her breast, and pillow, and about her bed, there may be slips of holly, and berries, and such free green things ... I want it to express the most beautiful repose and tranquillity, and to have something of a happy look, if death can.'

Charles wrote the fatal passages with tears streaming down his face and splashing on to the paper.

'She was dead. Dear, patient, gentle Nell was dead. There upon her little bed, she lay at rest.'

All over the world readers wept with him. Strong men in club-rooms broke down and cried. The fiery Daniel O'Connell burst into tears and threw the book out of the window. Californian miners sobbed round the camp-fire, and crowds on the quay at New York shouted to a British vessel 'Is Little Nell dead?' But he, her creator and murderer, was the most heart-broken of all, for, as he told Forster, old wounds bled afresh with Nell's death. 'Dear Mary died yesterday, when I think of this sad story.'

Before the year was out he stood by Mary's grave, now re-opened for her brother George, and another had recently been filled in on the other side, her grandmother's. Pale and sad, twisting her ring round his finger, Charles looked down at the coffin.

'Dear Mary, my dearest love,' he whispered, 'shall I take you away to wait for me somewhere secret? A private place where we shall never be parted? No. Dearest love, I can't steal your poor dust from your own family, much as I want to. In any case, I know that our spirits will not be kept from one another by our separation in the mouldy earth. But dear heart, it feels as if I am losing you for the second time.'

There was a rosebud in his hand. He kissed it, and dropped it on the coffin lid.

'Goodbye, my soul, my only love. Goodbye for ever.'

The mourners were approaching, a sad little band in black; Catherine on her father's arm, the twins crying, Mrs Hogarth almost hysterical, as she had been at Mary's funeral. But among them the startled Charles saw only one face, young and bright; sleek dark hair beneath a black bonnet, blue eyes meeting his with a look of recognition. All the blood seemed to drain from his heart.

But it was not Mary, or her ghost: only her sister Georgina.

CHAPTER TWELVE

The door of Number One Devonshire Terrace had shut behind them; they would not enter it again for six months, for they were off to America. The house had been let to General Sir John Wilson, and Charles had rented a furnished one in nearby Osnaburgh Street for the children, who were to live there under the avuncular supervision of Fred, with daily visits to the house of Charles's actor friend, William Macready, their temporary guardian. Catherine had cried very much at parting with the Darlings, and Charles had cried too, but his tears had dried quickly as they piled into the carriage that was to take them on the first stage of their journey to the 'Merrikas'.

Catherine waited in what Charles jokingly called the conjugal stateroom aboard the Cunard packet *Britannia*, in Liverpool docks. Their cabin was, in fact, rather smaller than a hackney-coach or a coffee-room booth. It had two bunker beds, one above the other: an arrangement Catherine viewed with a certain satisfaction. Their large double bed at home offered unlimited opportunity for marital dalliance, and she could hardly believe her luck in having reached this month of January, 1842, without having another Darling on the way. Walter had been born eleven months before, and since then she had remained miraculously free from pregnancy and its malaises.

Of course, Charles had been unwell for a good deal of the time, after the agonising operation for the removal of the fistula which had troubled him for so long.

Fanny Burnett, Charles's sister, who had come to see them off, was looking queasy with the gentle rocking of the ship at moorings. Not long delivered of a delicate son, she seemed far from well herself. It had been rather thoughtless of Charles to demand her presence, but he had been determined to make this a ceremonial gathering of all the friends and relations he could summon together; not so much because he envisaged a possible eternal parting from them if the Atlantic were in a bad temper, but because it was an irresistible opportunity for a party. They were having it now, he and the others, at the Adelphi Hotel. Catherine and Fanny had not, of course, been invited. Catherine was glad that the few possessions so far unpacked by Anne Brown, her splendidly efficient new maid, included a bottle of brandy. Her hand went up to her cheek, but furtively, so as not to worry Fanny. Fanny's restless eyes caught the gesture.

'Is it coming on again, Kate?'

'No, oh no. Just a wee bit swollen still.'

Before they had left London she had developed a toothache. There was no time to visit the dentist, and she was in any case so preoccupied with last-minute preparations that it hardly registered with her except as an irritation. Only when they were on their way to Euston Station did the first real pang hit her. The journey to Liverpool was a nightmare of wretchedness, horrible stabs and throbs of pain tearing through her head and puffing out her cheek to balloon-size. The invaluable Anne had brought along a small bottle of oil of cloves, and between applications of this and sips of brandy she survived without disgracing herself. Charles so hated tears, even of pain, though he was kindness itself when one was really ill.

Arriving in Liverpool had seemed like the perfect cure. It was such a bustling place, full of ships sailing to romantic, far-away places, and of exotic, spicy, tarry smells. The air was fresh after the stagnation of London, reminding her of her native Scotland. Charles's excitement communicated itself to her, and her spirits rose. Of course the Darlings would be all right with Fred and the Macreadys to look after them, and Charles had warned Mrs Macready that Morgan the nursemaid was inclined to be careless. Catherine began to look forward to America. There were beautiful new gowns to be unpacked when they got there, new scarves and gloves, and even jewellery, for Charles had decreed that she must outshine

168

everyone, even at the White House, and no expense spared.

Above the deck noises, the shouts of sailors, and the morose mooing of the cow which had been taken aboard to provide milk for the voyage, there came a familiar ringing voice.

'My dear, dear fellow, I can't tell you how much it has meant to me . . .'

Charles and the festive party were back from the Adelphi. She heard her name and Fanny's loudly called; together they climbed the steep companion-ladder to the small deck, littered with provisions and luggage, to join the men who clustered round Charles, slapping his back and shaking his hand: his brother Alfred, Forster, Mr Thompson of Broadstairs memories, others who had been collected along the way. Forster saw her and affectionately drew her into the circle.

'Quite recovered Mrs D? But I can see you are.'

Charles pulled her to him, showing her off to the others. The wind had whipped a lovely colour into her cheeks, paling the inflammation in the swollen one, and her eyes were sapphires beneath her fur-lined bonnet.

'Behold her, gentlemen!' He smelt, not unpleasantly, of gin today. 'Wife to the Inimitable, bound for the Americas! The best, the brightest, the bloomingest, the Beloved! In glorious spirits, an't she? Our boat is on the shore, our bark is on the sea, but before our parting's o'er, here's a triple health to she.' Then there was kissing and hand-shaking, and an invitation from the Captain to take a glass with him in the Saloon, before the final moment came when the jolly-boat containing their friends was receding towards the dockside, and they stood together on deck, Catherine waving her handkerchief, Charles, suddenly grave and withdrawn, raising his hand in solemn farewell.

The crossing was terrible, though not terrible beyond description. Charles, who was several times in real fear for their lives, and as sea-sick as everybody else, was busy making notes for convulsingly funny letters to be written home. Catherine's account of the voyage to Fanny was more realistic.

'We were eighteen days on our passage, and experienced all the horrors of a storm at sea, which raged frightfully for a whole night, and broke our paddle-boxes and the life-boat to pieces. I was nearly distracted with terror, and don't know what I should have done had it not been for the great kindness and composure of my dear Charles. It was very awful. I thought we should never see another day, but, thank God, we were spared, and you may imagine our relief and happiness when, towards morning, it gradually lulled . . . we were all very sick, and, to crown all my miseries, I had a most awfully swollen face, and looked quite an object.

'To turn to the brighter side of the picture, the reception Charles has met with is something not to be described. He is perfectly worshipped, and crowds follow him in the streets even. It will be the same, they tell us, all through America.'

So it was, their progress suggesting to Charles a strong likeness between themselves and the Queen and Albert. Balls, parties, receptions, speeches, and even nocturnal serenades were organised for Boz and his consort. There was less enthusiasm for Boz's emphatically expressed opinions on the subject of International Copyright. His vehement speeches urging America to exert herself in the matter as England had done were received with coldness and mockery. He was disgusted at the lack of freedom of opinion in the Land of the Free, and at the piles of pirated copies of his own works to be seen in the bookshops. He was even more disgusted at the universal American habit of spitting, at the miseries of American railroads, the horrors of American jails, and the 'accursed and detestable system' of slavery. Catherine suffered with him all the verbal and published vituperation, as well as the numerous discomforts of travel, and kept as cheerful as she could, longing more and more, all the time, for Devonshire Terrace and the Darlings. Charles didn't take kindly to complaints.

There were introductions to celebrities who had only been names to them in England: the poet Longfellow, Washington Irving, R. H. Dana, men who would become lifelong friends. One of them would not, though Charles would certainly never forget the pale, black-haired, haggard-faced young man who arrived at the United States Hotel, Philadelphia, one night when Charles was feeling particularly worn out after a day of alternately being lionised and arguing with the forceful critics of his opinions. Catherine had gone to bed with a headache; Charles only wished he could do the same, but here was the writer Mr Edgar Allan Poe, gushingly intense in his praise of Charles's works, first refusing and then accepting a glass of Madeira. After three bottles had been consumed, Charles congratulated his literary acquaintance on giving a damned good impression of a serious drinker.

Their adjournment to an opium den, where Mr Poe partook freely of rye whisky and proclaimed himself a miserable decayed dog, but a genius, confirmed Charles's suspicion that he was out with a very queer fish indeed. His own faculties began to cloud. He had, through the fumes of the stinking apartment, a dim idea that Poe was talking about their meeting being one of phrenological significance, whatever that might mean.

'I believe,' he went on, fixing Charles with a glittering eye, 'I am intended to communicate to you the substance of the most shattering experiment of my life – for you must know, dear sir, that my entire life has been and is devoted to a series of spectacularly dangerous experiments at the very edge of madness and destruction. Will you make yourself available at midnight tomorrow?'

Did he, he was to wonder in years to come, make himself so available? *Was* there ever a strange journey taken on a bitterly cold night with one who was rapidly assuming the air of a maniac, who babbled of mesmerism and of his recent most dangerous experiment, no less than the mesmerism of a man *in articulo mortis*, at the point of death? They seemed to be standing at the bedside of the subject of this experiment, a ghastly skeletal figure which still breathed, though it seemed hardly possible that breath could come through the sunken lips, from the collapsed lungs.

Poe was questioning it. Faint, groaned replies came from the terrible body. It had slept, it said, but now it was dead. Its body was but the shroud of its soul. It begged Poe to free it, until Charles frantically intervened and added his pleading.

'Wake him, for God's sake, Poe!'

Hurriedly the mesmerist obeyed. A groan of 'Dead! Dead!' came from the skull-like face, and to Charles's utter horror the sheet covering the thing on the bed suddenly writhed into life and slid to the floor, revealing a maggot-ridden, corrupting corpse.

Did any of it happen, or was it a nightmare born of verbal wrangling and too much Madeira taken too late at night? Charles's interest in mesmerism remained, but he would never care to dwell at length on his meeting with Poe. Later that year, back in England, he wrote to Poe on literary matters, adding politely:

'Do not for a moment suppose that I have ever thought of you but with a pleasing recollection.'

By the end of June they were home again. No more journeys across limitless distances, no more parties for the 'Boz and Bozess', no more ceremonial of taking out Maclise's picture of the children as soon as they arrived at a new hotel, and Charles playing *Home Sweet Home* on his accordion. Their welcome was tumultuous. At Osnaburgh Terrace the two elder Dickens children, on their way to bed, were suddenly hustled downstairs by Uncle Fred and their nursemaid and hurried down the garden path. From the hackney-cab which had just stopped a figure jumped out and ran towards them; and then little Mamie was kissing her father through the bars of the gate and everybody was laughing and crying at the same time. Then they were all upstairs, getting the two younger Darlings out of bed, Catherine cuddling baby Walter and little Katey, who had been very miserable under the Macreadys' austere rule, wild with delight, almost throwing off sparks like a real Lucifer Box.

As for five-year-old Charley, the sensitive little boy who still wore low-cut frocks like a girl, he could say nothing but 'I'm so glad to see you, Papa, Mamma, I'm so glad, too glad!' And too glad indeed he was, for he fell into violent convulsions, causing Dr Elliotson to be summoned urgently to the half-delirious child.

There was another familiar face among the welcomers – the calm, pretty face of Georgina Hogarth, who had become 'Aunt

Georgy' to the children in their parents' absence, telling stories to them, taking them for walks in the Park, reading out interesting bits from their parents' letters. Charles, submerged in the embraces of his family, had no time to notice that her likeness to Mary was merging into something which was wholly and entirely Georgina.

The first excitement was over, and they were back at Devonshire Terrace. The nursery floor was littered with the toys brought back from America; Georgina, acutely sensitive to her brother-in-law's moods, saw his exuberance turn into irritation at the general state of chaos, a condition he abhorred.

'Now!' she said brightly. 'Who wants buns and cream cakes?'

Amid the chorus of assent she turned to Catherine. 'I thought we'd have tea downstairs. Morgan has it ready.'

'Of course!' Catherine beamed. 'You really do take to arranging things, Georgie.'

'I like it.' she said truthfully.

Catherine had a bright idea. 'You must stay and keep on doing it. Would you like that?'

'Oh, I would, if . . .' she looked towards Charles, who was compulsively tidying up.

'I'm sure Charles would love to have you here as much as I would.'

Georgina's pretty face was alight with pleasure. She began to shepherd the children. 'Well then – come on, all.'

In bed that night, happily tired, Charles put his arm round his wife's plump shoulders and stroked the dark plait that strayed over them.

'Home, Kate, home!'

'Yes.' She sighed, but it was a sigh of contentment. She had been so homesick, and now it was over. Only one thing spoiled her pleasure. She was pregnant again, and it would all be as it had been before, sickness, exhaustion, ugly weight-gain, children demanding to be played with when she only wanted to rest, Charles being irritable and behaving as though it were all her fault . . . He was cheerful now, however, planning away.

'I shall make a tremendous assault on the *American Notes* tomorrow. I shall finish them, and they'll sell thousands of copies and we won't have a debt in the world.'

She turned towards him. 'Charles.'

'Mm?'

'I've been thinking.'

'Don't damage yourself, my dear.'

'No, seriously.'

'Even more dangerous.'

She knew that when he teased her, however unkindly, he was in a good humour.

'I think it would be very nice if Georgina lived with us. You see – this is really a very big house, and I have such a lot to see to, and Georgina is so good at these things. And now with the new . . . I shall need some help. May I have Georgina, Charles? Please let me have Georgina.'

'Well . . .' Something in him was questioning, uncertain, afraid of the awakening of memories that were so sweet and so painful. The likeness had struck him forcibly, the night they had come home.

'It will be *so* nice, Charles, just like the lovely old days, with you and me and . . .' She stopped, seeing Charles's remembering eyes. But he answered gently, 'If Georgina wishes to live with us, I shall be very happy. She's an angelic child.'

'I don't know about that,' said Catherine, conscious of far from angelic memories of her sisters in their youth. 'But she's certainly useful about the house.' She let the suggestion sink in before turning her back on him. 'I'm going to sleep now.'

Next day he came upon Georgina seated at a writing-desk, her ringlets falling over a household account-book and a pile of bills methodically impaled on a spike at her side. He watched her with a smile before looking over her shoulder.

'What are you doing, little Georgy?'

'The household accounts. Kate asked me to.'

'Really? I hope your arithmetic is better than hers. I'm quite convinced that Kate honestly believes that two and two don't necessarily make four. Now I know why our book-keeping has become so magically efficient.'

Georgina looked alarmed. She usually knew when Charles was being funny, and laughed accordingly, but sometimes his humour was elusive.

'I hope you don't mind,' she said. 'I like to do it, and Kate doesn't, so . . .'

He patted her shoulder. 'Dear girl, I'm delighted to have you here and happy for you to do whatever makes you happy while you are with us.'

She looked even more alarmed, her cheeks noticeably paling.

'Why, what is it?' he asked. 'Why do you look like that?'

'Oh, it's nothing.' She pleated a fold of her dress nervously. 'Just silliness.'

'Come and sit down with me and tell me the silliness. Now. Tell me what made your little face so pale and now makes it so pretty and pink.'

It was a moment before she told him. 'You said "while I am with you".'

'Of course. For as long as you are here you . . .'

Her eyes were on his, earnestly pleading. 'I want always to be here.'

'My dearest child! Of course you shall be with us, for just as long as . . .'

'For ever! I never want to leave you, *never*. And – and Kate and the children, of course.'

He was a little worried, a little puzzled, but smiled down at her.

'But, dear child, the time will come when you yourself will want to . . .'

'Promise me I can stay, Charles. Oh, please promise!'

'Of course you shall stay – as long as you wish.'

She was clutching his sleeve. 'For ever!'

'And a day, if you like, dear Georgy.' Gallantly he detached the small hand and raised it to his lips. On the hand that held hers Mary's ring sparkled. Her eyes dwelt on it, and as their fingers parted she began, hesitantly, to say something tremendously important to herself.

'I know that – I know that I can never understand your work as *she* did. She was so much cleverer than I am.'

175

He did not comprehend, until he saw her eyes still fixed on the ring.

'But I'm better at household things than either her or Catherine. And I *am* good with children. And I'm far, far better at arithmetic than either of them,' she ended defiantly.

His smile at this naïve piece of self-advertisement was sad. Little Georgy was trying to suggest herself as a replacement for the loved, lost Mary. It was sweet, and pathetic, and quite hopeless. That encounter at the graveside in Kensal Green had been his first and last identification of the living with the dead.

'Dear girl,' he said, 'Kate is herself, and Mary was her quite unforgettable self, and you are your own very sweet and wonderfully helpful self – and very good at arithmetic too.'

It was not quite the answer she had hoped for – if, indeed, she clearly knew what that answer was; but she was pleased, and played her last card in this present game.

'Charles . . . you may, I hope, feel inclined to talk to me about your work sometimes. You know, I read every word you write – and I'm sure Kate doesn't.'

Amused and touched, he said, 'Of course. We shall talk about my work, and you will give me the benefit of your opinions and we shall be a very dear brother- and sister-in-law indeed.'

The conventional response did not come; only an unmistakable look of disappointment. Charles frowned. Women were the devil to understand, even nice little Georgy. He shook his head impatiently.

'Well, my dear, we must both get on with our appointed tasks. My mind is so exercised over these ridiculous Americans I can think of very little else.'

He had reluctantly taken Forster's advice and let *American Notes*, with all its condemnations of native institutions, go to the printer's without an apologetic introduction. Much better, as John said, to let it stand on the strength of its accuracy and truth. The American public was touchy, very touchy indeed, as he had discovered when he was there, but surely they would appreciate plain speaking and an honest desire to suggest reforms. He could foresee criticisms, but what of them? He feared nobody's brickbats.

What he could not foresee was that an employee of Bradbury and Evans' printing firm would sell proof sheets of the *Notes* to an American journalist. With utter horror he stared at the front page of the *New York Herald* which Forster had brought him.

'My God! It's impossible. It's disgusting!' He flung the paper across the room.

'Disgusting indeed. The *Herald* sold fifty thousand copies in two days. They published within nineteen hours of getting the copy, our friend tells us.'

'Bloody, bloody thieves and pirates!' Charles raved.

'The same swine who sold them the proof sheets sold them to someone who not only sold them to the *Herald* but to at least three publishers – perhaps four – who've been flooding the United States with copies at six cents a piece.'

Charles groaned. 'Six cents a piece. Even if they hate it – at that price, what a bargain! So much for my campaign for international copyright.'

Forster, never noted for his tact, bumbled on. 'As if it wasn't bad enough, the American press is enraged.'

'I know.' Charles retrieved the paper and gloomily scanned the editorial. '"The book is all leather and prunella . . . not worthy of a sensible man's persual". And *I* am that famous penny-a-liner with the most coarse, vulgar, impudent, and superficial mind that ever had the courage to write about their original and remarkable country. My view is that of a narrow-minded, conceited Cockney. The *Notes* are the essence of balderdash reduced to the last drop of silliness and inanity. What do you think about that? No more! To hell with money and critics! I'm going out to play with my children.'

He strode out of the study, leaving Forster shaking his head over the invective in the *Herald*.

For all the frustration he had suffered over the pirating, Charles's spirits recovered with the news that English readers, at least, had welcomed the *Notes*. Three thousand copies had been sold in the first week after publication, with the likelihood of the work running into three or four editions within the year. At his Club, the author celebrated with Forster, Maclise, and the artist Clarkson Stanfield. His eyes bright, he looked round the company.

'I've a proposal to make,' he said excitedly. 'A trip, gentlemen, a trip!'

'Where to?' asked Forster, sleepy after many toasts.

Charles banged on the table. 'Damn where to! Just a wonderful mad trip, without publishers and pirates and petticoats and popinjays and pussycats and precious little pets. Just the four of us adventurers, galloping into the night!'

'Sounds like a good idea,' murmured Stanfield.

'I must put it on record . . .' began Forster.

'Forster agrees,' Charles broke in. 'And you, Maclise?'

'Carried – an-anonymously.'

Charles leapt on to his chair, one foot on the table, his glass raised.

'Onward, my brave buckos, onward!' he cried.

The brave buckos did not reply to the toast. They were all asleep.

In spite of the somewhat lukewarm reception given to Charles's proposal, the three-week trip into Cornwall was an uproarious success, a time of relaxation, of gales of laughter, of sight-seeing and great drinking and eating and good fellowship; and, for Charles, an escape from the domestic ties which delighted and irked him in almost equal proportions. Even better, it was a time in which the notion for a new novel came to him. Back in London, he talked over the details with Forster, and they exchanged ideas for the hero's patronymic, mostly of grotesque character.

'How does this take you, John? The Life and Adventures of Martin Chuzzlewig, his family, friends, and enemies. Comprising his wills and his ways. With an historical record of what he did and what he didn't. The whole forming a complete key to the house of Chuzzlewig.'

'First class,' said Forster. 'Though I still prefer Chubblewig.'

The book which finally emerged as *Martin Chuzzlewit* was a

disappointment. Charles knew it was good, the most mature work he had yet produced, with at least two wonderful comic characters in the hypocritical architect Pecksniff and the monthly nurse Sairey Gamp, whom Forster declared to be his best invention since Sam Weller. Not surprising, of course, that the book was hated in America, to which land Charles had sent his hero Martin to experience the sort of abuses he himself had witnessed there. Mr Hall, not happy with the profits from the book, enforced a penalty clause by which, should sales be disappointing, the author had to repay the publisher fifty pounds a month out of the two hundred pounds payable to each issue. Infuriated, Charles declared to Forster his intention of deserting the old firm for that of Bradbury and Evans.

'Damn it, John! I'm bent upon paying Chapman and Hall *down*, and when I've done that, little Mr Hall shall have a piece of my mind that he will never forget. I shall buy back *all* my copyrights.'

Forster looked despairing. 'But how, Charles, how?'

'What do you mean, how? By writing, that's how. What other magic lamp do I own?'

'I agree, I agree. But weren't you just saying you were too irritated, too burning in the head and so on, to write?'

'That was *then*!' Charles snapped. He assumed, realistically, the gin-laden tones of Mrs Gamp. 'When will you learn, Mrs 'Arris, that *then* is one thing and *now* is another? So just leave the bottle on the chimley-piece, and don't ask me to take none, but let me put my lips to it when I am so dispoged. And always remember, Mrs 'Arris, that if I could afford to lay all my fellow-creeturs out for nothink I would gladly do it, sich is the love I bears 'em. And pertikerly remember, Mrs 'Arris, Messrs Chapman and Hall, for I shall lay *them* out for nothink but sheer love, I swear it!'

Forster broke into laughter. 'My God, Charles, I cannot understand why every person who can read English doesn't take *Chuzzlewit* to his heart.'

His mood sunny in a flash, Charles grasped his friend's arm.

'Dear, dear John. I know very well that if there were one hundred thousand John Forsters in this country the Dickens children would want for nothing. You are truly a friend, John.'

Forster growled with pleased embarrassment. 'Well, then. Have you some thought of a new story?'

Charles smiled and laid a forefinger to his nose. 'My dear fellow, I am hourly expecting something of a quite extraordinary nature to turn up.'

The elder Dickens children, playing ball in the garden, were unaware that they were being benevolently observed over the gate by a middle-aged gentleman with a cheerful, shabby-genteel air about his clothes and a rakish slant to his tall hat. His somewhat prominent nose was red, as with much fine old Madeira. His eyes shone with pleasure as the small Charley ran towards him, clutching the ball his sisters were trying to capture. Katey stopped in full tilt, her eyes wide.

'Grandfather!'

John Dickens swept into the garden and scooped her up.

'My dearest little lovekins! Granpa it is, dearest grand-children. I have turned up! In short, I am here!'

CHAPTER THIRTEEN

The children had gone back to their playing, and their grand-father was standing in front of their father's desk in the study, just as one of them might have done if sent for after some misdemeanour. He had shed his air of jauntiness under Charles's irritable frown.

'But *why*, Father, why?' Charles was asking. 'You're supposed to be happily ensconced at Alphington.'

John shifted his feet uneasily. 'I know it, dear boy.'

'Well, then?'

John met his eyes with a look of limpid candour. 'It's a divine place, my boy. Oh, yes. The country, with its rural pleasures and its rustic virtues – I love it, I freely confess, and can barely drag myself away from it. But needs must when the devil drives, eh, my boy?'

'And which particular devil is driving at the moment, Father? Oh, sit down, sit down,' he snapped, suddenly unable to bear the abject attitude of the man before him looking like a guilty schoolboy before his headmaster.

John subsided on to a chair, murmuring something about it being uncommonly civil of him, and sighed deeply.

'If you *could* find the dregs of an old bottle of Madeira, my boy, I do believe I could force it down, even without the assistance of a biscuit. Dry weather, very.'

Charles glanced out of the window. It had been raining before the children had gone out to play. Resignedly, he went to the decanter which stood ready against his occasional need of a quencher when writing, and poured a glass for his father, who drained it at one gulp.

'Oh yes indeed,' John rambled on, 'nothing would drag me from that little Eden, where your sainted mother, about whom you haven't yet had time to ask me . . .'

'How is Mother?' Charles asked patiently.

'Ah, the country has brought out the last vestiges of goodness in her, and she is, one may say, more than fairly well.'

At least that was one complaint he would not have to listen to, Charles thought. 'I'm glad to hear it,' he said truthfully. 'And you look uncommonly well yourself.'

John beamed, sensing himself to be talking his way back into favour. 'I? My dear boy, I'm always well – blessed with one of those sanguine dispositions which remains unchangeably high, regardless of the weather.'

'So there are not pressing problems?'

'Pressing? Not pressing, certainly not.' He waved his empty glass about significantly. 'Excellent Madeira, this . . .'

Charles brought over the decanter, of which John took possession, placing it within easy reach.

'So, Father, you simply decided to pop up to town?'

'Exactly so. It seemed time for a little chat.'

Charles's frown returned. 'Chat? About what?'

'About – ? Oh, nothing in particular, you know. Mind you, your sainted mother gets a little bored from time to time. We are essentially town creatures after all, we Dickens.'

'Personally, I am always delighted to get out of it.'

'And delighted to get back to it, no doubt.' said John waggishly.

Charles laughed. 'No doubt.'

'No, indeed. There *is* the vexing question of your brother Alfred, of course. An excellent accomplished civil engineer like Alfred should have more suitable employment than he has at present.'

'What is that? I'm afraid I've rather lost touch with Alfred.'

'In a word, very little. Your mother was wondering whether you could not perhaps mention his accomplishments in that area to one of your many influential friends.'

Charles sighed. 'Well – no doubt I could. So that's brother Alfred.'

From brother Alfred, the conversation moved on to brother Fred, who, though his Treasury salary had been increased, had been living in a sadly extravagant manner, in proof of which his father passed over one of Fred's unpaid bills. Charles added it to a neat pile which already contained other accounts not settled by Fred. He then poured himself a drink, for he could foresee a trying interview ahead.

'No,' continued John, 'nothing is pressing, but there are these little troublesome details of family life, and we, Charles, you and I, heading the tribe of Dickens, are expected to solve them, are we not, my boy? Yes.' He poured himself another glass of Madeira. 'It's a task which requires both of us to be constantly vigilant, Charles, and it is very difficult for us to fulfil this responsibility when half of us (even if it is only, admittedly, the lesser half) lies locked in the arms of the bucolic countryside, listening day after day, night after night, to those infernal bloody noisy birds and bees and other damned creeping creatures of the rural backside of this great country of ours. Not,' he added less vehemently, 'to put too fine a point on it.'

Charles shook his head, half-impatient, half-amused. There had been something of this earlier in the year, when his parents, whose lease of the Alphington cottage had expired, had moved in with their landlady next door, and had inspired her with even more suspicion at close quarters than she had entertained before. In John's words, their preparatory demonstrations of migration had led to what might be considered a vote of want of confidence, and as usual Charles's solicitor, Mitton, had been asked for a cheque to reassure her. Now the migration had become a fact which no further cheques would cancel out.

'I am bored, my boy, I am bored.' John was saying. 'I'm not really old enough to be put out to pasture or sent to the knacker's yard, am I?'

'Of course not, Father.' What else could one say?

'Well, then, my dear son, save me from this crushing boredom, not to mention the constant complaints of your magnificent mother, who – not to put too fine a point on it – is driving me mad with her constant endless complaints.' His voice throbbed with melodramatic appeal. 'Save me, my son, save me! The heavens look down down and smile upon a son who respects his ageing parents!'

It was so blatant, so irresistibly theatrical, that Charles turned away to hide a smile. 'Well.' he said, 'I don't know. In Alphington you have lived very satisfactorily within your income – hardly a debt to speak of . . .'

'Hardly a debt to speak of and hardly anything else to speak of, either! I would be even more economic in my grave, would I not? I assure you, my son, that the activity of the worms would give me more to laugh about than I have in blessed, boring little Alphington.'

Charles laughed out loud. In his father's position his own sentiments would have been exactly the same. Ignoring John's offended protests, he laughed uncontrollably until he was able to speak again.

'Then what do you suggest, Father? You have something in mind, haven't you?'

'Well – since you ask – there has been brought to our attention a leetle, leetle house which is going in Blackheath for a quite ludicrously small rent, and which would suit your martyred mother and my modest self perfectly. May I tell you about it?'

Charles leaned back. 'You may.'

'Well, then.' John beamed, having won his point. 'As you request it, I will. A mere seventy pounds will obtain for us a delightful town cottage perfectly suited to the requirements of a genteel, happily ageing town couple. May I show you the exquisite and modest property?'

Charles groaned. 'I suppose you may . . .'

'Since you insist, I will. But first, dear boy, let us relax.' He looked hard at the decanter. 'My dear, dear Charles! What joy and pride your achievements bring to your loving parents in their declining years.'

'I'm glad of it, Father.' He indicated the manuscript on his desk. 'But I have the next instalment of *Chuzzlewit* to complete . . .'

'My dear boy, forgive me. I know that I am a tedious intrusion on your immortal labours.' He began to get up, but the pull of the decanter was too strong; sitting down again, he refilled his glass. 'I assure you that as soon as we have killed the bottle I will leave you to your significant works. Oh, what a fortunate, happy, happy family we are in these fortunate and unhappy days. The hungry 'forties, they're calling these years, Charles. But never mind, eh? Never mind. God bless us all!'

The delightful town cottage at Blackheath did not materialise, though Charles put up the money for it when he discovered that the migration from Alphington was a fait accompli: John was living in cheap London lodgings and his wife staying with friends. But the couple did not prove acceptable to the Blackheath landlords, and they finished up in rooms at the Manor House, Lewisham, an old dilapidated half-timbered building at the foot of Lewisham Hill, owned by an accommodating friend of Charles's.

From this address, to Charles's mounting fury, begging letters to Chapman and Hall and the solicitor Mitton were sent with monotonous regularity, and forwarded to Devonshire Terrace. He could not restrain his feelings on receiving such demands. In the following February he was writing to Mitton: 'I quite agree in opinion with you touching my father, who, I really believe, as Sam Weller says of someone in *Pickwick*, "has gone ravin' mad with conscious willany". The thought of him besets me, night and day; and I really do not know what is to be done with him. It is quite clear that the more we do, the more outrageous and audacious he becomes.'

In September he was almost rendered speechless when he received a forwarded letter from Chapman and Hall, in which his father blandly requested a free season ticket from the Watermen's Company to allow him to travel to and from Lewisham by the Greenwich steamer.

'As I am to be an independent Gentleman, how am I to get rid of my time? Two or three hours a day, two or three days a week at the Museum, would be a great relief, but to walk to London and back to accomplish that object is rather more than I can do with ease and rheumatism at sixty. If you would be my surety to the Watermen well and good, and I should be grateful; if not why then I must doze away the future ("who talks of future whose existence is already of the past?") in my arm chair, in re-reading the works of Boz.'

Charles crumpled the letter up and flung it away from him.

'Confound him, and all of them! They look on me as a Something to be plucked and torn to pieces for their advantage. My soul is sickened – yes, sickened! – at the thought of them!'

Hastily he scribbled a note to Mitton.

'If you should see my disinterested and most affectionate parent, will you undertake to tell him that his letter has disgusted me beyond expression; and that I have no more reference to anything he wants or wishes or threatens or would do or wouldn't do, in taking on myself this new burden, than I have reference to the Bell of Saint Paul's Cathedral or the Statue at Charing Cross.'

But still the drag-chain pulled at him, and still he wearily wrote out cheques: cheques for his father's wretched debts, for his brother Alfred, who was out of a job and whom he took on as secretary, for Fred's tailor's bills, for young Augustus's support. There was another Dickens baby on the way, due early in 1844, and the tumult at Devonshire Terrace was such that Charles rented himself a rural retreat at Finchley, Cobley's Farm, where he could work away at *Chuzzlewit*. At least some good money was coming in, from his *Christmas Carol*, the little book into which he had thrown himself with such passionate energy after a horrifying glimpse into the misery and degradation of slum children. His public laughed and cried and shuddered at Scrooge the miser, the Ghosts of Past, Present, and Future who changed his way of life, the poor clerk Bob Cratchit and his crippled child, Tiny Tim, and those other deformed children, the goblin forms cowering beneath the robe of Christmas Present: 'yellow, meagre, ragged, scowling, wolfish . . .' and dangerous.

'This boy is Ignorance. This girl is Want. Beware them both, and all of their degree, but most of all beware this boy, for on his brow I see that written which is Doom.'

The *Carol* was a commercial success, and he would need money increasingly as the years went on: writing, ever writing, to support his 'petticoats', Catherine and Georgina, the ever-

growing brood of children, the brothers who were turning out
to have the streak of extravagant fecklessness in them which he
would struggle so hard to discourage in his own sons, even his
father-in-law, George Hogarth, now fallen on poor times. And,
for another nine years after the flight from Alphington, there
would be his chief pensioner, his father: ebullient, self-confi-
dent, shameless, treading the flowery path which his son had
carved out for him, dipping into that son's pocket as cheerfully
as the growing cuckoo grabs food from its harassed foster-
parents.

Charles could not spare the nervous energy to be con-
tinuously angry. When another debt came in, or a breezy visit
from the debtor to pick up anything that might be going, he
was exasperated; less so as time went on, and he resigned
himself to the fact that there would be no more Alphington,
and that his parents were back in the old pattern of moving from
one lodging to another as soon as their rent got too much in
arrears.

'To think,' he said wryly to John Forster, who was writing
earnestly away at the work which would one day be the first
and most famous *Life of Charles Dickens*, 'to think that when
he and I used to walk to Gad's Hill, in my childhood, he would
urge me "to be very persevering and to work very hard".
What work has *he* done? How persevering has *he* been?'

'Why not give him some work?' Forster suggested. 'The
very thing he needs, perhaps.'

Charles stared, then clapped him on the back. 'Capital,
John! Admirable! The Dim Design – that shall be it. He shall
be sat down to a desk and put to some employment that will
keep him out of mischief.'

When the Dim Design took shape as the magazine *Household
Words*, with Charles as its half-owner and editor, his father was
taken on to the staff, editing the supplement which covered his
old ground, Parliamentary proceedings. It was something, if
only a little. There was something else in Charles's eye, when
he looked at his father; the image of a man like him, with all his
faults and weaknesses and comicalities, that should capture
readers as Pickwick and Pecksniff had captured them. The

figure began to take shape, to weave itself into the fabric of the novel that was beginning in his mind. It would be the most important, the greatest novel he had ever written, for it would be the story of his own life, with everything revealed that he longed to say, but that must never be said of Charles Dickens – only of David Copperfield. Maria Beadnell would be in it, and Mary, and Georgina – perhaps as the same person – and something of Catherine and their crumbling marriage, and the wound inflicted on him, never to fade, at the blacking warehouse.

'I shall take the whole world into my confidence, John.' he told Forster, 'and only you will understand.'

Forster, reading, understood. The child David, rejected by his evil stepfather, was sent to drudge in a warehouse on the river. It was at Blackfriars, not by Hungerford Stairs, and the bottles on which the boy drearily pasted labels were wine-bottles, but the place was unmistakable. So was the stoutish, middle-aged person, David's landlord, who entered the story in Chapter Eleven.

'His clothes were shabby, but he had an imposing shirt-collar on. He carried a jaunty sort of a stick, with a large pair of rusty tassels to it, and a quizzing-glass hung outside his coat – for ornament, I afterwards found, as he very seldom looked through it, and couldn't see anything when he did . . .

'"My address, said Mr Micawber, "is Windsor Terrace, City Road. I – in short," said Mr Micawber with the same genteel air, and in another burst of confidence – "I live there . . . Under the impression that your peregrinations in this metropolis have not as yet been extensive, and that you might have some difficulty in penetrating the arcana of the Modern Babylon in the direction of the City Road – in short," said Mr Micawber in another burst of confidence, "that you might lose yourself – I shall be happy to call this evening, and instal you in the knowledge of the nearest way."'

Forster smiled as he read on. Charles had taken every foible of his father's, every flourish of speech and shade of manner. The exuberance of the man was there, the fantasy, the desperation when things were going well, and the soaring optimism when they were darkest. Micawber was maddening, stupid, and selfish; his wife and children suffered through his monstrous extravagance; there was something a little strange and cold in his relationship with the child Copperfield, whom he seemed not to regard as a child; yet the character was head and shoulders over the rest. Whatever John Dickens had owed Charles throughout his life, it was fully repaid now, and would be, over and over again, in the sales of the book. 'I would be even more economic in my grave, would I not?'

'Don't you think,' Forster said to Charles, 'it may be just a little . . . well, offensive to him?'

Charles laughed. 'My dear fellow. He won't recognise himself – wouldn't, in a million years. People don't. Look at my mother, flatly denying that any such person as Mrs Nickleby could have existed. Why, I could draw *your* likeness, John, and you'd see it only as a clever invention no more like you than Uriah Heep.'

Copperfield was finished, had been published in monthly serial numbers and in book form, rapturously acclaimed, when illness struck the Dickens family. The new baby, Dora Annie, was not well. Catherine was so ailing with a nervous disorder that Charles took lodgings for her at Malvern Spa, leaving her there in Georgina's care while he returned to London to visit his father, who lay in shabby lodgings near the British Museum. He was feverish, sometimes rambling, in constant pain from the bladder disease which had troubled him for months, yet irrepressibly cheerful. He had been very ill, Charles's mother said, but seemed to be mending. Charles went back to Malvern.

A day or two later a message from his mother recalled him. On the railway journey to London his mind was a theatre, a stage on which the actors were his father and himself. He was a child again; they were in the Navy-Pay Yacht, *Chatham*, sailing on the Medway. Now they were at the Mitre, Charles rendering *The Cats'-meat Man* on the table, John beaming and clapping. The table had changed to the one in their home; the dreaded Deed was lying on it, the Deed that would send them to London. He was in the sordid lodging in Camden Town, ill in that narrow little bed which would soon be sold, and his father was sitting beside him, feeding him with slices of orange and making him laugh in spite of his pain. Now they were in the Marshalsea, and somebody was weeping – who? There were tears running down Charles's face, into the beard he had newly grown. On and on rolled the scenes like pictures in a Diorama, turning as the wheels of the train turned, bearing him towards London and what he knew would be the last scene of all. 'I assure you, my son, that the activity of the worms would give me more to laugh about . . .'

The hansom-cab from Praed Street Station got him to Keppel Street within fifteen minutes. His mother's face was swollen with weeping when she let him into the lodging. He kissed her, and followed her upstairs to the untidy room where his father lay, changed since the last time he had seen him. He was staring at the ceiling, smiling sometimes, muttering to himself.

'I came as soon as I heard,' Charles said, his shocked eyes on the changed face. 'Is he . . . ?'

His mother shook her head mechanically. 'Not a word – not a movement – for hours.' She began to weep again. 'But I will never desert him . . . never.'

He had not felt so tender towards her for many years. Perhaps the coming death of John drew them together, or perhaps he had written out his bitterness towards her in translating her into Emma Micawber, loyal, trusting, put-upon, as she herself had been. He drew her to him. 'There, Mother. You rest for a while – I'll sit with him.'

'He was brave, Charles. He was dreadfully brave, for it was a terrible thing, and must have troubled him for so long, the doctor said, but he was brave and never said a word about it, to anyone, but laughed and joked and kept everyone so jolly. Didn't he, Charles?'

'He did, he did. Go and rest now,' and he gave her a gentle push towards the door. He looked down at his father's almost unrecognisable face, the Mask that had haunted him but without the horror of that childhood memory.

'Oh, father, have they silenced you at last?' he whispered.

All night Charles sat by the bedside, putting a cup of water to the dry lips, dampening the burning forehead. For many hours, a night and a day, he kept vigil, until the time came when the occasional muttering ceased and the dying man lay quiet, seemingly already out of pain. His breathing was so faint that Charles bent over him to hear whether breath still came and went. The eyelids lifted.

'Who's there?' asked John feebly. The old familiar jaunty smile came back. 'Oh, Charles, my boy.'

Charles's clasp tightened on the cold hand. 'Father.'

Another murmur. 'Tell me . . . something.'

'What? Slowly now, take it slowly.'

'Micawber is me . . . ain't he?' At his son's nod he smiled again, nodded in satisfaction, and died.

Clods of earth fell slowly, rhythmically, on the coffin in the newly-dug grave in Highgate Cemetery. The young trees round it were in April green; in a nearby field lambs were playing. In Charles's mind two phrases rang, turn by turn. He created me, I created him: Charles Dickens and Micawber, Micawber and Charles Dickens. Under the fast-disappearing coffin-lid lay John Dickens, mortal. Might his other self, Micawber, be among the immortals?

'Earth to earth, ashes to ashes, dust to dust,' the vicar was saying, as the clods fell, 'in sure and certain hope of the Resurrection to eternal life, through our Lord Jesus Christ; who shall change our vile body, that it may be like until His glorious body, according to the mighty working . . .'

A sudden sharp gust of wind swept up from London, making Charles shudder and pull up the collar of his great-coat. He hated funerals, a part of himself was always buried with the coffin.

He was thirty-nine; already more than half of his life was over.